"Maybe I should to have a look at this."

"Nonsense. Not much he can do for this, and I've had worse."

Stubborn woman. "Let me at least run some cool water over it and have a look."

Mitch led Cora Beth toward the sink then extended her hand under the spigot. Holding her slender wrist, inhaling her cinnamon and honey scent, hearing that sudden catch in her breathing as the water hit her hand, he was suddenly sharply aware of her as a woman, a woman whose company he enjoyed perhaps a little more than he should.

He gave his head a mental shake. That kind of thinking was wrong for any number of reasons. Not the least of which was the solemn vow he'd made after Dinah's death to never marry. With God's help he'd made peace with that aspect of his future years ago.

Or thought he had.

Books by Winnie Griggs

Love Inspired Historical

The Hand-Me-Down Family
The Christmas Journey
The Proper Wife
Second Chance Family

Love Inspired

The Heart's Song

WINNIE GRIGGS

is a city girl born and raised in southeast Louisiana's Cajun Country who grew up to marry a country boy from the hills of northwest Louisiana. Though her Prince Charming (who often wears the guise of a cattle rancher) is more comfortable riding a tractor than a white steed, the two of them have been living their own happily-ever-after for more than thirty years. During that time they raised four proud-to-call-them-mine children and a too-numerous-to-count assortment of dogs, cats, fish, hamsters, turtles and 4-H sheep.

Winnie has held a job at a utility company since she graduated from college, and saw her first novel hit bookstores in 2001. In addition to her day job and writing career, Winnie serves on committees within her church and on the executive boards and committees of several writing organizations, and she is active in local civic organizations—she truly believes the adage that you reap in proportion to what you sow.

In addition to writing and reading, Winnie enjoys spending time with her family, cooking and exploring flea markets. Readers can contact Winnie at P.O. Box 14, Plain Dealing, LA 71064, or email her at winnie@winniegriggs.com.

WINNIE GRIGGS

Second Chance Family

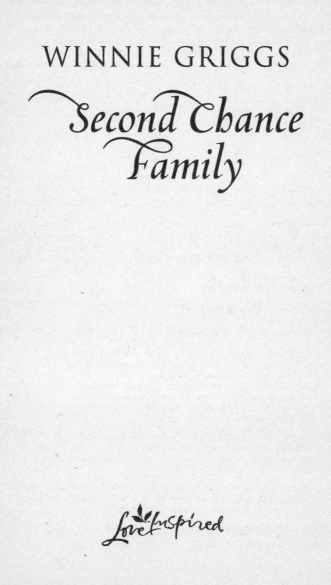

Love Inspired

Recycling programs
for this product may
not exist in your area.

LOVE INSPIRED BOOKS

ISBN-13: 978-0-373-82877-7

SECOND CHANCE FAMILY

www.LoveInspiredBooks.com

Printed in U.S.A.

"For My thoughts are not your thoughts,
neither are your ways My ways,"
declares the Lord.

"As the heavens are higher than the earth,
so are My ways higher than your ways
and My thoughts than your thoughts."
—*Isaiah 55:8–9*

To my husband, Ronnie, who supports me
in all aspects of my life, even when it's not such an
easy thing to do. God truly blessed me when
He sent you into my life.

Chapter One

September 1893
Knotty Pine, Texas

"Hey, let me go! I ain't done nothing wrong."

Sheriff Mitchell Hammond wasn't buying that for a minute. The furtive way the boy had been sneaking out of the boardinghouse garden had guilt written all over it. In fact, Mitch's gut told him this kid was more than likely the culprit responsible for the rash of petty thefts that had plagued the town the past week or so. "Stop your squirming, son. I think maybe we need to talk about that bunch of carrots you have stuffed in your shirt."

"Them's my carrots."

The kid's voice had more than a touch of bluster to it.

Mitch tightened his hold on the boy's collar. "You don't say? Well, here comes Mrs. Collins now. Since she runs this boardinghouse and this here is her garden, why don't we see what she has to say about that."

Cora Beth Collins was hurrying toward them. Even in the early morning light, he could make out the concerned look on her oh-so-readable face, could tell that her honey-brown hair was pulled back in its usual tidy bun, could appreciate the way her crisply starched apron was tied around her trim waist.

Mitch frowned as he realized where his thoughts had strayed. He'd always considered Cora Beth a fine lady and a good friend. But lately he'd begun to feel something a little warmer than mere friendship when he caught sight of her.

And that was definitely *not* a good thing.

"What's all this commotion about?" Her breathless voice held an accusing tone that he was certain was aimed more at him than at the young scoundrel in his grasp.

Mitch tipped his hat with his free hand. "Morning, Cora Beth. Sorry if we disturbed you." He tilted his head toward his still-squirming captive. "I caught this boy raiding your garden."

Consternation flitted across her face and then she gave Mitch a challenging look. "It's not raiding if he has my permission."

He wasn't surprised by her quick defense of the boy. Cora Beth had the softest heart in town—she'd give up her last crust of bread if she thought someone else needed it more. Especially if that someone was a kid. But he also noted that she hadn't actually claimed to have given the kid permission. And he hadn't missed the surprise and relief that flashed across the boy's face—a dead giveaway that his captive hadn't expected her to back him up.

"And did he?" It would be interesting to see how she answered him—she was too honest to out-and-out lie, no matter how much she wanted to rise to the kid's defense.

But to his surprise, she looked him straight in the eye, her expression free of evasiveness. "Actually, he's been weeding the garden in exchange for whatever produce he can carry." Then she glanced back at the boy and gave him an encouraging smile. "And a fine job you've been doing of it, too, young man."

That gave Mitch pause. Had he been a little too quick to judgment with the kid?

The boy mumbled something that might have been a thank-you, then glared up at Mitch, renewing his efforts to get free. "See, I told you I wasn't stealing. So, you gonna let me go now, mister?"

But despite Cora Beth's staunch defense, Mitch wasn't quite ready to believe the boy was totally innocent. "It's sheriff, not mister. And hold still. I'm not through with you just yet."

"Go easy." Cora Beth put out a hand but stopped short of touching either of them. "He's just a boy, not some hardened criminal." Her expression softened as she turned to his captive. "What's your name?"

Mitch raised a brow. "Now that's mighty interesting. He works for you, but you didn't bother to learn his name."

Cora Beth's expression reflected a mix of guilt and bravado, but she refrained from responding.

Keeping his amusement in check, Mitch turned his attention back to the closemouthed youth. "The lady asked you for your name, son."

"Ethan." The boy dug a toe into the ground and his tone was surly, grudging.

"Got a last name to go with that?" Mitch asked.

No response other than a tightening of the lips.

Cora Beth placed a hand on her supposed-gardener's shoulder. "You know, my brother Danny is twelve years old. I'll bet you're just about the same age, maybe a little older."

"I'm eleven." The boy's suddenly straighter posture bespoke a pride that was no doubt due to the fact that she'd erred on the plus side.

Which, knowing Cora Beth, she'd likely done deliberately.

"Is that right?" she said. "Well then, you're a very *mature* eleven." She cocked her head to one side. "Have you had your breakfast yet?"

The boy shook his head, and his rebellious expression shifted to hunger for a flash before he guarded it once more.

From the looks of the kid, Mitch guessed it'd been a while since he'd had a decent meal. But he'd landed on the right doorstep, figuratively speaking, to take care of that. If there was one thing Cora Beth could do exceptionally well, it was cook.

Sure enough, she straightened and gave a nod toward her back porch. "Well, we're going to do something about that. You come on inside. I just took the biscuits from the oven and it won't take more than a few minutes to scramble up some eggs."

Ethan scowled up at Mitch. "I don't think the sheriff'll let me go."

Cora Beth tossed Mitch a look. "Well then, I guess we'll have to invite him to join us."

Mitch touched the brim of his hat, giving her an answering smile. "Now, how could I turn down such a gracious invitation?"

She placed a hand on the boy's shoulder, her gaze still locked on Mitch. "You can let go of him now. He's not going anywhere, at least not until he's had his breakfast." She gave Ethan a smile. "Are you?"

"No, ma'am."

Mitch repressed the urge to roll his eyes at the boy's overly docile tone. Cora Beth might trust him not to make a break for it but Mitch wasn't so gullible. Maybe because he had more experience with individuals who wore Ethan's hunted look. Likely as not, the kid would bolt at the first opportunity.

He kept a close eye on the boy as he let the two of them precede him. Stepping inside the large kitchen of the boardinghouse, Mitch removed his hat and hung it on a peg by the door. "Nothing like the smell of fresh baked biscuits to get a man's stomach to rumbling."

That earned him a smile from Cora Beth. "You men-folk take a seat at the table and I'll have your eggs and bacon cooked up quick as a cat's pounce."

Mitch smiled a thank-you before he pulled out a chair, careful to seat himself between the boy and the door. "You're in for a treat." He kept his tone friendly. "Mrs. Collins is the best cook in these parts."

"Smells good."

The boy seemed a little more relaxed now. Was he ready to answer a few questions? "You're not from around here, are you?"

"No."

The bitter edge to the boy's tone was unexpected. Mitch filed that impression away to mull over later and continued his questioning. "So where *are* you from?"

The boy shrugged, not meeting his gaze. "Here and there. We move around."

So he wasn't traveling alone. "Who all makes up that *we?*"

Ethan clamped his lips shut, then looked past Mitch. "Is there something I can do to help you, ma'am?"

Cora Beth smiled over her shoulder. "Why thank you, Ethan, but I have it all under control."

Mitch reclaimed the boy's attention. "I asked you who you were traveling with."

He saw Ethan's internal struggle play out on his face. "My pa likes to travel," he finally blurted out.

Something in the boy's demeanor gave Mitch the feeling that Ethan was holding something back. But before he could press further, Cora Beth looked over her shoulder again.

"Your mother doesn't travel with you as well?" she asked.

"My ma's dead." There was no heat in his answer this time—only a starkness of tone and expression.

The sounds of Cora Beth's utensils against the pans stopped. "Oh, Ethan—" her voice carried a caresslike sympathy "—I'm so sorry."

Ethan looked up to acknowledge her concern. "Thank you, ma'am. I miss her a lot."

Mitch, who'd lost his own mother at a young age, felt a tug of matching sympathy for the boy. But he couldn't let his feelings get in the way of his job. Learning what he could about the boy's situation—not feeling sorry for him—was the best way to help him. "And where is your pa right now?"

Ethan glanced back at the table. "Our camp is set up a couple miles outside of town."

Before Mitch could press further, Cora Beth set a plate in front of each of them. "That's enough with the questions for now, Sheriff. Let the boy eat."

Ethan reached for a biscuit and scooped up a forkful of the scrambled eggs at the same time.

"Ethan." Cora Beth used that voice most mothers acquired instinctively, the one that was gentle yet uncompromisingly firm at the same time. "In this house we always give thanks before we eat."

Ethan tensed for a moment, rebellion tightening his jaw. But he set down his fork and gave her a pinched-faced apology. "Yes, ma'am. Sorry."

She touched his shoulder before taking a seat beside him. "I know you are." Then she turned her moss-green gaze toward Mitch. "Sheriff, would you say grace for us, please?"

He nodded and bowed his head, oddly touched that she had turned to him to perform that service. "Father, we thank You for this food and for the one who so generously prepared it. We ask that You watch over us this day as we go about our business. And we also ask that You keep a special eye on this young man sharing the table with us since he seems to be in need of Your guiding hand. Amen."

Cora Beth and Ethan echoed his amen. Ethan sent him a glower as he looked up, but then dug into his food without comment.

Mitch frowned as Cora Beth stood and headed back toward the stove. "Aren't you going to join us?"

"The others will be down for breakfast soon. I've got several more plates of eggs to fix."

The "others" included Cora Beth's family—three daughters, a younger brother and an uncle—and her three regular boarders. He wondered what it would have been like to grow up with such a large extended family. His own parents had passed on when he was barely six and he'd been raised by his grandmother who didn't believe in socializing much outside of church. Thank goodness he'd had school to get him out of that oppressive house for a time.

"You go ahead and eat your fill." Cora Beth's words

brought his straying thoughts back to the present. He glanced up to see that her smile was directed at Ethan. "There's plenty more if you're still hungry when you eat that up." Then she glanced Mitch's way. "That goes for you, too, Sheriff."

He studied her for a moment as she worked, then reluctantly returned his attention to his table companion. "Just where is this camp of yours?"

"Like I said, a couple of miles outside of town."

"I was looking for something a bit more specific."

"A couple of miles *south* of town."

Well, there was another way to get the answers he needed. "After breakfast, I think I'll give you a ride back to your camp."

The boy paused with his fork poised halfway to his mouth. This time he met Mitch's gaze head-on. "No need. I *like* walking."

"No doubt." Mitch gave him a broad, companionable grin. "I did my share of walking all over these parts when I was your age. Lots of interesting places to explore." He reached for his glass. "Still, I'd like to see this camp of yours for myself."

Ethan shoved the forkful of eggs into his mouth, his glower deepening.

"Besides, I like to meet the folks who spend time in Knotty Pine, welcome them to the area and get to know a little about them." He caught and held Ethan's glance. "I'd like to meet your pa. Seems strange that he would let you wander off so far on your own."

"Pa knows I can take care of myself."

Mitch let that one go unchallenged. "Is your pa planning to stick around Knotty Pine awhile?"

Ethan shrugged.

"Don't want to discuss that subject either?" Mitch

planted his elbows on the table. "Then let's try a different one. Do you know anything about a shirt and sheet that went missing from Mrs. Johnson's clothesline Monday, or a pie that disappeared from Mrs. Evans's windowsill yesterday, or some damage inside Mrs. Oglesby's greenhouse?"

The boy's shoulders hunched but he didn't look up from his plate.

Mitch stabbed a forkful of eggs, trying to keep his irritation in check. The boy was looking guiltier by the second. The question was, had he been stealing out of mischief or genuine need? "You're about as forthcoming as a fence post, aren't you, boy? A person might think you aren't talking because you have something to hide."

That only earned Mitch a glare.

Time to be more direct. "Look, Ethan, I'm willing to listen to your side of things, but in order for me to do that you need to do some talking. So either you start answering my questions here and now or we can go down to the jailhouse to finish this conversation." There—direct but reasonable.

Cora Beth didn't seem to agree. She plopped down a platter of sizzling bacon on the table with a little more force than absolutely necessary. "I know you have a job to do, Sheriff, but Ethan's not a criminal—he's just a boy. No need to scare him like that."

That drew Ethan's shoulders back and slapped an indignant frown on his face. "I'm *not* scared."

Mitch locked gazes with the boy. "Then answer my questions."

Ethan licked his lips, then tilted his jaw defiantly. "We're not planning on settling here. Probably be moving on today or tomorrow."

Not the question he'd been referring to, but Mitch decided it was a start. "Where are y'all headed?"

Ethan shrugged again. He seemed to be fond of that gesture. "Wherever I—we can find work."

Interesting slip. "What kind of work are you looking for?"

Instead of answering, Ethan grabbed his glass of milk and began gulping it.

"Don't you know?"

The boy set down his glass with enough energy to make the liquid slosh wildly. "Course I know. Thing is, my pa can do just about anything. Mostly, though, he does carpentry work."

Mitch leaned back, giving the boy a challenging look. "Well, in that case maybe he *should* consider sticking around here for a while. I reckon Knotty Pine could use a good carpenter."

"That's right," Cora Beth added brightly. "Why I was just telling Mrs. Plunkett the other day that some of the railings on the front porch need replacing. But now that school's started back up, my brother Danny's too busy and Uncle Grover's not up to that kind of work anymore. I'd be glad to hire your father to do the job for me."

Ethan's expression took on a trapped look as he stared back down at his plate. "I'll sure enough tell him, ma'am. But I think he's not really interested in settling down hereabouts."

The kid's answers took on a different tone when he responded to Cora Beth. She had a knack for dealing with kids, no doubt about it.

A sudden cry from Cora Beth followed by the clattering of a dropped spoon had Mitch out of his chair and across the room in a heartbeat. "What is it?"

Cora Beth clutched her left hand against her chest.

"I'm such a ninny, I burned my hand on the skillet." Her tone was light, but her attempt at a smile had more than a touch of grimace to it.

"Let me see." Mitch gently tugged on her injured hand, cradling it in his own as if it were a baby bird.

"It's nothing, really." But her strained expression belied her words.

"Now, aren't you the one who always says talk like that is more foolish than brave?"

Cora Beth gave a shaky laugh. "No fair turning my words back on me." She tried to draw her hand away. "I need to finish—"

"Breakfast will keep." He made quick work of moving the skillet away from the heat, then frowned as he studied the angry red streak on the side of her left hand. "Maybe I should fetch Doc Whitman to have a look at this."

"Nonsense. Not much he can do for this and I've had worse."

Stubborn woman. "Let me at least run some cool water over it and have a better look."

He led her toward the sink, then extended her hand under the spigot. Holding her slender wrist, inhaling her cinnamon and honey scent, hearing that sudden catch in her breathing as the water hit her hand—he was suddenly sharply aware of her as a woman, a woman whose company he enjoyed perhaps a little more than he should.

He gave his head a mental shake. That kind of thinking was wrong for any number of reasons. He'd made a solemn vow after Dinah's death, a vow to never marry. It had been a bitter pill to swallow, but when he'd been faced with the reality and consequences of his own shortcomings, it had been his only choice. It hadn't been easy, but he'd finally made his peace with that aspect of his future a long time ago. Or thought he had.

Lately, he wasn't so sure.

"See—" Cora Beth's words drew his thoughts back to the present "—it's not so bad. You're making a fuss for nothing."

"What I *see* is that this burn of yours is going to make a very nasty blister."

Ethan appeared next to them, holding the crock of butter. "My ma used to say that butter was good for a burn."

The smile Cora Beth gave the boy seemed softer and more genuine than the one she'd attempted earlier. "Thank you, Ethan. My mother used to say the same thing."

With a nod, Ethan set the crock on the counter beside them and returned to the table.

While Mitch was slathering butter over Cora Beth's burn, carefully telling himself that she was no different from any other citizen in town, the door to the hall opened. Cora Beth's younger brother Danny stepped inside, then stopped as he took in the scene before him. "What's going on? Why's the sheriff here? You okay, Cora Beth?"

"Your sister burned her hand on the skillet," Mitch answered.

Danny quickly crossed the room. "Is it hurt bad? Are you gonna have to get Sadie to come in and help again?"

Cora Beth laughed. "Don't be silly. It's just a little burn. I'll be right as rain in no time."

Danny glanced Mitch's way. "Then why are you here?"

"Nothing to do with your sister. I caught—" Mitch

looked around, scanning the room. His jaw tightened as he realized he'd been outfoxed by an eleven-year-old boy. "Hang it all, the kid's slipped out on me."

Chapter Two

Cora Beth felt guiltily relieved that Ethan had gotten away. She admired Sheriff Hammond's integrity and sense of duty, of course, but sometimes a gentler hand was required, especially when youngsters were involved.

She stared at the door, wondering how Ethan had managed to slip out without either of them noticing. "I hope he's going to be okay."

"Who?" Danny stared at her, then at the sheriff.

"A kid I found prowling around outside." The sheriff's drawl was roughened by an edge of irritation.

"He was *not* prowling," Cora Beth insisted. "He knew he was welcome to that little bit of produce he harvested." She turned to her brother. "His name is Ethan and he's about your age. Sheriff Hammond spotted him over by the garden and thought he was up to mischief." She shot a stern look Mitch's way. "But the sheriff was mistaken. So I invited them both in for breakfast while we tried to get it all straightened out."

Her would-be-doctor shook his head. "And he repaid you by running off without so much as a thank-you."

"Not true. He thanked me very nicely when I invited him in."

Danny's brows drew down as he tried to follow their conversation. "I never heard of any kid named Ethan around these parts."

The sheriff nodded as if Danny had come down on his side. "Exactly."

Oh for goodness' sake. She deliberately turned away from Mitch and toward Danny. "He and his family aren't from Knotty Pine, they're just passing through. And I think it falls to us as good Christian folk to be neighborly and welcoming while they're here. Including—" she gave Mitch a sideways glance "—making certain they have enough to eat."

She raised her good hand to forestall whatever grousing the sheriff seemed primed to offer. "Now, the sun's up and school'll be starting before you know it. Danny, please make sure the girls are awake and about, then tend to your chores. I've got to finish getting breakfast ready before everyone comes down looking for something to eat."

"Before you do that," the sheriff interjected with a glance toward Danny, "fetch me something I can use to bandage your sister's hand, would you?"

With a nod, Danny left the room.

Silence descended and suddenly Cora Beth was acutely aware that the sheriff was still holding her hand. Feeling her cheeks warm as if she were a schoolgirl rather than a matron of twenty-seven, she drew away and turned toward the stove. "I should get back to my cooking." She was pleased to find her voice was matter-of-fact.

"That can wait a few more minutes." Sheriff Hammond took her elbow and guided her to the table. "At least let me bandage that hand first."

Cora Beth nodded and wordlessly allowed him to pull out her chair.

Did the silence seem as awkward to him as it did to her? Goodness, what was *wrong* with her?

She was actually relieved when Danny returned. He handed some strips of cloth to Mitch, swiped a crisp slice of bacon from the platter on the table, then gave a wave and headed back out to the hall again.

Mitch quickly unrolled the cloth. "Now, let's see about getting you taken care of."

Cora Beth studied the slight wave in his dark brown hair as he wrapped the cloth around her palm. The tickle of warmth in her chest no doubt came from the novelty of having someone tending to her for a change. She loved her family dearly, and loved taking care of them, but every once in a while she liked to feel she wasn't just a mother or a caretaker.

"Do you think Ethan's going to be okay?" she asked.

"More'n likely." He paused his ministrations and gave her a long look. "You do realize he's probably a thief?"

Why couldn't he stop thinking like a sheriff for just a few minutes? "If he's a thief it's only because he's desperate. Did you see how thin he was? And those bruises on his arms?"

He went back to bandaging her hand, but not before she caught a flash of something unreadable flicker in his expression. "I saw. Looks like he's had a rough time of it." He tied off the bandage and sat back, meeting her gaze head-on. "That's one reason why I need to find out who or what he's running from and why. I know you feel sorry for him, and yes he's just a kid, but my job is to uphold the law and to protect the citizens of this town."

He seemed to hesitate just a heartbeat before continuing. "And I figure the 'upholding the law' part of my job includes figuring out who is responsible for the boy and making sure they take that responsibility seriously."

Cora Beth smiled. She shouldn't have doubted Mitch—he *did* care about Ethan's welfare. "Of course."

"That's assuming he wasn't lying about traveling with his pa."

Had he always had that suspicious nature or had his job made him that way? "Why ever would he lie about a thing like that?" she asked.

"He could be a runaway."

"A runaway. Oh my goodness, do you think he's in some sort of trouble?"

Mitch shrugged. "Don't know. But I aim to try and find out."

"If he did lie about traveling with his father—oh, Mitch, he could be an orphan. What if he doesn't have anyone to look out for him?"

"One way or the other, he needs to be under the care of an adult. If there's no one to take him in, I'll see about getting him into an orphanage." He must have read something in her expression, because he gave her a sympathetic look. "I'm sorry if you don't like hearing that, but there are worse things out there for an orphan than being institutionalized."

What did he mean by that? Then Cora Beth bit her lip. She'd almost forgotten that Mitch himself had been orphaned young, though he'd had a grandmother to take him in. But still, why would he say—

Then she remembered some oblique comments about his grandmother. From all accounts, Opal Todd had not been an easy woman. But Cora Beth wasn't sure exactly what that had meant for Mitch as he was growing up.

"You know as well as I do," he continued, obviously unaware of her thoughts, "running around the countryside, stealing for his meals, is no way for any kid to live. The next time he gets caught raiding a garden, the owner might not be as understanding as you were."

It was hard to argue with that kind of logic. Still, an orphanage...

She straightened. "Do you think he'll be back?" If only she could speak to Ethan again, perhaps get him to trust her.

Mitch gave her that crooked grin of his. "After getting a taste of your cooking, he'd be crazy not to." Then he sobered. "If he *does* come back, though, I want your word that you'll let me know right away."

Cora Beth hesitated. Mitch obviously made Ethan skittish. It would be so much easier to get the boy to relax if—

"I mean it." His I'm-the-lawman-around-here tone was back. "I can see you like the kid, but we don't know anything about him. You need to trust me to handle this my way."

She gave a reluctant nod. "All right. I promise." And truly she did trust his intentions, if not his methods.

She pushed back from the table and stood.

He followed. "Don't know if you noticed, but he slipped a couple of biscuits in his shirt when he thought no one was watching."

The man didn't miss much. A requirement of his job,

she supposed. But more importantly, he'd seen what Ethan did and hadn't called his hand on it. Mitch was more sympathetic than he'd have her believe.

"He's welcome to them," she said. "Poor boy was probably worried about where his next meal's coming from." Then she tilted her head to one side and studied him. "You weren't really going to arrest Ethan, were you?"

"Depends on just how much mischief he's been up to and what his motives were. Right now I'm more concerned with finding him and getting to the bottom of his situation."

"What do you mean?"

"Whether you want to believe it or not, there's the possibility that he's a troublemaker on the run, in which case I aim to see he faces whatever he has coming to him. He's young enough so that, if we can make him learn he has to bear the consequences of his actions now, it might set him on the straight and narrow going forward."

"True, as long as we temper those consequences with mercy."

"That depends." He gave her a long, steady look. "Sometimes the greater mercy is disguised as discipline. Of course, if he *is* running from trouble, it could be that it's not of his own making. That's a whole different story and, depending on what kind of trouble it is, he might need a lawman in his corner to straighten things out."

She hadn't thought of that. "He'd be lucky to have you at his side."

He ignored her compliment. "Then again, he could have been straight with us about traveling through here with his pa. In which case I'd sure like to have a word or two with the man to make certain he understands his responsibilities as a parent."

Cora Beth had no trouble at all picturing Mitch leading that conversation. "You left out one possibility—that he's an orphan trying to make it on his own."

"If that's the case, then I aim to see he finds a new home, one way or the other." He tugged on the cuff of his sleeve. "The point is, a kid on his own like that is trouble, any way you slice it."

She thought about Danny. What would have happened to him if her folks hadn't been willing to take him in when his own folks died? "Ethan's just a boy."

"Don't go feeling too sorry for him just yet. I still haven't ruled out the troublemaker scenario."

She held her bandaged hand to her chest. "I don't believe that for one minute, and I don't think you do, either." When he didn't dispute her statement she softened her voice. "He's a good boy at heart, I know it."

Mitch shook his head. "Now how on earth can you know that? He stole those carrots from your garden. And I'd stake my badge that he's behind a half dozen other thefts that have taken place around here lately."

"I told you, he didn't steal anything from me. He earned those vegetables by pulling weeds."

Mitch raised a brow. "You mean he really did that?"

She stiffened. "Mitchell Hammond, did you think I was *lying* to you?"

He rubbed the back of his neck and shifted slightly. "Not lying exactly, just maybe stretching things a bit."

"Well, I'll have you know it was the gospel truth."

He crossed his arms. "You want to tell me how you hired that kid without even knowing his name?"

It was her turn to shift a bit. "When I went out to

the garden yesterday, I found someone had pulled all the weeds from the row of pole beans. And it was well done—not some halfhearted, higgledy-piggledy job. I figured the few scraggly tomatoes that were missing were fair payment to whomever did the work." She refused to let the expression on Mitch's face make her feel guilty. "I left a note on the gate saying so in case whomever it was came back."

"Well, it sure would have been helpful if you'd said something to me about it yesterday."

There was no need for him to get so riled up. "I didn't figure it was anything I needed to bring a lawman in on."

"Hang it all, it's my job to know all the comings and goings around here. How can I keep a proper eye on Knotty Pine if my own townsfolk are hiding things from me?"

She decided to ignore his question—it was probably rhetorical anyway. "The point is, he didn't just *take* my vegetables—he did his best to earn them. I wouldn't be the least bit surprised if you went back to whomever claims they were robbed and find some kind of payment was left for them, as well."

"Even if that were true, it's still stealing if the owner didn't agree to the trade. Rita Evans was mighty upset about her cherry pie going missing—seems she'd made it as a treat for Alfred's birthday. Not to mention how livid Mayor Oglesby's wife was over the damage done inside that glass plant house of hers. Not only were several pots tipped over but it seems one of her prize plants was missing."

Cora Beth smothered a groan. "Oh my goodness—please don't tell me it was her orchid." Nelda Oglesby was downright fanatical about that plant. When she'd first received it, she'd spent almost all of the social hour at the Ladies' Auxiliary meeting going on and on about how beautiful and delicate the plant was, how much cosseting it needed and how much special care had been required to get it shipped to Knotty Pine from whatever exotic place it had come from. And the members of the committee had been given weekly updates ever since.

Mitch raised a brow. "I do believe that was the name she mentioned—about twenty times."

"Oh dear. Poor Ethan. If he's the culprit, she won't forgive him easily."

"Poor *Ethan*. He's not the one who had to listen to a tirade on just how special that plant was and how particularly heinous a crime it was to steal it. You'd think the blooming thing was sprouting diamonds and rubies, the way she carried on."

A smile tugged at Cora Beth's lips. "I believe listening to citizen complaints is part of your job, too, sheriff."

He glowered at her. "I take back my comment about your softheartedness. You are one hard woman."

Cora Beth chuckled outright at that, enjoying the teasing. "So what are you planning to do now?"

"Well, right this minute I'm going to help you get breakfast on the table." Mitch rolled up his sleeves as he moved toward the stove. "How many more eggs do we need to scramble?"

Surely he wasn't serious? "Oh, no, you don't have to—"

"No arguments or I *will* go fetch the doctor."

Her lips twitched. "Mighty high-handed of you."

His grin was unrepentant. "Comes with being a lawman."

"Do you even know how to cook?"

He shot her an aggrieved look. "I may not be able to set as fine a table as you set, Cora Beth Collins, but I can certainly scramble eggs and fry up bacon. Just show me how much is left to be done."

Before she could comply, Uncle Grover stepped into the kitchen. "Danny told me you had an accident. Are you all right?"

His obvious worry touched her. "I'm fine, Uncle Grover. Danny shouldn't have worried you."

"Nonsense, Danny did just as he should." He waved a hand toward Mitch. "And I may not be as spry as the sheriff over there, but I'm here to help."

Just what she needed, another man trying to do her job. "That's very sweet of you, Uncle Grover, but—"

"I'm finishing up the cooking," Mitch interrupted. "Why don't you find me some platters to dish it up on?"

The older gentleman smiled as he pushed his spectacles up higher on his nose. "Of course."

When had she lost command of her own kitchen? It seemed her place had been temporarily usurped by one determined lawman.

She watched Mitch crack several eggs into a bowl and then stir them up with a great deal of vigor. He looked surprisingly at home. Her late husband had been a dear man and hard worker, but he'd never willingly gone near a cookstove except to serve up his plate.

Her three daughters came skittering into the kitchen, seven-year-old Audrey in the lead. "Mama, are you okay?"

"I'm fine, girls." She adjusted five-year-old Pippa's pinafore, then checked twin Lottie's hair ribbon. "Say hello to Sheriff Hammond."

"Hello, Sheriff Hammond." The greeting rang out in unison from all three.

"Good morning, girls. Don't you all look pretty this morning."

While Pippa and Lottie clamored to examine their mother's injury, Audrey approached Mitch. Cora Beth answered the twins' questions as she kept part of her attention focused on her more brash offspring.

"How come you're cooking breakfast?" Audrey asked.

Mitch smiled down at her. "Just helping out your mother."

"But I didn't know men could cook."

He pointed the spatula at her. "I cook my own meals all the time."

"Don't you have a mommy to cook for you?"

"Afraid not."

"Oh. Then you need a wife."

Cora Beth cleared her throat. "Okay, girls, time to get the table set."

"Yes, ma'am." They obediently moved toward the dining room, ready to tackle the morning chore.

Uncle Grover chuckled. "They're pretty wound up this morning. I'd better go supervise."

"Thanks, Uncle Grover." Cora Beth grabbed the dirty dishes from the table and headed for the sink. "Sorry about Audrey's stream of questions," she said over her shoulder to Mitch. "She hasn't quite figured out what's appropriate and what's not."

He smiled. "I like a girl who speaks her mind."

Nice to know. "Earlier, when I asked what you were going to do, I meant about Ethan."

"I know." Mitch didn't bother to turn around this time. "I'll take a ride and talk to some folks on the farms outside of town, see if anyone has spotted him, and look around for the camp he mentioned. Though to be honest I'm not even sure there *is* a camp."

Cora Beth had no doubt he would meticulously comb the area looking for Ethan. And he'd keep searching until he either found the boy or ran out of places to look.

Because Mitch Hammond was just that stubborn.

And just that caring.

He'd make a fine family man someday. The very thought caused a little flutter in Cora Beth's stomach, which she did her level best to ignore.

Chapter Three

"Knock, knock."

Cora Beth looked up from her clumsy attempts to polish the tea service to see a familiar petite form standing at her back door. "Sadie, hi. Come on in."

Sadie Reynolds stepped inside and removed her bonnet. "I saw Sheriff Hammond a little bit ago and he told me what happened to your hand."

Cora Beth rolled her eyes. "You mean he stopped in at your place and asked you to come by and check on me. That man can be worse than a mother hen sometimes."

Sadie grinned. "Especially when it comes to a certain boardinghouse proprietress."

Cora Beth ignored the warmth creeping into her cheeks as she shook her head. "Nonsense. He cares about everybody around here, you know that." Still, it had been mighty nice having him fuss over her this morning.

Sadie's mouth turned up in a smile. "True, but I think he favors a certain someone just a wee bit more than the others."

Sadie seemed to be having fun at her expense. "Don't

be silly," Cora Beth said. "And he really shouldn't have worried you with this."

Sadie removed her bonnet and set it on the counter. "I guess he just figured since I helped you out around here once before, I could do it again."

Last spring Sadie had spent a couple of weeks at the boardinghouse to lend a hand when Cora Beth sprained her wrist. That's when Sadie had met Eli Reynolds, the man who would become her husband a few short weeks later.

"That was different," Cora Beth explained. "This is just a little burn, nothing worth making a fuss over. Not that I'm not happy to see you, but I'm perfectly capable of doing my own housework." She gave her friend a knowing look. "Besides, if Mitch knew your happy news I doubt if he'd have bothered you with this." Just last week Sadie had announced that she and Eli were expecting their first child. So far, they were only letting family in on the news. Cora Beth had been touched that Sadie considered her part of her extended family.

Sadie grinned. "You're probably right. Men can be so over-the-roof protective when it comes to dealing with women who are expecting. As if we were made out of glass." She laughed. "Eli won't even let me saddle my horse anymore."

Then she sent a pointed look toward Cora Beth's hands and turned the conversation back to her original topic. "Are you really going to try to handle that tea service one-handed?"

Cora Beth grimaced. She was holding down the creamer with her left forearm while she tried to polish with her right hand. "I'm managing."

"Of course you are." Sadie gave her a mock pout. "Are you sure you're not refusing my help because you're worried I'll botch it like I did last time I came to help."

"Fiddlesticks—you were a big help." At Sadie's skeptical expression, she grinned. "But I concede that your true talents lie elsewhere."

"That's a very polite way of putting it." Sadie crossed her arms. "Now, I know how very capable you are, but seeing as I'm already here and since the Ladies' Auxiliary is meeting in your parlor this afternoon, I insist that you put me to work. I might be all thumbs, but since you're having to polish that tea service one-handed I figure I can do near as good a job as you today."

Cora Beth gave in with a smile. "Have it your way. Grab a rag and help yourself."

As Sadie joined her at the table, Cora Beth nudged the silver polish toward her. "Did the sheriff tell you anything else about what happened this morning?"

"You mean about your sunrise prowler? Yes, he told me, though I suspect I didn't get the whole story. He did ask me to keep a lookout for the boy."

"The boy's name is Ethan and I'm not convinced he's motivated by anything other than necessity. He's only eleven, for goodness' sake, and the poor thing is thin as a twig."

Sadie held up her palms in mock surrender. "Okay, I'm convinced—he's a good kid."

Cora Beth smiled sheepishly, realizing she'd been a touch too vehement. "Sorry. But it's so frustrating not knowing what his situation is, not knowing if he even has enough to eat."

"Well, you can rest assured, unless he's hitched a ride on a wagon headed out of town, the sheriff will find him."

Cora Beth fiddled with her locket. "The problem is,

Ethan doesn't want to be found. Sheriff Hammond put the fear of the Almighty into him this morning."

"He was just doing his job."

"I know, and he's mighty good at it." Cora Beth didn't want Sadie to think she was being critical. "But sometimes a softer touch is required."

"Perhaps the sheriff just needs a good woman to set the example for him."

And there were plenty of single ladies in town willing to take on that job. Many a miss had set their cap for the good sheriff. Cora Beth made a noncommittal sound and moved toward the stove, hoping to turn the conversation to a different topic.

But Sadie wasn't to be deflected. "I often wonder why a man with as much to recommend him as Mitch never married. I mean, I know he's no hermit and he doesn't lack for partners at the town dances or invites to Sunday dinners. It almost seems like he goes out of his way, though, not to spend too much time with any one eligible lady."

Sadie had been in Knotty Pine less than a year, so she wasn't familiar with everyone's histories the way the locals were. And Cora Beth certainly didn't want to start digging it all up for her. "I'm sure Mitch has his reasons."

"But you'd think he'd want to settle down with a family of his own." She gave Cora Beth an arch look. "Goodness knows there's any number of young ladies around here who'd be tickled pink to receive an offer from him. After all, in case you haven't noticed, in addition to his other fine qualities, there's some who'd consider him handsome to boot."

Oh yes, she'd noticed. But Cora Beth refused to

be baited so she held her peace as she opened the oven door.

Sadie went back to her polishing, a musing look on her face. "I just can't figure why a man like our sheriff wouldn't have landed himself a wife by now."

Looked as if she would have to go into this a bit after all. "Actually, he *was* engaged to be married, once."

Sadie sat back in her chair, polishing forgotten. "Oh my goodness, he was? What happened?"

Cora Beth kept her back to her friend, taking her time checking the batch of cookies. "Dinah, his fiancée, died a few days before the wedding. It was a freak accident and poor Mitch was devastated." She remembered the horrible darkness that had seemed to envelop him, the way he'd withdrawn into himself for a time. "I don't think he's ever quite gotten over the loss," she finally added.

"Poor Mitch. How awful for him." Sadie's voice softened in sympathy. "How long ago was this?"

Cora Beth finally turned to face her friend. "Nearly ten years now."

"Ten years?" Sadie stared at her incredulously. "You made it sound as if it were more recent. Ten years is a very long time to grieve. It's past time he moved on with his life."

Cora Beth winced at her friend's cavalier tone. "A body doesn't ever stop truly grieving for a loved one. I lost my Phillip five years ago and I still miss him."

"Oh, Cora Beth, I'm sorry." Sadie rose and gave her a tight hug. "Of course you miss your husband," she said as she stepped back. "But that doesn't mean you'd never marry again, does it? I mean, if the right man came along?"

Cora Beth thought about that for a moment. Would

she? She'd loved Phillip dearly but he was gone now. And she'd really *liked* being married, having a help-meet at her side, someone to share her joys and burdens, someone to be a father to her daughters, someone to cherish and be cherished by in return. "If someone came along whom I loved and who loved me, then yes, I would marry again."

Sadie gave a satisfied nod as she took her seat again. "Quite right. And the same is likely true for Mitch. He may just need a push from the right woman to help him realize he should take a chance on love again."

Cora Beth wasn't so sure of that. A few years ago it had looked like Harriet Elkenberry would finally get him to take that walk down the aisle, but in the end she'd given up and gotten hitched to Roger Baker, with Mitch standing in as best man.

For all his popularity and friendliness, Mitch seemed quite happy with his bachelor status. Which, after all, was his business and no one else's.

Cora Beth glanced up to find Sadie studying her with a look that made her feel as if her friend could read her thoughts. But she was rescued from further unwanted discussion when the hall door swung open.

"Cora Beth, I—" Beulah Plunkett halted when she saw Cora Beth wasn't alone. "Oh, hello, Sadie." She turned back to Cora Beth. "Sorry for the interruption, I didn't know you had company."

Mrs. Plunkett, one of Cora Beth's three long-term boarders, was a tall, imposing woman with a hawk-like nose and a steel-gray bun that perfectly matched her no-nonsense personality and commanding voice. The starchy widow had rented rooms for herself and her daughter Honoria at the boardinghouse for over a dozen years. Cora Beth had learned a long time ago that beneath her severe, outspoken exterior, the woman had a heart of gold. She'd also suspected for a while now that Beulah Plunkett had a soft spot for Uncle Grover.

"You're not interrupting," she said waving the woman into the room. "Sadie and I were just indulging in a bit of idle chatter. Was there something you needed?"

"Mr. Collins told me about your little accident this morning."

Cora Beth hid a smile. Mrs. Plunkett was the only person in town who called Uncle Grover by his more formal appellation.

"It's unfortunate that you allowed yourself to lose focus on your task that way," she continued reprovingly. "But no doubt it was due to the distraction caused by your unexpected early morning visitors." She clasped her hands in front of her, which in no way detracted from her severe shoulders-back posture. "Since the Ladies' Auxiliary will be meeting here this afternoon, I thought I'd offer my services to help in getting everything ready." She cast a look Sadie's way. "However, I see that someone else was before me, so I will leave you ladies to your work."

Mrs. Plunkett, normally a stickler for protocol, rarely set foot in the boardinghouse kitchen and normally seemed more apt to give orders than take them so Cora Beth was truly touched by the offer of assistance. She also sensed that Mrs. Plunkett was disappointed to not be needed.

"Oh, please don't go," she said impulsively.

Sadie exchanged a meaningful look with Cora Beth and set down her polishing rag. "Actually, if you don't mind taking my place here, I really should get back home."

Mrs. Plunkett moved toward the table. "Well, if you're certain you're not leaving on my account."

"Not at all." Sadie stood. "I promised Eli I would attend to the household accounts before he came home from the bank this afternoon."

Sadie gave Cora Beth a quick hug, then moved to the door. "Keep an eye on her, Mrs. Plunkett," she called back over her shoulder. "She shouldn't be doing too much with that hand." Then, with a final wave, Sadie was out the door.

When Cora Beth turned back to the table, Mrs. Plunkett was already busy polishing the creamer. Was she really just here to lend a hand, or was there something else on her mind? At any rate it looked like it was going to be up to her to initiate the conversation. "How is Honoria liking her new job?"

This past summer the townsfolk had decided Knotty Pine had outgrown its schoolhouse and had built an additional room onto the building. Which meant Mr. Saddler, the schoolteacher and another of Cora Beth's longtime boarders, needed some help. To everyone's surprise Honoria Plunkett, Beulah's daughter, had applied for the job. So, when the children of Knotty Pine had started back to school this fall, Mr. Saddler had taken the older children and Honoria had taken the younger group.

"She seems to be enjoying it very much," Mrs. Plunkett replied. "It has given her a reason to get out of the house and spend time with other folks besides her old mother. Between her hours at the schoolhouse and her time at home working on papers and planning lessons I barely see her at all anymore."

Ah, she was lonely. Cora Beth's heart went out to her. "Well, she appears to be doing a good job. My girls certainly enjoy having her for a teacher." Danny was in Mr. Saddler's class so he didn't share classroom time with the girls now. Ethan would be in there with him if he stayed here in Knotty Pine.

"I would expect nothing less of her."

Cora Beth hid a smile at that. "Yes, of course."

Mrs. Plunkett rubbed the creamer with increased vigor. "I was wondering, is Mr. Collins really your uncle?"

Interesting change of subject. "My late husband's uncle, actually."

"And he's been living with you for some time now?"

"Uncle Grover came to live with us when Audrey was still a baby, so I guess it's been nearly six years now. Before that, he lived up in Indiana." Where was all of this going?

"He's a widower, is he not?"

"Yes, though I never met his wife. She died before Phillip and I ever married. Unfortunately they were not blessed with children."

"But he has you and your girls."

Cora Beth smiled. "And we have him."

"I suppose you are wondering why I am prying into your family's personal life."

"I don't mind." Then she grinned. "But you're right, I did wonder."

Mrs. Plunkett allowed herself a smile, though her expression quickly returned to its normal schoolmarm severity. "I've reached a decision and I thought it only proper that I inform you of it."

"Oh?"

"I have decided to court Mr. Collins."

The outrageous declaration caught Cora Beth off

guard. For the life of her she couldn't form a proper response.

Fortunately, Mrs. Plunkett didn't wait for one. "I realize that it is unorthodox," she continued. "But I have tried to let the gentleman know of my interest without being too forward, and he appears to remain oblivious. Since I am no longer in my prime, I have decided not to waste what years are left to me by being coy."

Cora Beth had trouble keeping her expression appropriately sober as she tried to picture Mrs. Plunkett being "coy."

"So, do I have your blessing?"

"Of course you do." Fascinated by this side of her normally staid boarder, Cora Beth joined her at the table. "May I ask how you intend to go about this courtship?"

"I intend to insert myself into his life at every given opportunity." She pursed her lips primly. "I am, however, open to suggestions."

"You know about his fascination with insects." Uncle Grover fancied himself an entomologist and had an extensive collection of specimens he had gathered himself.

"Yes, of course. One can't be around your uncle for any length of time and not be aware of his unusual hobby." She drew back her shoulders. "I'm afraid it quite put me off when I first met him. But I confess, if one pays proper attention to his discourse on the subject, his passion and knowledge of the subject make it all rather intriguing."

"Then how do you feel about hiking?"

"Hiking? I'm not at all certain that it is a suitable pastime for a genteel lady."

"That's unfortunate. Uncle Grover likes to explore

the fields and wooded areas around here for new specimens. I'm sure it would make his treks more enjoyable
if he had company."

"I see. And come to think of it, I do recall Dr. Whitman saying that vigorous walking is good for one's con-
stitution. Perhaps I will rethink my stand on hiking."

"And if I might make another suggestion?"

"Please do."

"Everyone likes to feel useful, to feel needed. Perhaps if there was some project of your own that you
could ask for his assistance with. Something of a long-
term nature perhaps."

Mrs. Plunkett gave her a measured look. "A very sensible suggestion. I will have to think on that."

"Well then." Cora Beth stood. "I believe you've polished that creamer well enough. Thank you for your
help."

"Thank you, my dear. We may need to have little
chats like this more often."

"You're welcome in my kitchen any time."

Cora Beth smiled as the door closed behind Mrs.
Plunkett. The woman had surprised her, but in a happy
way. This little campaign of Mrs. Plunkett's, regardless
of how it all worked out, would be good for both Mrs.
Plunkett and Uncle Grover. One could never have too
much romance in life.

Even when it ended in tragedy, the way hers had. And
the way Mitch's had.

Was she ready for another go at it herself? She'd told
Sadie that perhaps, if the right man came along, she'd
consider marrying again.

The thing of it was, when she thought about that
"right man," one very specific image came to mind.

Dear Father, I know You already gave me one

wonderful man to love and partner with in this life, but he was taken away from me so soon. I know You have Your reasons, and that those reasons are always perfect, but I sure would like a second chance at marriage, at finding a loving husband, a helpmate to share my joys and burdens with. I have a certain someone in mind, but I'm willing to follow Your will in this.

She thought a minute and then decided to add a postscript to her prayer. *If not a husband, then maybe just a little something to add a bit of excitement or a touch of the unexpected to my life.*

A smile teased at her lips. Wouldn't folks be surprised if they knew that no-nonsense, matter-of-fact Cora Beth Collins longed for excitement and romance in her life?

The question was, though, was she brave enough to help make it happen?

Chapter Four

Cora Beth placed the last of the tea cakes on the cart and nodded to Mrs. Plunkett. "That's everything."

The older woman raised a brow. "I should think so. You have enough here to feed half of Knotty Pine."

The business portion of the regular Wednesday afternoon meeting of the Knotty Pine Ladies' Auxiliary had adjourned and the group had moved into the visiting portion. Mrs. Plunkett had followed Cora Beth into the kitchen, insisting on helping her with the hostessing duties.

Now Cora Beth nodded absently in response to her comment. "I accidently doubled the recipe for the lemon bars and since some of the ladies don't like pecans, I made one batch of shortbread cookies with nuts and one without."

Truth was she'd been so distracted all day that it was downright surprising she had anything edible to serve at all. How was Mitch's search going? She'd hoped he'd ride back into town at lunchtime, but if he had, she'd missed him. Not that he was obliged to check in with her, of course. But surely he knew how anxious she was to hear whatever he'd discovered.

Was he still out there because he'd found some sign of Ethan that he was following? Ethan seemed a clever boy, but if anyone could track him down it would be Mitch. Hopefully the boy hadn't had time to get into any further mischief. Goodness knows the next person he ran into might decide to press charges, or worse.

Perhaps Mitch had already found the camp and maybe met Ethan's father. Or not. It was just so frustrating not knowing.

Heavenly Father, I know I've been calling on You a lot today, but please guide Mitch in his search, and please, please, watch over Ethan. Beneath that bravado, I can tell he's a scared little boy trying to make his way. He's taken a wrong path, somehow, and I'm afraid he might be in serious trouble. But You know all of that better than me. Just please let him realize he's not alone and help him to feel the comfort of Your presence. Amen.

Feeling a bit calmer, Cora Beth focused back on Mrs. Plunkett to find the woman studying her with an expectant look. Uh-oh, caught daydreaming again. "I'm sorry, did you say something?"

"I just asked you to open the door while I push the cart." She gave Cora Beth a probing look. "Is there something on your mind?"

Cora Beth nodded. "I just offered up a prayer for a friend in need."

Mrs. Plunkett nodded as if that settled matters. "Then you're helping your friend in the best way you can right now."

"I know. But I've never been very good at waiting."

"Patience is a virtue, my dear. You must learn to wait on the Good Lord's timing."

"Yes, ma'am." Feeling properly chastised, Cora Beth

meekly followed her boarder down the hall and into the parlor.

Once Mrs. Plunkett had pushed the cart into the room, Cora Beth touched her arm. "Would you mind presiding over the teapot today?" She lifted her bandaged left hand. "I wouldn't want to risk making a mess of things."

"Of course, my dear, I would be honored."

Seeing the sparkle in the older woman's eye, Cora Beth was pleased she'd made the offer. She hadn't realized before how Mrs. Plunkett, without a home of her own as such, might have felt about not being able to play the role of hostess in these weekly gatherings. She'd have to see if she could find a way to work something out with her for future gatherings that wouldn't hurt her pride.

Then Cora Beth's smile wavered as she saw Nelda Oglesby approaching with a determined look on her face.

"I hear Sheriff Hammond caught a thief raiding your vegetable garden this morning." Nelda seemed to hold Cora Beth responsible for the presence of a thief in their midst.

Cora Beth pasted the smile back on her face and strove for a mild tone. "Actually, it was a misunderstanding. The boy he found was just doing some work for me."

Nelda didn't seem reassured. "Is that so? Then why is the sheriff searching high and low for that vagrant even as we speak?"

Alice Danvers and Ida Van Halsen, two of Nelda's closest friends, drifted over. Cora Beth tried not to feel ganged up on. "Because we're concerned the boy might be out on his own and need some help," she answered.

"On his own? Ah, a runaway is he?" Nelda gave a ladylike sniff. "Running from some kind of trouble of his own making no doubt. This probably isn't the first bit of hooliganism he's been up to. I hear several ladies here have experienced thefts this past week."

Other conversations had tapered off by this time and most of the ladies in the room were openly listening to the discussion about Ethan now. At that last comment, Patsy Johnson stepped forward to join them. "That's right. A couple of items from my laundry went missing on Monday."

Cora Beth raised a hand before anyone else could list their grievance. "But that doesn't mean Ethan is responsible. And besides, he's just a boy."

The mayor's wife drew herself up with a huff. "That's easy enough for you to say. After all, that little hooligan only took a few vegetables from you." Her voice took on a tone of genteel outrage. "But he stole my prize orchid. And he made a mess of my greenhouse in the process."

Ida tsked, patting Nelda's arm sympathetically. "After all the work you put into that beautiful plant. It must be such a heartache for you."

"I tell you, I could hardly take it in." Nelda had her hand over her heart. "I stepped into my greenhouse and I near swooned right there on the threshold. As I told Sheriff Hammond, anyone who would do such a terrible thing had to be a blackhearted scoundrel."

Cora Beth tried to reason with them once more. "But you can't be certain it was Ethan."

"That's right," Sadie added. "Perhaps some animal got inside and made that mess."

Nelda looked down her nose. "Only an animal of the two-legged variety would carry off a whole plant, pot an all. And, if not this Ethan, then who else could it be? Surely you don't think it was someone here in town."

Mrs. Plunkett handed a cup of tea to Sadie. "I hear you told Sheriff Hammond you thought it was the Colfax boy."

Ruby Colfax, Andy Colfax's mother, stiffened and Nelda had the grace to look embarrassed. "I was distraught. I didn't know what I was saying."

Ida patted her arm. "Of course you were. Anyone would be."

Sadie moved to stand beside Cora Beth. "I think we should leave this to Sheriff Hammond. I'm certain he'll get to the bottom of the matter and handle it in a way that is fair to all parties."

"He'd better. After all, we pay the man to handle crimes of this sort."

Was that intended as a slight to Mitch? "What we pay Sheriff Hammond to do is uphold the law," Cora Beth said firmly, "but as I'm sure anyone in this room can attest, he does so much more than that for this town." She gave Nelda a smile she hoped appeared reassuring. "And I have every confidence he'll get to the truth of the matter. Whatever that may be."

Determined to end this line of conversation, she turned and waved a hand toward the tea cart. "Now, please, everyone have some refreshments. I tried a new recipe for the shortbread cookies and I'd love to hear what you all think."

As the ladies complied, conversations turned to other topics and Cora Beth offered up another prayer—this time for courage for Ethan. Looks like he'd have some unpleasant music to face if Mitch succeeded in finding him.

And she was determined to see he didn't face it alone.

Mitch paused a moment as he stepped onto the back porch of the boardinghouse. Maybe he should have taken time to clean up a bit before stopping by. It had been a long, hot day and he had more than a little trail dust clinging to him. But he knew Cora Beth would be eager to hear any news he could bring her.

Then Cora Beth spied him through the screen door and took the decision out of his hands.

"Oh, Sheriff." Was her welcoming smile for him or for the report she was hoping for? "Don't just stand there, come in and tell me if you found out anything about Ethan."

Well that answered that. Removing his hat, Mitch opened the screen door but didn't enter. "I can talk from here. I don't want to track my dirt into your kitchen."

"Nonsense, that's what brooms are for. And you look like you could use a tall glass of lemonade. Get in here and let me pour some up for you."

Mitch stepped into the kitchen and hung his hat. "That sounds good." He moved closer. "How's the hand?"

"Barely remember I burned it." She reached inside the cupboard for a glass. "Well, don't keep me guessing. Did you find any sign of Ethan or his camp?"

He grabbed the pitcher before she could lift it. The woman sure didn't seem to be letting that burn slow her down any. "I spent most of the afternoon searching the likely places south of town and there wasn't hide nor hair of him to be found. I'm beginning to think he wasn't being exactly truthful when he told us where he'd pitched camp." Not that that surprised him, but he knew Cora Beth had a lot of faith in the kid. Sure enough, she immediately rose to his defense.

"And who could blame him. He's just a boy. The poor thing was probably afraid you'd haul him in and put him in jail if you found him."

Her accusing tone stung. "Now, Cora Beth, you know good and well I—"

"Oh, I didn't say you'd do it." She handed him a glass, her expression softening. "But *he* doesn't know that. You can be mighty intimidating when you put your mind to it."

Did she disapprove? "The boy's been stealing things." He managed to keep the defensiveness from his tone. "Someone has to take him in hand before he gets into some real trouble."

She let out a soft sigh. "Sorry if I sounded critical— I know you're doing what you think is best for Ethan. And given time, he'll see that for himself."

"Like as not we'll never know. Chances are he's moved on."

He could see she didn't like that idea at all. "Surely he couldn't have gone far." She sat at the table and waved him to a seat across from her. "I'm worried about him. I keep wondering, what if Danny had found himself in that situation? I'd want someone with a good heart looking out for him."

He'd figured she'd make that comparison sooner or later. But Ethan wasn't Danny and she could get hurt if she started thinking that way. "I know you like to think the best of everyone, but you can't really be sure what kind of kid Ethan is. If you aren't careful, you're likely to get disappointed, or worse. Some things just aren't worth taking that risk over."

Her expressions softened. "Oh, Mitch, people are always worth taking those kinds of risks over."

There was no reasoning with her when she was like this. "Remember your promise to let me know if he comes back."

She met his gaze, worry etching a vertical line above her nose. "You wouldn't *really* put him in jail, would you?"

"Not unless I had no other choice. But, assuming I do find the boy, *something* will have to be done with him. As you admitted yourself, he's got no business living on his own."

"So you don't believe he's traveling with his dad?"

"It's possible." Just not very likely. "But if his pa is with him, why'd he let the kid roam lose at all hours of the night and day?"

"Maybe the man is ill or injured."

Or something a bit less innocent. No need to worry Cora Beth with that possibility though. "The sooner I find where he's holed up, the sooner we can get our questions answered."

He pondered a moment over whether or not to give her the other bit of news, then decided she needed to hear it. "I sent a telegram to the orphanage up at Casonville this morning and they've already responded. There's room for him there if that's what's needed."

"No."

He didn't like the decisiveness of her tone or the stubborn set to her jaw. "It's a well-run facility," he said, keeping his tone neutral. "From what I hear, they take real good care of the kids."

"Maybe so. But that's not the same as being part of a real family."

"Not everyone gets to be part of a real family." He should know. "Danny was lucky he had your folks to take him in. And Uncle Grover was lucky he had *you* to take him in. The orphanage is there to take care of those who aren't so lucky." He held up a hand to stop her response. "At any rate, I just contacted the orphanage as a precaution. He might not be an orphan at all."

"Which would mean he's a runaway."

Not necessarily. But again, there were some things he'd prefer not to point out to her.

She didn't seem to notice his lack of response. "What if he had a real good reason to run away? I mean, there's some folks who aren't fit to be parents. And there are worse dangers than the physical ones."

He noticed she'd cradled her burnt hand against her chest. Was she even aware she'd done it? "The law is clear that a minor belongs with his parents or guardian."

"Well, I think there should be some flexibility in the law where kids are concerned."

"Not if he isn't in mortal danger." He rubbed the back of his neck, uncomfortable with this line of talk. "Regardless of my personal feelings, I've sworn to uphold the law, and that's what I'm bound to do." No matter what it cost him personally.

"Of course. I'd never ask you to do otherwise."

He could tell she hadn't made peace with this. "Look, there's no sense in borrowing trouble. We don't even know that he *is* a runaway. I may stumble on him tomorrow, camped with his pa, just like he said. Or I may never see him again, which makes this whole conversation pointless."

Some of the tension seeped from her expression. "You're probably right. But just so you know, before I let you put Ethan in an orphanage, I'll adopt him myself."

Cora Beth was normally a levelheaded woman. But when her much-too-soft heart was involved, common sense seemed to fly out the window. "You haven't been in that boy's company for more than thirty minutes and you don't know anything about him. What makes you think he's someone you'd want to take responsibility for, much less have sharing a house with your daughters?"

"Because I'm convinced he's a good kid who just needs someone to give him a chance, someone to believe in him." She took a deep breath. "But you're right, we need to stop going round and round this way. After all, it's in God's hands and we need to have faith that He will work it out for the best, whatever that is." She gave him a soft smile. "Would you pray with me for Ethan's well-being?"

"Of course." He watched her slide her hand across the table and after only a heartbeat, he took it in his own. Bowing his head, Mitch forced himself to focus on his prayer. "Almighty God, we ask that You keep a close watch on Ethan, that You keep him safe and lead him to those who can help him. And if that someone is not one of us, that You also give Mrs. Collins peace in the knowledge that You, who look after even the smallest of sparrows, will be watching over him. Amen."

Cora Beth echoed his amen, and he had a few moments to study her bowed head before she looked up to meet his gaze.

"Thank you." Both her words and smile were soft and intimate. It was almost as if she saw something special in him, something—

Abruptly he released her hand and pushed back his chair. "Thank you for the lemonade, but I'll be on my way." He stood, rubbing the back of his neck again. "I need to tend to some paperwork before I make my nightly rounds."

He saw the puzzled surprise in her expression but was grateful that she left her question unvoiced.

"Thanks for stopping in to tell me what you found," she said instead. "And for praying with me."

With a nod he crossed the room in a few quick strides, retrieved his hat and made his exit. Once outside he paused and took in a few deep breaths.

Man, he had it bad. For a minute in there, when she'd given him that warm smile, he'd thought that there wasn't much he wouldn't do to earn another one like it from her.

Heavenly Father, I know these feelings I'm having about Cora Beth are inappropriate. We both know I'm not a till-death-do-us-part kind of man, no matter how much I wish I were. And a lady like Cora Beth deserves someone whose love for her will stand the test of time, someone who won't hurt her like my granddaddy did my grandmother. Or like what I almost did to Dinah before You took her. So please, help me to hold my distance and to not do anything to cause her distress.

He hadn't asked God for something for himself in a long time. The last time he'd done so, the result had been a disaster. Would God help him this time?

Trouble was, keeping his distance from Cora Beth was the last thing he wanted to do. Either way, he couldn't win.

Cora Beth watched as Mitch made his hasty exit. She hoped her earlier words hadn't upset him—she hadn't meant to be critical. Sometimes she needed to stop and think before speaking. Knotty Pine was blessed to have such a conscientious man as Mitch for their sheriff and next time she saw him, she'd make a point to tell him so.

She moved to the sink, where she could look out the window and watch him walk away. His stride was purposeful, confident and had just a touch of a masculine swagger. He looked solid. And dependable.

And alone.

Alone? Now where on earth had that thought come from? Mitch had lots of friends—of both the male and female persuasion. He was well respected and well liked by most everyone in Knotty Pine. He was welcomed everywhere and his standing as a bachelor was obviously through choice rather than lack of opportunity.

Yet ever since she'd had that conversation with Sadie this morning, she couldn't shake the thought that there was another layer to his long-term bachelor status. And now that the idea had insinuated itself into her thoughts, it was hard to shake it. He lived alone, had done so since his grandmother had passed on nine years ago. She herself couldn't imagine what it would be like not to be surrounded by family.

As if to punctuate that thought, the door burst open behind her and her three daughters shot into the room, clamoring for her attention. She smiled as she patiently listened to their excited chatter. What with these three, Danny and Uncle Grover, she was truly blessed to have such a warm and lively family. But there was always room for more.

Perhaps she would make a point to invite Mitch over to join them for supper occasionally.

After all, it was the neighborly thing to do.

* * *

Early the next morning, Cora Beth quickly descended the stairs, tying an apron around her waist as she went. She was up earlier than normal hoping that, despite what Mitch believed, Ethan would return. In fact, she'd throw a few extra eggs in the skillet, just in case.

Humming, she stepped into the kitchen, lit the lamp and headed for the stove. As soon as she stoked the fire she'd check the garden to see if—

A sudden urgent banging on the back door jerked her head around. "Coming." When she opened the door it was Ethan himself standing there, looking scared and more than a little worried.

She quickly pushed open the screen door. "What is it? Is something wrong?"

"It's Cissy, my little sister," he blurted out. "She's real bad sick and I don't know how to help her."

Oh mercy, he had a sister out there somewhere. "Where is she? Is she alone?"

"Scout is with her. He's a real good guard dog, but she needs someone who can do some healing. I wanted to bring her here, but she was too sick to walk and I knew I couldn't carry her this far."

The anguish in his face tore at her heart.

"I promised I wouldn't be gone long," he continued, "and that I'd bring someone who could help her get better. Please, ma'am, you got to come with me."

Cora Beth's mind was racing. The fact that he'd taken the chance to come to her for help was enough to convince her this was serious. And he hadn't mentioned anything about his dad—did that mean the children had no adult to help them? "Come on in and tell me what's wrong with her while I get a few things together."

"You don't understand. She's mighty sick. We gotta hurry—"

"I know, Ethan, and I promise I'll go as quickly as I can. But I need to gather a few things before I run off. And I want to get my brother to hitch up the buggy so we can reach her quicker and have a way to get her back to town if we need to." She laid a hand lightly on his shoulder. "Don't worry, Ethan, we're going to take care of your sister."

"Please hurry."

"I will." She needed something to distract him from his worry. "Do you know how to empty the ash box and stoke a stove properly?"

His brow drew down in a puzzled frown. "Yes, ma'am."

"Well, I'd appreciate it if you'd take care of that little chore for me while I go wake my brother. The kindling is here and the firewood is right out there on the porch."

With a nod, he moved to the stove.

She noted the heaviness in his slumped shoulders and her heart went out to the boy. At his age he should be going to school and playing with friends, not acting as sole provider for himself and a sibling. How ill was his sister? And how old was she? Please God, let it be one of those childhood ailments that seem more serious than they really are.

Cora Beth sent up a prayer for both children as she rushed up the stairs. She rapped on Danny's door, then stuck her head inside before he had a chance to respond. "Get dressed," she told her still-groggy brother. "I need you to take care of something for me."

"Now?"

"Right now."

Something in her tone must have caught his attention because Danny was suddenly alert and scrambling from his bed.

She rushed down the hall and tapped on another door. This time she waited for a response before she opened it. "Uncle Grover, something's come up and I could use your help downstairs right away."

As soon as she was satisfied he understood, she fetched a large carpetbag from her room and headed back to the kitchen, aware that every minute counted.

By the time she reentered the room, Ethan had the stove nicely stoked and ready for her—not that she'd be doing any cooking this morning. The boy looked as if he were standing on a hot griddle himself. The worry over his sister was stamped on his whole being.

"Thank you. Now, tell me what's wrong with your sister while I gather up some supplies."

"She was complaining about her stomach hurting when she went to bed last night. Then she woke up about an hour ago and her head was burning up and she was crying." The boy's concern for his sister was palpable. "Can we go *now?*"

"In just a few minutes. How old is your sister?"

"Seven."

So young—Audrey's age.

Danny came in still buttoning his shirt. "What's going—" His worried frown turned to man-of-the-house alertness when he spotted Ethan.

Before Cora Beth could say anything, Uncle Grover joined them, his sparse gray hair still spiky from sleep.

"Who's he?" Danny asked.

"This is Ethan." Cora Beth turned to their guest.

"And Ethan, this is my brother Danny and the gentleman behind him is my Uncle Grover."

Ethan nodded to the new arrivals but didn't say anything.

"Fellows, Ethan needs our help. He and his sister are camping outside of town. His sister took sick last night and he's worried about her. She's the same age as Audrey and she's out there right now with only a dog for company."

She saw them both come to attention at that. "Danny, I need you to hitch up the horse and buggy as quick as you can and bring them here. Uncle Grover, would you please head over to Doc Whitman's and let him know his services may be needed shortly? Then go over to Sadie's and ask if she can spare Mrs. Dauber to come fix breakfast for the boarders this morning."

Danny nodded, gave Ethan one last measuring look, then headed for the front door.

"Don't you worry about anything here," Uncle Grover said. "You just see to that little girl. As soon as I take care of your errands I'll get the girls up and make certain they get to school on time."

"Thank you." Cora Beth patted the older gentleman's arm. "I knew I could count on you." Then she had a quick thought. "Mrs. Plunkett was very helpful to me yesterday. I'm sure she'd be willing to help you get things organized this morning, as well."

Uncle Grover looked a little surprised at her suggestion, but nodded. As he passed by Ethan, he gave the boy a reassuring smile. "Don't you worry, son. You're in good hands with Cora Beth. She's got three daughters of her own and knows all about tending to their hurts."

Bless him, Uncle Grover was a dear sweet man, even if he could be forgetful at times. She'd never once regretted taking him in, even after her husband died and she was worried about how she was going to make it.

She turned back to Ethan. "While we're waiting for the buggy, I'm going to gather up a few things I might need to make your sister—Cissy, was it?—more comfortable until the doctor can get a look at her. I'm sorry I haven't had a chance to start cooking breakfast this morning but there's some pie left over from last night's supper there on the counter. Feel free to serve yourself up a piece. And in the meantime, tell me just where this camp of yours is." Anything to keep his mind focused on something other than his worry.

While Ethan talked and ate, Cora Beth grabbed whatever herbs and powders she figured might be needed. She also gathered up a blanket, some clean strips of cloth and a flask of water, and stuffed them all into her carpetbag. Just as she finished, she heard the whinny of a horse.

Goodness, that was mighty quick, even for Danny. But she wasn't one to question the blessings sent her way. "Sounds like the buggy's here. Ready?"

Ethan didn't have to be told twice. He was up from the table and holding the kitchen door open for her before she'd finished her sentence. He reached the door ahead of her and threw it open.

Then he halted on the threshold.

As soon as she looked past his shoulder she saw why. There was no sign of the buggy, just a lone figure astride a horse, silhouetted in the shadowy predawn light.

She'd know that form anywhere. Mitch Hammond. And he didn't look happy.

Chapter Five

Mitch touched the brim of his hat, feeling a tad irritated at the guilty, caught-in-the-act expressions worn by the pair standing on the porch. Did they think he was here to confront Ethan when there was a little girl at risk? "Morning, Cora Beth, Ethan."

Cora Beth recovered quickly and placed a hand firmly in the boy's back, propelling him forward with her. "Good morning, Sheriff. What a welcome surprise."

He could almost believe she meant it. "I ran into your Uncle Grover on his way to Doc Whitman's place and he told me what was going on." Mitch dismounted and met the two of them at the steps. "Thought I'd see if I could lend a hand."

"As a mater of fact, you can." Cora Beth turned from him to Ethan, moving her hand to the boy's shoulder. "This is an answered prayer, Ethan. If you got up on that horse with Sheriff Hammond, the two of you could ride on ahead and be there to check on your sister in no time flat."

Mitch was as startled by her suggestion as Ethan seemed to be. It wasn't that he didn't want to help, but he'd figured that helping meant escorting the two of them to the kids' camp, maybe driving the buggy and doing whatever heavy lifting might be required. He certainly didn't know anything about dealing with sick kids on his own. Surely a few extra minutes…

Ethan shot him a wary glance. "Maybe we should just wait on the buggy."

"The boy's right. I'll go help Danny—"

"Nonsense." The look Cora Beth gave him was schoolmarm stern. "There's a sick little girl out there who needs tending to, and even if Danny got the buggy here in the next minute or two, your horse can go cross-country and that's a lot faster."

That brought him up short. She was right of course. Whether he was good with kids or not wasn't the issue. Making sure that little girl got help of some sort as soon as possible *was*.

Cora Beth turned to Ethan. "And you need to go with him so your sister knows he's there to help and doesn't get frightened. I'll follow along in the buggy as soon as I can so we can bring her back to town more comfortably, but I think we'll all rest easier knowing someone is with her."

Mitch was already turning back to his horse. "If Ethan goes with me, how will you know the way?"

"He told me where it was earlier." She set the carpetbag down. "If I understood his directions, they're camping in the woods just past the Caster place, near Little Pine Creek. The sun'll be up in a few minutes so that won't be a problem. I can take the old creek trail to get there but I'm not sure how close to the camp itself I can get."

"You won't be able to see it from the trail." Ethan

made it sound like that was a good thing. "I wanted to make sure no one would spot us."

Mitch nodded to himself as he mounted up. Definitely runaways.

Cora Beth gave the boy a reassuring smile. "Don't worry. Either I'll find you or you'll find me. God is looking out for us." Then she made shooing motions with her hands. "Well? Don't just stand there, there's a sick little girl waiting on you."

Mitch stared down at the boy, trying to gauge what he was thinking. "You ever rode double before?"

"Not since—" The boy swallowed. "Not in a long time."

"Well, looks like you're about to get reacquainted with the practice." Mitch reached down. "Let's go see about that sister of yours."

Ethan hesitated then squared his shoulders and took Mitch's hand. Once he was settled in the saddle behind Mitch, the boy cleared his throat. "There's something you ought to know about Cissy. She has a limp."

Cora Beth's brow drew down in concern. "She hurt her leg, too?"

"No." He shifted in his seat. "I mean, yes. Only it was years ago, back when she was just a baby. She can walk, and doesn't want folks babying her or anything, but her left leg doesn't work so good." His tone took on a defiant edge. "But that don't mean she ain't every bit as good as anyone else."

"Of course it doesn't." Cora Beth gave the boy that reassuring smile that could make a dying man feel he was going to be okay. "Now go on with Sheriff Hammond and see to your sister. I'll be there as quick as I can."

Mitch gathered the reins and looked down at Cora

Beth. "You sure you'll be okay handling the buggy on your own?"

She put both fists on her hips. "Mitchell Fredrick Hammond, my dad owned a livery stable, remember? I learned how to handle a buggy before I started school. Now stop all this shilly-shallying around and go on with you."

Interesting how her face lit up when she was riled. "Yes, ma'am," he said with a tip of his hat. Then he turned the horse and headed east toward Little Pine Creek, setting a quick pace. The priority right now was getting to that little girl and making sure she was okay.

They rode in silence for a while, with Ethan sitting very stiffly in the saddle. The sky was brightening by the minute—soon it would be full daylight. Mitch let his passenger adjust to his perch and the horse's loping stride before he finally spoke. "I take it your pa isn't at that camp."

There was a long moment of silence. "No."

"Want to tell me what you and your sister are doing out in those woods without your parents?"

There was no hesitation this time. "No."

The boy's honest response drew a grudging smile from Mitch. But he was careful not to let it color his tone. "Tell me anyway." He didn't expect to get a lot of information, but this talk would give them both something to think about other than what might be happening with his sister right now.

"Our folks are dead."

The stark, matter-of-fact statement touched Mitch in a way a more self-pitying one would not have. "You got any other relatives?"

"None that want us."

This time Mitch winced. If that was true, it was no wonder the kid had such a big chip on his shoulder. It appeared that telegram to the orphanage hadn't been a wasted effort after all. How serious had Cora Beth been about taking Ethan in? Whatever her intentions, he knew the addition of a younger sister would strengthen rather than weaken her resolve.

"So, I guess this means you've been leaving your sister alone while you go out scavenging for supplies."

"Scout was with her." His tone was defensive. "And I made sure to only be gone a few hours each day."

"Who's Scout?"

"Our dog. He wouldn't let anything happen to Cissy."

"I see."

Another long silence, this time broken by Ethan. "I didn't like taking them things, you know. My ma taught me that it's wrong to steal and I did try to leave something in exchange." He squirmed a bit and then continued. "But I gave Ma my word before she died that I would watch over Cissy, no matter what. There weren't no other way I could see to do it."

The kid seemed to have his own brand of honor. "You could have just asked. There's lots of folks around here who would have been glad to help out."

"And there's folks who'd just as soon spit on you as look at you. I wasn't taking no chances after—" He halted, biting off the rest of what he'd been about to say.

The cynical, bitter words drew Mitch up short. What in the world had these kids been through and how long had it been going on? "After what?"

"Nothing." The words were mumbled, grudging. "We just wanted to be left alone, that's all."

There was definitely something the kid wasn't telling him. "So where exactly did y'all come from?"

Ethan hesitated for a moment, as if weighing the risks of revealing too much. "Back when both my folks were alive we lived near Howerton."

Howerton? That was almost fifty miles away. "How in the world did you two kids travel such a far piece on your own and end up in the woods outside of Knotty Pine?"

He felt the boy's shrug. "Same as anybody else, I reckon. Little bit of riding, little bit of walking."

There had to be more to it than that, but it was obvious he wasn't going to get much in the way of details. Not right now anyway.

"Can't we go any faster?"

"Homer's a good horse but he's carrying two of us." Mitch shared Ethan's sense of urgency, however, and nudged the horse to a slightly faster pace. "Where were you and your sister headed to?" Best to keep the boy talking.

"No place in particular. Anywhere I can take care of me and Cissy without folks trying to poke their noses into our business."

Another conversational dead end. Why was Ethan so set on he and his sister going it alone? What wasn't he saying?

This time Mitch let the silence draw out until they reached Little Pine Creek. "Where do we go from here?"

The boy pointed to the right. "Follow the creek for a little ways. I'll tell you when to head into the woods."

Mitch obediently turned the horse.

They'd only traveled a few minutes when Ethan

motioned ahead to the left. "There's a pig trail just up there—hard to spot unless you're really looking for it."

"I see it." Though calling the barely visible gap in the trees a pig trail was giving it more credit than it deserved. It was going to be a tight squeeze getting the horse through the undergrowth. He led the animal up to the mouth of the trail then stopped. "How far is it to your camp?"

"Not far."

"Then I think we should walk from here." Leaving the horse here would also serve to let Cora Beth know where to wait if she arrived before they returned.

They quickly dismounted, and Mitch tethered the horse to a bush while Ethan watched impatiently. Mitch waved a hand toward the almost nonexistent trail. "Lead the way."

As if he were a hunting dog who'd slipped his leash, Ethan took off at a run.

Mitch matched his pace. *Please, Lord, let that little girl be okay.* He wished again that Cora Beth was here with them. Her quiet competence, compassion and maternal experience would serve the sick little girl much better than his inexperience with children.

"Cissy, I'm back!"

Almost before Ethan's words died out, the thicket opened up to a clearing the size of a large room. Mitch was relieved to hear a response to Ethan's hail—a good sign that things were not quite as dire as he'd feared.

Ethan's progress was momentarily hampered by the enthusiastic greetings of a gray and black spotted hound. Ethan gave the animal a perfunctory pat, with an absently uttered "Good boy, Scout" but his focus was obviously on the makeshift shelter the animal had been guarding.

The dog immediately gave way and turned a much less friendly eye toward Mitch.

Ethan disappeared inside the structure and Mitch could hear him speaking to his sister. As soon as he made a move to follow, however, the dog bared his teeth and let out a low, menacing growl.

Mitch halted. "Easy boy. I'm here to help."

Ethan stuck his head back out. "It's okay, Scout. Let him by."

The dog stopped growling but his suspicious gaze never wavered from Mitch.

"How's your sister?" Mitch asked as he approached, giving the animal a wide berth.

"She's really hot and still feeling sick."

The structure, built out of stout branches and a large sheet of canvas, looked like a cross between a tent and an open lean-to. Mitch had to bend almost double to get inside and it wasn't much better once he was in. Not only was the roof low, but there was barely room to contain the three of them. His eyes went immediately to the little girl lying on a blanket to one side. Even he could see she didn't look well. Her cheeks were flushed and she was drenched in sweat. As he watched, her shoulders fluttered in a shiver.

The little girl studied him with wide frightened eyes and her hand snaked out to grab her brother's.

Mitch tried to adopt a friendly tone. This would go easier if he could calm her fears before he tried to carry her out of here. "Well now, Ethan, you didn't tell me what a pretty little buttercup your sister is." He knelt down beside her. "Your name is Cissy, right?"

"It's really Cecilia," she said. Her voice sounded thready and her free hand plucked at her sheet. "But Cissy is easier."

"Well, Cissy, I'm Sheriff Hammond and I hear you're not feeling so good. Both your head and tummy hurt, do they?"

She nodded.

He rested his arm on his legs as he considered his next words. Cora Beth would know what to say. "You know, I've had my share of headaches and tummy aches and they're just not any fun at all," he said, feeling his way. Then he had an inspiration. He pulled a wax-paper-wrapped lemon drop out of his pocket. "I find when I'm feeling poorly one of these usually helps to make me feel a tiny bit better. Would you like to try one?"

Her eyes lit up at the sight of the treat. She shot a quick glance toward her brother, and at his nod she turned back to Mitch. "Yes, please. Lemon drops are my favorite but I haven't had one in a very long time."

"They're my favorite, too." He unwrapped the candy and handed it to her. "That's why I always have a few in my pocket."

He leaned back on his haunches again. "Did your brother tell you about the nice lady he met yesterday?"

"The one who gave him those biscuits and bacon for me?"

So that's why the boy had taken the extra. "That's the one. Well, she's headed this way with a buggy so we can take you where there's a doctor. You'll like her and Dr. Whitman. Between the two of them, they'll have you all fixed up in no time."

Her expression turned uncertain, and she glanced back at her brother. "But, Ethan, we aren't supposed to go to town where folks can see us."

"Why's that?" Maybe the girl would be more forthcoming than her brother.

"Because *he* might—"

"Don't worry, Cissy," Ethan interjected. "We just need to see about getting you better right now. And Mrs. Collins is a real nice lady. She'll see nothing happens to us."

Now who was this "he" Cissy was afraid of? And what did Ethan mean by Cora Beth seeing nothing happened to them? Was someone after them? Well, they'd have to come through him to get to them. But now was not the time to start interrogating the boy again.

"The thing is," he explained to Cissy, "Mrs. Collins's buggy can't come here to your camp. So, if it's okay with you, I'm going to carry you out as far as the trail. And," he added quickly, "at the same time, you can protect me from that ferocious guard dog you have out there."

That drew a little giggle from the girl. "Scout isn't ferocious."

Mitch pretended surprise. "He isn't? I don't know, he seemed pretty ferocious to me. I'd feel a whole lot safer if you agreed to keep an eye on him for me. So is it a deal? If I carry you to the buggy, will you make sure your dog doesn't try to find out what my ankle tastes like?"

She giggled again and nodded. "It's a deal."

"Thanks. Now I'm gonna pick you up, Buttercup, real easy like." He scooped her up, sheet and all, frowning over how hot she was. The child was burning up. He was surprised, too, by how light she was. Too light, too fragile. He could understand why Ethan had resorted to stealing to care for her.

With a great deal of effort he managed to make

his way out of the confined space without jostling her too much.

As soon as he straightened, Scout started growling, hackles raised, teeth bared. Ethan had been right about what an effective guard dog the animal was. Mitch gave Cissy an aggrieved look that was only partially feigned. "See what I mean?"

"It's okay, Scout," she coaxed. "Sheriff Hammond is a friend. He gave me a lemon drop." She said that as if it was the mark of his worth.

The animal stopped growling, but there was no doubt he was keeping an eye on Mitch.

Mitch turned to Ethan. "You need to gather up anything here you want because you might not be back for some time." Actually there was no *might* about it—he planned to make sure these two kids didn't live like this anymore. But no need to add to the boy's worries any more than necessary right now.

He saw the mutinous look on Ethan's face, then saw him glance at his sister. The boy's shoulders sagged and with a nod, he ducked back inside the structure.

Mitch used the time to study the small campsite. It was surprisingly well tended.

Someone had put quite a bit of effort into fixing the place up. Much of the area nearby had been cleared of the thickest of the brush. A small area off to one side of the lean-to, a safe distance away, had been cleared down to the bare dirt. In the center, a circle of stones and bed of ashes topped by a crudely constructed spit marked where the youthful squatters cooked their meals. There was a pile of twigs and small branches nearby, cut into firewood-size pieces. A low tree branch on the perimeter bore a change of clothes for each child, a sign that they were keeping up with everyday chores such as laundry.

Ethan really had done a remarkable job of creating a home for his sister.

The boy reappeared from the lean-to, carrying a small, lumpy tote sack that seemed barely a third full. He crossed the clearing to grab the clothes from the makeshift clothesline, then looked around as if lost.

Finally he squared his shoulders, turned back to Mitch and nodded. "Let's go." Without so much as a backward glance, the boy led the way up the trail to where they'd left the horse.

Mitch followed, with Scout bringing up the rear.

When they arrived back at the road, there was still no sign of Cora Beth and the buggy. Cissy was shivering again and her eyes were closed. The arm she'd draped around his neck had gone slack and she was shifting fretfully in his hold.

"My head hurts," she said in a pitiful whisper.

"I'm so sorry, Buttercup. Just hold on, our ride will be here soon." What did he do now?

"Ma used to sing lullabies to us when one of us got sick," Ethan said. "Cissy always liked that."

Sing? Mitch didn't know any lullabies. Then a long forgotten memory of his own mother singing him to sleep at night came to him. How had that song gone? He hummed for a few seconds, trying to capture more of the memory. Slowly the words came back to him, a few at a time.

> *Good night, happy dreams,*
> *my sweet little one.*
> *Close your eyes, go to sleep,*
> *while I sing you this song.*

The daylight has faded,
God's creatures now rest,
snuggle down my sweet child
In your own little nest.

Mitch was surprised to discover that the song, even with his stumbling rendition, really did seem to calm her a bit. He searched his memory for more of the words.

Good night, happy dreams,
my sweet little one.
You played and you laughed,
but now day is done.
We've said our prayers and
I've tucked you in tight.
Day is done, God is nigh,
time to wish you good-night.

Cora Beth scanned the tree line. Surely it wasn't much farther. Unless she'd gotten the directions wrong. *Heavenly Father, please don't let that be the case.*

A moment later the road turned and she sighed with relief when she saw the group waiting for her just up ahead. Then the unexpected sound of singing caught her attention. She couldn't catch the words from this distance, but the soft crooning was unmistakable. Mitch was singing a lullaby.

Mitch sat on the ground with a child cradled in his lap. Ethan stood nearby, a dog at his heels.

The family-like tableau tugged at her heart. She'd never seen Mitch so, well, so *fatherly* looking before. But it suited him.

He caught sight of her a moment later and the singing stopped. He got to his feet, taking obvious care not to jar his precious burden.

"Mrs. Collins is here, Buttercup," she heard him say. "You just hold on now. We're going to get you to the doctor and he'll fix you right up." But the worry in his voice told Cora Beth a different story.

She pulled on the reins, bringing the buggy to a halt and set the brake. "I came as fast as I could," she said as she hopped down. "How is she?"

Rather than answer directly, Mitch gave his head a little shake. "If you'll take her, I'll—"

"No." Cissy's tone was groggy and petulant. "I want Sheriff Lemon Drop to hold me."

Sheriff Lemon Drop? Cora Beth smiled as she saw Mitch's discomfort. His well-known predilection for the sweet treat had caught him out, it seemed.

"We talked about what a nice lady Mrs. Collins is, remember?" Mitch's tone was gentle but coaxing. "She's the lady who made those nice fluffy biscuits you mentioned. She's going to hold you while I drive the wagon—"

"No, I want you."

Cora Beth recognized that tone from experience. Tears were imminent if they didn't head this off quickly. "That's all right, Cissy. The sheriff can hold on to you while I drive the buggy."

She stroked the little girl's head. Poor thing, her forehead was burning up and her eyes were glassy.

Glancing up at Mitch, she gave him a reassuring smile. "Y'all hold on just a few minutes while I turn the buggy around."

"Maybe I should—"

Cora Beth shook her head. "It won't do to get her

worked up right now. You're taking care of what's most important. I can handle the buggy."

She turned to Ethan. "As soon as I get the buggy turned, I need you to tie the sheriff's horse to the back. Think you can do that?"

Ethan was already headed toward the horse. "Yes, ma'am."

"Good."

Cora Beth climbed back up on the seat, glad to see the trail was wide enough to make turning the buggy a simple matter. Once she'd accomplished her task, she set the brake and climbed down again while Ethan took care of Mitch's horse.

Gently brushing Cissy's hair from her forehead, she gave the child her most reassuring smile. "Cissy, you need to let me hold you for just a little while so Sheriff Hammond can climb up in the buggy. I promise to let him have you back just as soon as he's settled in."

The little girl gave her a suspicious look. "Promise?"

Cora Beth traced an *X* across her chest. "Cross my heart."

Cissy looked up at Mitch and repeated her question. "Promise?"

"Absolutely."

Apparently satisfied, the child held out her arms for Cora Beth.

Mitch handed over the feather-light patient, gave Cora Beth a look she couldn't quite interpret, then climbed quickly into the wagon and reached back down.

"Here you go, sweetheart." Cora Beth gave the child a little squeeze before handing her up to Mitch. "Right back in the sheriff's arms where you'll be all safe and sound."

Seeing the way the little girl snuggled trustingly back into Mitch's arms was heartwarming. "You should slide over to the middle," she told Mitch. "Ethan and I will take the ends and help support you."

By this time Ethan had finished taking care of the horse and had fetched a cloth sack that he now tossed behind the seat.

Cora Beth glanced down at the dog. "There's no room for him in the buggy. Will he be all right?"

Ethan nodded, patting the dog's head. "Yes, ma'am. Scout's pretty fast. He'll follow along without any problem."

"Good. Then let's climb on up and we'll be off."

Ethan nodded. But before Cora Beth could boost herself up, he stopped her. "I know how to drive a buggy, ma'am. I can handle the reins so you can help the sheriff watch my sister, if you don't mind."

Cora Beth hesitated, not sure how adept the boy actually was. But her brother had handled larger carriages at a much younger age. And Ethan probably needed to feel as if he were doing something to help instead of just sitting around. She stepped back. "That would be mighty helpful, Ethan. Thank you."

She ignored Mitch's frown and moved around to the other side while Ethan scrambled up and took the reins. Once she indicated she was settled in, Ethan released the brake and set the horse in motion.

After a few minutes of observing the way the boy handled the reins, she gave a satisfied nod. Her faith had not been misplaced—he could handle a horse and buggy just fine. She relaxed and turned to Mitch and Cissy.

The child had fallen into a fitful sleep, stirring restlessly but keeping a hand against Mitch's chest. "I think you've made a lifelong friend, Sheriff Lemon Drop," she said quietly.

Mitch shifted, obviously uncomfortable with her words. "I gave her a piece of candy to ease her fears a bit," he said self-consciously. "She's a sweet kid," he added in a softer tone.

And you're a very sweet man. But saying that out loud would only serve to make him uncomfortable so she refrained and little else was said on the ride back.

When they reached town, Cora Beth directed Ethan to Doc Whitman's office. She was surprised to see children still straggling into the schoolhouse—it seemed so much later in the day than that.

Once Ethan set the brake, Mitch eased Cissy into Cora Beth's arms while he stepped down. She worried at how warm she was to the touch, how restless and fretful she acted even though she didn't open her eyes.

Mitch reached back up for the child and their gazes locked for a second. She read her own worry mirrored in his face. Then he turned to Ethan. "Make sure you help Mrs. Collins down." Then, without a backward glance, he strode quickly up the front walk. Doc Whitman, who'd obviously been on the lookout for them, held the door open.

As Ethan helped her down, Cora Beth could tell he was anxious to follow his sister inside. But there wouldn't be news or anything he could do for several minutes. "You saw the livery we passed when we came into town?" she asked him.

"Yes, ma'am." He nodded without taking his gaze off his sister.

"I need you to bring the buggy and Sheriff Hammond's horse there," she continued firmly. "The man who works there is named Freddy. Tell him I sent you.

Then you can come back here and wait to see what the doctor has to say about Cissy."

Ethan didn't look happy, but with one last glance toward the clinic door, he obediently climbed back up and did as she'd directed.

When Cora Beth entered, Mitch was standing alone in Dr. Whitman's outer office, twisting his hat brim in his hand, looking every inch the worried father.

"Ethan's taking your horse and the buggy over to the livery." She glanced toward the closed door to the examining room. "Did Doc say anything?"

Mitch raked his fingers through his hair. "No, he's checking her out now."

"Is Lucy with him?" Doc Whitman's daughter often helped him out.

But Mitch shook his head. "Barney Waskom came by with word that Annielou's baby's coming. Lucy's tending her until Doc can get away."

Cora Beth moved to the door. "Then I'd better see if I can lend a hand." She checked for a moment as she passed him, reaching out to touch his sleeve. "Don't worry, Doc's going to take good care of her."

Chapter Six

Mitch watched Cora Beth disappear into the examining room. Just like back there in the woods, he felt useless, unable to help in any way that mattered.

Lord, please take care of that little girl.

He was almost relieved when Ethan burst through the outer door.

"How is she?" The boy stared at the examining room door as if, if he just tried hard enough, he could see through it.

"Doc Whitman hasn't come out yet. I'm sure he'll let us know as soon as he's able."

"Can I see her?"

"Not yet. Mrs. Collins is in there with Doc. We'd only crowd them if we went in." He searched his mind for something to distract the boy. "Where's Scout?"

"Sitting outside." Ethan finally glanced his way. "He won't bother nobody, promise."

"I'm sure—"

The examining room door swung open and Cora Beth stepped out. She wore an encouraging smile that eased Mitch's worse fears.

Ethan craned his neck, trying to look past her. "Is Cissy gonna be okay?"

"She's a very sick little girl, but the good news is Doc says she should be fine as a springtime robin in a couple of days. Assuming she gets proper care, that is."

Some of the tenseness eased from the boy's muscles. "Just tell me what I need to do."

Cora Beth placed a hand on his shoulder. "Your sister needs lots of bed rest and lots of nourishment to help her get better. And she won't get that out in the woods."

"I can see that she eats and rests," he said stubbornly.

"I have a better idea." Cora Beth gave him an encouraging smile. "I would really like for the two of you to stay at the boardinghouse with me."

It was an offer Mitch had expected her to make. But Ethan seemed reluctant.

Before the boy could say anything, however, she held up a hand. "It's admirable that you want to take care of things yourself, Ethan. But right now you need to think about what's best for Cissy. She'll recover a whole lot quicker if she has a comfortable, dry place to stay and plenty of nourishing food to eat. At least agree that you'll stay with me until she gets better."

The boy looked down at the floor. "I can't afford to pay you," he said gruffly. "And my pa always said a body shouldn't take charity as long as he can fend for himself."

Mitch raised a brow. So how did stealing fit into that picture?

But Cora Beth smiled in agreement. "Sounds like your pa was a practical, honorable man. But I'm not talking about charity. I'd expect you to do some chores around the place to earn your keep."

Ethan was silent for a moment, studying the floor as if the answer were written there. Then he squared his shoulders and looked up. "If that's what's needed to get Cissy better again, then I reckon I can agree to that. You just tell me what needs doing and I'll take care of it."

"Agreed."

"But only until Cissy gets better. Then we need to be on our way."

Not if Mitch had his way. But before he or Cora Beth could say anything, Doc Whitman stepped out of the examining room.

"Hello, young man," he said when he spotted Ethan. "I suppose you must be this Ethan my patient has been calling for. You can go back there and sit with her for a while if you like."

Ethan didn't wait to be told twice. A moment later it was just the three adults in the outer office.

"Thank you for seeing to her, Dr. Whitman," Cora Beth said. "Please send me the bill."

He waved her words aside. "I'll have no talk of that. Just bake me up one of those special fruitcakes of yours next time you're in a baking mood and we'll call it even." He rolled down his sleeves. "Now excuse me while I get a powder that you can give her to help with her fever. Just mix it up with water and have her drink it twice a day until her fever is gone."

The doctor peered at her down the bridge of his nose. "And I notice you've got yourself a nasty looking burn on your hand. I'll get you some salve for that, as well."

"Thank you, but—"

He cut her off with a shake of his head. "Don't forget who the doctor is around here. Now, you're welcome to leave the little girl here for a bit, but you'll need to sit with her yourself. I'm heading over to the Waskom farm to help bring Barney and Annielou's new addition into the world."

"If it's okay to move her, I think we'll go ahead and bring Cissy over to my place. It'll be easier for me to keep an eye on her there." She turned to Mitch. "If you'll help me move her?"

"Of course. No farther than it is to your place, I can carry her there."

"Good." Dr. Whitman handed her the powders and the ointment. "Probably best to get her settled into a more comfortable bed, anyway. I'll plan to come by to check on her in the morning, but if you need me before then, just send someone to fetch me."

"Thank you, Dr. Whitman."

"You're welcome. Now I'm headed out. Just pull the door closed when you leave."

Mitch noted the smile Cora Beth gave Doc didn't reach her eyes and that her brow was still furrowed in worry. He gave her a probing look. As soon as they were alone, he voiced his question. "Is there something you didn't want to say in front of Ethan?"

"Oh, Mitch, that poor little girl."

His chest constricted at the sight of the pain in her eyes. Was Cissy's outlook worse than she'd made it sound?

"It's awful." Her voice almost broke. "The child's ankle," Cora Beth paused, swallowing hard. "There's an ugly welt, barely healed, that goes all around her left ankle. Mitch, I think someone *shackled* that child."

Mitch's gut tightened and his temper rose. What sort of low-down, miserable, slime-swilling toad would treat a little girl so harshly? If he knew who was responsible—

Seeing Cora Beth's stricken expression, he put a check on his temper. She needed some reassurances right now. His arms itched to cradle her, to stroke her hair and soothe away some of the pain he saw in her eyes. But that would only trade one kind of concern on her part for another. So he settled, instead, for taking her hand. "Well, she's safe now. And I promise I'll make sure she stays that way."

He did his best to ignore what the approval and gratitude in her eyes did to his composure as he released her hand. "Now, let's get that little girl over to the boardinghouse before I make my morning rounds."

And part of those rounds would be a stop at the telegraph office so he could contact the marshal in Howerton. One way or the other, he aimed to get to the bottom of whatever or *whoever* had hurt those kids and sent them into hiding.

Cora Beth watched as Mitch gently lifted Cissy, sheet and all, from the examining table. He appeared more at ease with the child than he had earlier.

"She seems to be feeling better." Ethan looked at Cora Beth as if for confirmation of the hope expressed in his words.

"She's certainly less restless than before," Cora Beth answered. "And that's a good sign." She waved to the far side of the room. "If you'll gather up her shoes and socks we'll get her over to my place so we can make her more comfortable."

As they stepped out onto the sidewalk a few minutes later, Scout greeted Ethan with a friendly bark and wagging tail. Hmm, she hadn't considered the dog in the mix when she'd decided to take on the two kids. Not that it changed her mind any—she'd just have to adjust her plans. Hopefully he wasn't a house dog.

They'd only taken a few steps when a familiar figure came quickstepping up to them. "Cora Beth, what's going on? Is everything okay?"

Cora Beth blinked at the sudden appearance of her sister. "Josie, what on earth—"

"I just dropped Viola at the schoolhouse and Danny was telling the other kids some wild story about an early-morning adventure you had."

Cora Beth shot her sister a warning look. "Danny tends to exaggerate. And I can't stop to chat right now." She gave a slight nod toward Mitch and the child he was carrying.

Josie wasn't to be dissuaded. "Then I'll walk with you."

As her sister fell into step beside her, Cora Beth quickly made the introductions. "Josie, this is Ethan, and the little girl the sheriff is carrying is his sister, Cissy. Cissy's not feeling so well right now so the two of them are going to be staying with us at the boarding-house for a while."

This time Josie took her cue and smiled down at the boy. "Hello, Ethan. I'm Cora Beth's sister, Josie. Glad to make your acquaintance."

Ethan nodded an acknowledgment and Josie turned to Mitch. "Hello, Sheriff. I take it you were part of my sister's adventure this morning?"

"Morning, Josie. How are things out at the ranch?"

Cora Beth hid a smile at the adept way Mitch dodged Josie's question.

Josie's raised brow indicated she'd noticed, as well. "Apparently not nearly as exciting as things are over at the boardinghouse." She glanced at the little girl who was shifting restlessly in Mitch's arms and her gaze softened. "Poor little thing. Is there anything I can do to help?"

Mitch looked past Josie and suddenly stiffened. Following his gaze, Cora Beth discovered why. The mayor's wife had spotted them and was headed their way, a determined look on her face. Cora Beth touched her sister's arm. "Josie, I promise to fill you in on the whole thing a little later, but right now I need to take you up on that offer of help."

"In what way?" Josie's voice held a note of suspicion.

"Nelda Oglesby is headed this way and I'd rather not have to answer her questions right now. Do you think you could distract her for me?"

Josie gave her a long look, then nodded. "Distract her how?"

"Ask her advice on something, anything. The latest fashions from back east or planting a flower garden would be good topics."

Josie made a face. "Not two of my favorite subjects."

Josie had always had a bit of the tomboy in her—Cora Beth supposed it came from all those years her sister was stuck running the livery to keep their family together. Her marriage to Sadie's brother Ry last year had softened her a little but her rough edges still peeked through from time to time.

With a martyred sigh, Josie nodded. "I'll do it, but you'll definitely owe me for this one."

"Thanks. I'll make sure I have a pot of coffee made and some pie sliced and ready when you come by."

"You'd better." Josie's frown plainly expressed

her feelings of martyrdom. "And I'll be wanting the complete unabridged version of the story."

Nelda was almost upon them by this time. Josie pasted on a big smile and stepped forward to close the distance before Nelda could get any closer.

She unabashedly linked arms with the woman. "Nelda Oglesby, just the woman I need to see."

Nelda blinked, obviously caught off guard. "Yes, yes, nice to see you, too, Josie, but I must speak to the sheriff—"

"Oh, I'm sure that can wait." She waved a hand toward their party dismissively. "You can see them any time but I'm only going to be in town for a little while before I have to get back to the ranch. Besides, as you can see, the sheriff is busy right now."

"But—"

Josie continued on as if Nelda hadn't spoken. "Now, I've been told when it comes to flowers you are *the* authority in town, is that right?"

Nelda paused. "Well, it's true that I do know a bit on the subject." She patted her hair. "I suppose I could spare a few minutes. What did you have in mind?"

Josie gently tugged Nelda back the way she'd come. "I thought I might try adding plants along my front porch and I noticed the ones you have at your place are so pretty."

"My azaleas?"

"Is that what they are? Do you think we might go take a look and you can tell me…"

By that time the gap between them had widened significantly and Cora Beth let out a relieved breath. She met Mitch's glance from the corner of her eye and they shared a guilty smile, but neither said a word.

Their little procession was the object of several

curious stares as they made their way to the boarding-house but they didn't pause for conversation—merely exchanged greetings and moved on with apologies.

A few minutes later Cora Beth led the way up the boardinghouse steps. Before she could reach the front door it opened and Uncle Grover stepped out, holding the screen door wide for them. "I take it this is your little sister, Ethan. Poor thing, she looks in need of some special cosseting. But don't you worry, cosseting is Cora Beth's specialty. She'll have her in the pink of health in no time."

He turned to Cora Beth. "I thought you might be needing the downstairs room so Mrs. Plunkett and I have it all fixed up and ready for the little one."

"Bless you, Uncle Grover, I don't know what I'd do without you to help me."

Cora Beth hurried down the hall and opened the door to the downstairs bedchamber. Sure enough, there were fresh linens on the bed and the covers were turned down and ready for the patient.

"If you don't need me," Uncle Grover said, "I'll get back to the kitchen. Mrs. Plunkett sent Mrs. Dauber home right after breakfast and has been tidying up the kitchen for you." He seemed a bit bemused. "An amazingly efficient woman."

Cora Beth hid a smile. It seemed Mrs. Plunkett was already making progress with her campaign. "Thank her for me. Oh and, if you don't mind, ask her if she'd be so kind as to put a pot of water to heating on the stove so I can make a broth. Ask her to use the big stock-pot."

When she turned back to the room, Mitch had already placed Cissy on the bed. The little girl opened her eyes and looked around.

"There you go." Mitch straightened. "Isn't that comfy? Mrs. Collins is going to take real good care of you and you'll be good as new before you know it."

"Aren't you going to stay with me, too?" Cissy's face puckered as if she were ready to set up a loud protest.

"Sorry, Buttercup, I have to get back to work. But I'll be back to check in on you this evening." He winked at her. "And I might just have a couple more lemon drops in my pocket by then. Would you like that?"

That seemed to mollify the little girl somewhat. "Uh-huh."

"I thought so. Now you get lots of rest and do just as Mrs. Collins says, okay?"

Cissy nodded and snuggled down deeper under the coverlet, closing her eyes.

Mitch stepped back, studying the child for a moment.

Cora Beth's heart was touched by the tender, protective look on his face.

When he turned to find her watching him, his expression shifted to a sheepish smile. Cora Beth decided to ease his discomfiture with a change of subject.

"I'm going to fetch her one of Audrey's clean nightgowns to help make her more comfortable." She was careful to keep her voice pitched low. "Then I'll fix a big pot of broth for when she wakes up again. Doc says it's important for her to get lots of food and liquids, and lots of rest."

Then she turned to Ethan. "There's a couple of vacant rooms upstairs. I'll make one of them up for you in a little bit, but if you want to keep an eye on your sister for a while, you can pull that chair over there up to the bed."

"Thank you, ma'am. But you don't need to fix me

another room. I can sleep on the floor in here with Cissy just fine."

"Nonsense. There's no need for you to sleep on the floor when there are perfectly fine beds sitting unused—"

"No offense, ma'am, but I promised my ma I'd look out for Cissy and I don't think I can do that if I'm all the way up on a different floor."

To her surprise, Mitch nodded. "A man needs to stick by his word, and it's always important to protect those in your care." He placed a hand on the boy's shoulder. "But, Ethan, your sister is going to be well cared for here."

Ethan seemed to plant his feet more firmly. "Are you telling me I *can't* stay here?"

Cora Beth gave in. "Oh, very well, if you feel so strongly about it, you can stay in here with her, at least until your sister's feeling better. Then we'll discuss it again. But I'll have none of this sleeping on the floor nonsense—not in my house. There are several cots in the attic that I pull out when we get more boarders than expected. I'll fetch one down for you."

"You get that change of clothes," Mitch said. "I'll fetch the cot."

Fifteen minutes later Cora Beth had changed Cissy into fresh clothes, left Ethan to watch over his sister, and headed for the kitchen. And walked in on Mrs. Plunkett slicing corn from a cob and Uncle Grover chopping carrots.

"Oh, hello, my dear," Uncle Grover said. "I hope you don't mind, but Mrs. Plunkett thought it would be a good idea for us to get the broth started." He smiled approvingly at the apron-clad woman. "She seems to know how it is done."

"I don't mind at all—in fact, I'm grateful." She crossed the room and grabbed another of her aprons from a wall peg near the back door.

"How's the little girl doing?" Mrs. Plunkett asked.

"She's sleeping right now. Dr. Whitman thinks she'll be fine in a few days."

"That's good to hear." Mrs. Plunkett sliced the last few rows of kernels from the cob and moved toward the stove. "We've got corn, carrots and turnips in the pot now. Anything else you want to add?"

"That's a good start. And you two have done more than enough for me this morning. I can take it from here."

"Are you sure?" Uncle Grover finished the carrot he was working on and Mrs. Plunkett transferred the slices to the pot. "We don't mind helping."

"I'll be fine." She tied the apron strings behind her and gave Mrs. Plunkett a meaningful look before turning back to her uncle. "Besides, if I remember right, you mentioned last night that you wanted to go over to Fuller Pond today and look for damselflies."

"Is that right?" Mrs. Plunkett picked up her cue with admirable smoothness. "You know, when I was a girl I had quite an interest in botany. I even had a scrapbook where I pasted samples of different leaves and flowers and did the research to identify them."

"The mark of a true enthusiast as opposed to a mere hobbyist is the time they put into doing the research."

"Very true." She lifted her chin. "Actually I find my interest in the subject has revived. I imagine a location such as Fuller Pond would have quite a variety of plant samples to study."

"Why yes, I imagine it does."

Not to be deterred, Mrs. Plunkett tried a more direct

approach. "It seems a fine day to begin my renewed studies. If your niece is certain she doesn't need my help, perhaps I could accompany you on your little expedition."

Uncle Grover nodded, looking slightly taken aback. "Why, yes, of course. I would be delighted to have a bit of company."

Cora Beth's amusement at the determination of the apparently love-struck Mrs. Plunkett faded once the two had left the room. As she raided her pantry for items to add to her stockpot, her mind kept replaying those awful scars she'd seen on Cissy's ankle. Did Ethan bear similar marks? What had happened to them and who was responsible? Should she ask Ethan about it or would that just push him to close himself off more?

"I've placed the cot in Cissy's room."

Cora Beth started. She'd been so lost in her own thoughts she hadn't heard Mitch step into the kitchen.

"Sorry. Didn't mean to startle you." He was holding his hat in his hands and looked uncharacteristically diffident.

"That's okay. It's what I get for woolgathering." She swiped the hair off her brow with the back of her hand. "Thank you for fetching the cot. I'll get the linens and make it up when I finish in here."

"I don't think Ethan is in any rush. He probably won't try to sleep until he's sure his sister is doing better."

Cora Beth nodded. "He's bound to be tired. I have a feeling that boy has been carrying a much-too-big burden for much too long."

"Give him time. He'll eventually learn to relax again."

She nodded her agreement. Then she smiled, remembering the way Mitch had been with the children today—especially Cissy. "That little girl has sure taken a shine to you."

His smile was self-deprecating. "It was the lemon drops that did it."

She sincerely doubted that was all it was. "It seemed to me she was as fond of the man as the candy." She went back to chopping the greens. "That lullaby you sang to her was nice. Don't think I ever heard that one before."

Mitch rubbed the back of his neck. "It's one my ma used to sing to me. I'd almost forgotten it until Ethan said something about singing being a good way to calm her down." He smiled crookedly. "Funny what desperation will do for your memory."

"Well, it was sweet." She smiled at his grimace and then went back to work. "Did you learn anything more about their history?"

"The only information I got out of Ethan was that both their parents have passed on. And it doesn't sound like there are any other relatives in the picture. As soon as I leave here I'm going to send a telegram to the sheriff over in Howerton and see if he can shed some light on things."

He sounded confident and in control again. Then he absently slid the brim of his hat between his fingers. "Are you going to be all right here? Should I have someone stop in to lend a hand?"

"For goodness' sake, of course I'll be okay. What do you think happens when I have extra guests here at the boardinghouse?"

He raised his palms. "You handle it with your normal efficiency. But your hand is still burned and your guests don't normally include sick little girls."

"My hand is doing fine and I have three daughters of

my own, remember? I've handled sick little girls before. Besides, Josie will be here soon, remember?"

He grinned. "But not necessarily in a mood to be helpful."

She returned his grin. "Josie is more than a match for Nelda."

As if to punctuate her assertion, Josie stepped through the hall door, with Sadie right on her heels. "Okay you two, after spending twenty minutes listening to Nelda expound on the relative merits of roses versus azaleas for showiness, I'm ready for that explanation I was promised. And I brought Sadie along so you only have to tell your story once."

Mitch nodded a greeting, then moved toward the door. "I believe your sister is more than capable of handling the explanations on her own. And since I wouldn't want to get in the way of any family talk, if you ladies will excuse me, I have morning rounds to take care of."

Cora Beth watched him leave with a raised brow. "It seems our sheriff would rather make his rounds than spend more time in my kitchen."

Josie grinned. "Don't worry, he's not getting off as easy as he thinks. When I left Nelda, she was ready to storm the sheriff's office and demand he give her an update on what progress he's made toward capturing some criminal who's apparently been vandalizing that fancy glass plant house of hers."

"Oh dear." Cora Beth stopped chopping for a moment. "Nelda's making much too much out of all this."

"Out of all *what?*" Josie's voice had a long-suffering tone to it.

Cora Beth waved her knife distractedly. "It's a rather

long story. You sure you don't want to take care of your weekly marketing first and tend to this at lunch?"

"Positive. That's why I brought Sadie with me—reinforcements in case you try to renege on our agreement. Now, Cora Beth Wylie Collins, stop chopping those vegetables so you can tell us just what's been going on. I take it there's a connection between those kids you had with you at Doc Whitman's office and what's put that bee in Nelda's bonnet, but I couldn't make a lick of sense out of her ramblings and I sure as Sunday didn't want to encourage her to explain."

Cora Beth laughed outright at that.

"I tried to fill her in." Sadie had removed her bonnet and grabbed one of Cora Beth's clean aprons. "But she said she wanted to get it straight from the horse's mouth."

"How flattering." Cora Beth surrendered her knife to Sadie and took the already chopped vegetables and moved toward the stove. "All right, have it your way. I'm making a broth for my young patient. Don't worry, I can talk and cook at the same time. And you, little sister, know where I keep everything. You can start a fresh pot of coffee brewing."

Sadie frowned. "Patient?"

"Hush, Sadie." Josie grabbed the canister of coffee. "Let her start at the beginning."

Cora Beth sighed. "All right, but Sadie already knows part of this." She gave a quick rundown of all that had transpired since Ethan had burst into her life yesterday morning.

When she was done, Josie shook her head. "Those poor kids. I hope Mitch finds the rotten dung beetle who's responsible for their misery and tosses his sorry hide in jail. Anything I can do to help?"

"Anything *we* can do to help?" Sadie amended.

"Thanks, but not right now. They're going to stay here with me for the time being."

"And once Cissy gets better?" Josie asked.

Cora Beth shrugged, not ready to answer that question just yet.

Josie narrowed her eyes. "I know that look. You're planning to take them in, aren't you?"

"It's a little early to be thinking of that," Cora Beth answered mildly.

"Big sister, you're not fooling me for one second. Can you honestly say you haven't thought about it?"

"All right, *yes,* if you must know, I've thought about it. But that's all—I'm not *planning* anything. We don't even have the whole story yet. We may find they have other options we don't know about."

Sadie dumped her vegetables into the stockpot. "Well, regardless of what happens, it's a good thing you're doing, giving those kids a place to stay. Don't let Nelda, or anyone else for that matter, give you grief about it."

Josie grinned. "She's right. Giving you grief is my job." She pulled three coffee cups from the cupboard. "And don't forget, Ry can help if the kids need any kind of legal assistance."

Ry Lassiter, Josie's husband and Sadie's brother, was a lawyer who'd left a successful practice in Philadelphia to come to Knotty Pine and start a horse ranch. Though there wasn't much call for a lawyer in town, he still provided legal advice from time to time.

"Thanks. I'll let you know if it comes to that."

Josie took her cup of coffee and moved back to the table. "Now, if we're ready for a change of subject, I have some news to share."

"What kind of news?" Sadie asked.

But as Cora Beth watched the pink creep into her sister's cheeks, she instinctively knew what was coming next.

"Well, when Sadie's baby makes his or her appearance, there'll be a new cousin following close behind."

Cora Beth was already halfway across the room. And her own joy at the news was echoed by the squeal Sadie let out.

She gave her sister a hug. "Oh, Josie, I'm so happy for you. And you're going to make a wonderful mother."

Josie's expression was uncharacteristically uncertain. "Do you really think so?"

"Of course. You've been wonderful with Viola."

"But Viola was seven years old when she came into my life as Ry's ward. This is a baby we're talking about."

"A sweet, precious little baby. And you're going to be a marvelous mother. I promise."

Josie gave her a fierce hug, then laughed as Sadie tried to squeeze into their embrace.

Cora Beth backed away, letting the two of them have their moment.

Sadie hugged Josie then stepped back as well.

"This is marvelous. We can work on our layettes together." Sadie giggled. "Oh my goodness, that brother of mine must be over the moon excited."

Josie laughed. "And then some. But he's already trying to treat me like a helpless ninny. Tried to make me put off my trip to town today because he couldn't come with me. As if I suddenly can't handle a horse and buggy."

Sadie grimaced. "He and Eli will make quite a pair these next few months. Have you told Viola yet?"

Josie shook her head. "I remember you said you and Eli were going to wait until our trip to Hawk's Creek next week to tell his sister, Penny, so she could have time to get used to the idea away from her friends before letting the whole town in on it. That sounded like a good plan so Ry and I are waiting, as well."

Hawk's Creek was the Lassiter family ranch situated near Tyler, more than sixty miles northwest of Knotty Pine. The two families were taking a trip there to visit Ry and Sadie's brother Griff for his birthday.

Cora Beth moved back to the stove. "Looks like there'll be more than a birthday to celebrate when you all get together."

Sadie nodded. "Actually, this turned out to be great timing for the trip. It was all I could do to convince Eli it was perfectly okay for me to travel at this stage of things. Goodness knows what he'll be like in a few months."

While Josie and Sadie traded stories on how foolish their husbands were being, Cora Beth quietly went back to her cooking.

It was such a joy to know Josie and Sadie were getting ready to bring new lives into the world, new additions to their family. It was truly a blessing. But for some reason, hearing them laugh fondly about their husbands and share plans for the coming months of their pregnancies, left her feeling left out, restless. Which was silly. She'd had her shot at marriage and had three beautiful daughters to show for it.

And now God had put Ethan and Cissy into her keeping for a while. What more could she ask for?

Yet she did find herself longing for more. For someone to make her family complete. To make *her* feel complete.

Chapter Seven

Cora Beth studied the four faces staring back at her from their seats around the dining-room table. As soon as they'd come home from school, they'd clamored to find out all about her early morning adventure. Cora Beth knew Danny had had some misgivings about Ethan when they'd met, though she wasn't quite sure why, so she wanted to make certain she explained the situation properly so that they all accepted the newcomers in a warm, friendly manner.

She said a quick prayer, then took a deep breath. "I wanted to let you know about some special guests we'll have staying with us the next several days."

"Is it new boarders?" Pippa asked. "Does that mean Danny has to share a room with Uncle Grover again?"

"No, they're not regular borders. It's a young girl and boy. Their names are Ethan and Cissy. Cissy is the same age as Audrey, and Ethan is about Danny's age. The thing is, Cissy is really sick and they need a place to stay while she gets better."

"Don't their ma and pa want to take care of them?" Audrey asked.

"They don't have a ma and pa," Cora Beth explained. "And they're all alone."

"We don't have a pa, either." Audrey sounded melodramatically forlorn.

"I know. But you have me, and Uncle Grover, and Danny and your sisters. You also have Aunt JoJo and Uncle Ry and Viola. Ethan and Cissy don't have anyone. So, for now, I'd like us to take them in. What do you think?"

Audrey gave a vigorous nod. "We can be their family. I'll be their sister."

Lottie and Pippa echoed Audrey's sentiment almost in unison.

That left Danny. She studied his demeanor. Of all of them, he should have been sympathetic to the runaways' plight. Orphaned as a toddler when his folks were passing through Knotty Pine, he'd had no one else when her parents took him in. Of course he'd been so young when it happened, he probably had no memory of that time. "What are you thinking?" she asked him.

"I just think you ought to be careful is all. That Ethan looks like a troublemaker. Sheriff Hammond caught him stealing, didn't he? And I hear he took some other stuff around town, too."

How much had her brother heard? "Ethan's not a bad kid. He was only trying to take care of his sister. I don't think any of us really know what we'd stoop to if we were in similar situations." She held her brother's gaze. "Jesus forgave the thief on the cross when he repented. Don't you think Ethan deserves another chance, too?"

"I guess." Danny's tone was more grudging than gracious. "If he repented."

"Then we're agreed. We're going to do our best to make them feel at home while they're here."

"How long are they going to be here?" Danny asked.

"As long as it takes for Cissy to get better."

"Where are they?" This came from Audrey.

"They're going to stay in the downstairs bedchamber for now. That'll make it easier for me to check in on Cissy from time to time." She smiled. "Oh, and I misspoke—they're not *completely* alone in the world. They have their dog Scout with them."

"They have a dog?" Audrey hopped out of her seat, and Pippa and Lottie's eyes shone with excitement. Her girls had always wanted a pet but Cora Beth had been reluctant to have one around in case it put off potential boarders.

"They do. Scout is—"

The door swung open. "Mrs. Collins, Cissy is—" Ethan, holding a small pitcher, halted on the threshold when he realized Cora Beth wasn't alone. "Sorry," he said, starting to back out. "I'll come back when—"

"Nonsense." Cora Beth waved him over. "Come in and meet everyone."

Ethan stepped into the room with all the eagerness of a prisoner entering a cell. "Yes, ma'am."

"You've already met my brother Danny. This pig-tailed imp is my oldest daughter Audrey. And these two look-alikes are Pippa and Lottie." She gave them all an encouraging smile. "Girls, this is Ethan."

Audrey had already popped up from her chair and crossed the room to meet the visitor halfway. "Hi." She stuck out a hand in a very grown-up gesture. "Welcome to our family."

Ethan gingerly took her hand and stared at her with a confused expression. "Excuse me?"

Audrey gave him a bright smile. "We decided, since

you and your sister don't have a family, you can be part of ours, at least while you're staying here. And your dog, too."

Ethan glanced from Audrey to the rest of the group and then focused on Cora Beth. "You did?"

She nodded. "We all did."

"Ma says your sister is sick," Audrey added. "But don't you worry, Ma knows just how to make kids feel better."

By this time Pippa and Lottie had joined Audrey, and the girls had the poor boy nearly surrounded. "Can we see your dog?" one of them asked.

Cora Beth took mercy on Ethan and called the girls back to the table. "You all get to work on your lessons now and let Ethan be. You can meet Cissy when she's feeling a little better. And you can meet Scout when your work is done."

She turned to Ethan. "Was there something you needed?"

Ethan shook his head as if to clear it. "Yes, ma'am. Cissy drank the last of her water. I was going to refill the pitcher."

"You go right ahead. And I'll bring in another bowl of broth in just a bit."

A few minutes later, when Cora Beth stepped into the sickroom with a tray containing a bowl of the promised broth, she found Ethan sitting beside the bed, wiping his sister's forehead with a damp rag.

She offered the little girl a cheery smile. "Cissy, I brought you something to eat." Then she turned to Ethan. "The family sits down to supper in about an hour. But I can fix you a bowl of broth to tide you over if you're hungry now."

Ethan shook his head. "I'd just as soon take my meals with Cissy if you don't mind."

Was he afraid he wouldn't be welcome? "But there's plenty of room at the table. I'll be glad to stay with Cissy while you eat if you're worried—"

"It ain't that." He drew his shoulders back. "You're an awful nice lady, and I sure do appreciate all you're doing for Cissy. But family should stick together, and no offense, ma'am, but nice as it was for your little girl to say what she did, Cissy is my family, not those folks out there."

Such a mature outlook for such a young boy. "I understand. But I hope you know that you would be truly welcome."

She set the tray on the bedside table and turned back to Cissy. "Now, how's the patient feeling? Ready for a bit of something to eat?"

"I'm not hungry." The child's tone was fretful, petulant.

"Why don't you try just a little," Cora Beth coaxed. "It'll help you get better quicker."

The child wiggled herself into a more upright position. "Is Sheriff Lemon Drop coming back?"

"He most certainly is. I think he's taken quite a shine to you."

That seemed to perk her up a bit. "Do you think he'll sing to me again?"

Cora Beth sat on the chair next to the bed and spooned up a bit of the broth. "Would you like him to?"

The child nodded. "He has a nice rumbly voice."

Cora Beth moved the spoon toward Cissy and the child opened her mouth automatically. "If you ask him, I know he'll be happy to sing for you."

A nice rumbly voice—yes, that was a good description. It was the kind of voice that resonated deep within a person. Deep and true, like the man himself.

Mitch stepped into Cora Beth's kitchen wishing he had better news for her and for those two kids. It had been a long day, and it wasn't over yet.

"So how did you fare with Josie and Sadie this morning?" It was cowardly to put off what he'd come here to say, but he wasn't in any hurry to give her the unsettling news.

"It went well. Told them all that I know about Ethan and Cissy, caught up on everyone's family news, had a nice little visit." She raised a brow. "How did you fare with Nelda?"

Mitch grimaced. "She's dead set on making someone pay, and pay dearly, for the loss of her precious plant."

A worry furrow creased her forehead. "Is she going to make trouble for Ethan?"

"I think I appeased her for now. But I'm afraid Ethan is going to have to eat quite a bit of crow."

That didn't seem to worry Cora Beth overmuch. "Eating crow is unpleasant, but can be good for one's character."

Time to quit procrastinating. "Thought you might like to know, I got a response to the telegram I sent to the sheriff over in Howerton."

She clasped her hands in front of her. "Oh?"

Ease into it. "Their last name is Prentiss."

"Prentiss." Her nose scrunched in concentration. "That sounds familiar."

"Remember about fifteen months back, Titus Brown returned from a trip with a wife and two kids?"

He saw the moment realization hit. Cora Beth sat

down hard, her expression stricken. "Oh no." The words came out almost as a whisper.

"I'm afraid so. The wife was Janet Prentiss, a widow, and Ethan and Cissy are her two kids."

Titus Brown was well known in the area for his drinking, his foul mouth and even fouler temper. There wasn't a woman in these parts who would have anything to do with the man, much less marry him. It wasn't surprising that he'd gone off to where he wasn't known to find him a wife.

"That poor woman." Cora Beth placed her interlaced hands on the table. Her knuckles had turned white. "The Ladies' Auxiliary made several attempts to visit her and invite her to church and into some of our homes, but Titus wouldn't have it. Last time we tried, he met us at the door with a shotgun and told us that we were trespassing and to get off his property." She met his gaze. "But that was no excuse for giving up."

He'd known she'd react this way. "Don't go blaming yourself. Titus never was one to tolerate visitors." If there was any blame to be dished out, a wagonload should be piled high at his door. It was his job to protect the citizens of this community.

"Does this mean she's dead?"

"It fits with what Ethan told us. But I aim to find out for sure. I'm going to talk with Ethan this evening, then ride out to Titus's place in the morning. And this time he *will* talk to me."

She reached a hand across the table but stopped short of grabbing his. "Whatever that man says, you *can't* send those kids back to him, Mitch, you just can't."

Didn't she know him better than that? "I agree. But I'm pretty sure it won't come to that. I'd be mighty surprised if Titus took the time to go through a legal adoption. And if that's the case, he doesn't have any claim to them. They're wards of the state."

Some of her tension eased. "So what happens to them now?"

He held her gaze. "I think you already know the answer to that."

"The orphanage?" At his nod, she leaned forward. "No. We can't let that happen."

When had she started thinking of them as partners in this? And how exactly did he feel about that? "I don't see as we have much choice in the matter. Unless we can find a blood relation who wants to lay claim to them. And the sheriff in Howerton didn't seem to think there was much chance of that."

"But you don't have to do anything right away, do you? I mean, Cissy is sick and Ethan is half starved and they're both near about worn to a nub."

He wished he could give her the reassurances she wanted. "I won't do anything definite about their future accommodations until Cissy is better," he temporized. "But I'd like to speak to Ethan about what I've found out and see what he has to add."

She stood. "I'll get Uncle Grover to sit with Cissy and then ask Ethan to join us here in the kitchen."

Mitch watched her leave and then stood and paced the floor. He understood her concerns—he felt the same. He was the town sheriff, hang it all, he was supposed to protect the folks around here.

He'd made a few trips out to Titus's place in the months since he'd brought his new family home—it was the sheriff's job to check on everyone in the community occasionally, even those who didn't want to be checked up on. He hadn't seen the kids on any of his visits but he'd seen the new Mrs. Brown a time or two.

She'd seemed nervous and withdrawn, but she hadn't given any indication anything was wrong, even when he'd asked. Of course Titus was always there, hovering around, telling Mitch they were fine and to get off his place and leave them alone.

Why hadn't he made more of an effort to check things out? He'd let Mrs. Brown down and now she was dead. He'd let those two kids down, as well. And there was no way he could come close to making it up to them, not with the terrible price they'd paid. It was something he'd have to live with for the rest of his days.

Five minutes later he was seated back at the table when Cora Beth escorted Ethan into the kitchen. The boy stared at him as if he were facing a firing squad. Another stab at Mitch's conscience.

"Don't worry, Ethan, you're not in any kind of trouble," Mitch said. "Have a seat, I just want to talk."

Ethan sat across the table from Mitch, perched on the edge of his chair. Cora Beth sat beside the boy.

Mitch decided it would be easier on all of them if he got right to the point. "I've been doing a little checking with the sheriff over in Howerton today and I've learned some things about you and your sister."

Ethan went very still. "What kind of things?"

"I've learned that your last name is Prentiss. That your mother is Janet Prentiss. That she was married to Jonathan Prentiss, a carpenter who died rescuing a kid from a charging bull."

"My pa was a brave man," Ethan said proudly.

Mitch nodded. He could see a touch of that same courage in the boy, now that he knew a little more of his story. "I also learned that your ma married Titus Brown about a year and a half ago and the three of you moved here to live on his place."

Ethan stood, knocking his chair over in the process. "We're not going back there! Not ever. I promised Cissy I'd keep her safe. If you try to make us, I'll find a way for us to run away again."

Mitch tried to calm the boy. "Nobody's going to make you go back to Titus. You have my word."

Ethan didn't look convinced. In fact, he looked poised to run. "Does that mean you're gonna just let us go on our way when Cissy gets better?"

The boy was definitely no fool. "Let's just see about getting her well first." Mitch wasn't going to lie to him, but he didn't want to add more worries to the kid's already full plate. "There'll be time enough to worry about where you go next when the time comes."

Ethan's mouth pinched into a tight, distrustful line.

He couldn't blame the kid and there wasn't much more he could do to reassure him, either. Time to push this conversation in a different direction. "Tell me what happened to your mother."

Some of the tension leeched from Ethan, replaced by an air of loss. He stared down at the floor as his Adam's apple bobbed for a moment. "About three months ago she got real bad sick." His voice was thick but steady. "Titus wouldn't send for the doctor, no matter how much I begged him to. He kept saying she was just trying to get out of doing all her chores. But my ma wasn't like that."

Cora Beth straightened the chair he'd knocked over. "I'm sure she wasn't," she said softly.

He nodded his acceptance of her sympathy. "She died a few weeks later. Titus just dug a hole on that little hill behind the house and buried her there. He wouldn't even send for the preacher."

Ethan's tone hardened, turned bitter. "Bad enough he

wouldn't let her go to church on Sundays even though she begged him to, but it just weren't right not to have a preacher there at her graveside to speak to her passing. Cissy and I did the best we could to give her a proper burial service. Cissy picked the flowers and I made a cross out of two branches. We said a prayer together, but it wasn't special like if a preacher had said it."

Mitch mentally berated himself. How could he *not* have realized what was going on out there? That woman might still be alive today if he'd tried harder.

This time Cora Beth lightly touched Ethan's arm. "I'm so sorry there was no one around to help you and your sister get through that sad time. But you must know that God hears everyone's prayers and was as pleased with yours as He would have been with even the finest of preachers."

"If God hears everyone's prayers, how come He didn't help us when we begged Him to?"

Mitch winced at the bitter, jaded question. He knew exactly how the boy felt—he'd asked himself that very question when his own world had shattered.

But Cora Beth didn't flinch away from the question. "Oh, Ethan, don't ever doubt that He hears all our prayers, and that He loves us deeply. That doesn't mean He's going to keep the hard times away, but it does mean He's always right beside us to help us through them. You just have to remember that He knows things we don't, things we may never know or understand till we get to heaven ourselves. You just have to have faith, you have to believe that there is nothing that happens here on earth that He can't somehow turn into a blessing down the road."

Mitch studied her face as she spoke. Did she really believe that?

When Ethan didn't say anything, Cora Beth took his hand. "I'm sure your mother would have been very touched to learn that you loved her enough to do your best to give her a proper funeral, all on your own, especially given the conditions you were dealing with. Any mother would be."

"Thank you, ma'am." Ethan sat back down at the table, and glanced at the locket she wore around her neck.

"Ma had a real pretty silver locket, too. She wore it all the time—said it was a wedding present from my pa. Just before she died she gave it to Cissy—put it around her neck herself. But after Ma died, Titus took it. Said whatever Ma had was his now. We never saw it again."

Mitch felt his temper rising anew. What kind of sorry excuse for a human being would treat grieving kids that way? Which brought to mind another question. "Ethan, why does Cissy have that scar around her ankle?"

Ethan's face contorted. "It's all my fault."

Cora Beth brushed the hair from his forehead. "I very much doubt that."

"But it is. I didn't like the way Titus treated my ma, and I kept telling her that we should leave him. I told her I'd find work and take care of her and Cissy. But Ma said I was too young for that and we didn't have anywhere else to go so we had to stay there."

Mitch hadn't thought he could feel any worse, but Ethan's words proved him wrong.

"After Ma died, I knew Cissy and me would be better off on our own so I told Titus that we were leaving. But he said we belonged to him, that he had paid good money to move us all to his place and he intended to get his money's worth."

Cora Beth's reaction to this was a sharp inhale.

"After Ma died, Titus said that Cissy had to stay to do the cooking and I had to keep helping with the field-work." Ethan's jaw tightened. "Since he knew I wouldn't leave without Cissy, and he needed me to work in the fields, he padlocked an iron shackle on her bad leg." Ethan's expression darkened even further. "Said it didn't matter since that leg wasn't much good for anything anyway."

Mitch felt his hands tighten into a fist as he thought about anyone treating that little girl so roughly.

"That doesn't make any of this your fault," Cora Beth protested.

There was a part of Mitch that wished Cora Beth were speaking to him, not Ethan.

Ethan continued as if she hadn't spoken. "Once a week, whenever he went into town for supplies and whiskey, he locked me in the root cellar just to make sure I didn't try to get her free while he was away."

The boy finally looked up and met Mitch's gaze, a hardened man-to-man kind of look. "I shouldn't have said anything to him about us leaving. I should have just up and done it when he wasn't looking. Then Cissy wouldn't have had to go through all that."

Mitch instinctively knew the boy wasn't ready to listen to anything that sounded like platitudes. "How did you manage to escape?"

"I used my work time to make my plans." Ethan's voice took on a more confident tone. "I worked with Beebob every chance I got, getting him used to me and used to carrying loads."

"Beebob?"

"Titus's plow mule. I knew we'd need a way for Cissy to ride since she can't walk too fast. Titus always took the horse and buckboard with him when he went to town, so Beebob was our best bet. He's a bit ornery, but I think that's because of the way Titus treated him. I fed him carrots and whatever I could find that I thought he'd like, brushed him extra careful with the curry comb, talked real gentle to him and after a while, he and I got to be good friends. Then I tried sitting on him whenever I knew Titus wasn't likely to see, just to get him used to having a rider."

Mitch had wondered how the two kids had managed to get so far from Titus's place in so short a time. And with so many supplies. "But how did you get out of the root cellar and Cissy out of her shackles?"

Ethan grinned for a split second before that hardened look came back. "Turns out the hinges on one of the root cellar doors could be lifted pretty easy. So after Titus left I'd come out and gather supplies, things I knew he probably wouldn't miss, and hide them down in that root cellar. Then I'd spend the rest of my time working to get Cissy free. I knew Titus would notice if I tampered with her shackles at all. But I figured he wouldn't notice if I worked away at the post that Cissy's shackles were secured to."

Clever kid.

"Titus always stayed in town until near dark, so when I knew it was closing on time for him to get back, I'd just clean up any sawdust and splinters I'd created, disguise my work as best I could and lock myself back in the cellar as if I'd never left."

"And Titus never noticed?"

Ethan snorted derisively. "He's not real smart and he never figured I could get out of the cellar. He only checked the lock where it was attached to Cissy's ankle—he never thought to look at the post. Though he did almost catch me once when he came home a little early. Lucky thing Scout started barking when Titus was still a ways off. I managed to slip out the back way and get in the cellar and put the door in place before he got close."

"But you did get the shackle off her."

"I grabbed a chisel and hammer before we left. First night out I made sure that thing came off and tossed it in the creek."

"What happened to the mule?" Mitch asked.

"We made camp that first night and when we got up the next morning he was gone." He rubbed the back of his neck. "Guess I didn't do a good enough job tethering him. Luckily I'd unloaded all our supplies. Anyway, that's why we were stuck here. I'd planned for Cissy and me to be far away from Knotty Pine by now."

"Where were you headed?"

"As far away from Titus as we could get."

"You were very brave and resourceful," Cora Beth stated. "Your sister is very lucky to have you to look out for her."

Mitch stood and moved around the table. "Ethan, I'm sorry I didn't do more to check on your family. I can't change that now, but you have my word you won't have to go back to Titus's place." He held out his hand.

To Mitch's relief, after a moment, Ethan stood, extended his own hand and they shook. It almost felt as if the boy were forgiving him. But Mitch still didn't know if he could forgive himself.

"Ethan," Mitch cautioned, "your sister's not up for another of your daring escapes. She's safe here. You need to let her stay put and rest so she can get better. Understand?"

The boy nodded.

"Do I have your word on that?"

After a slight hesitation, Ethan nodded again. "Yes, sir."

Good enough.

Ethan turned to Cora Beth. "Whenever you want to set me some chores to do, ma'am, I'm ready."

She smiled. "Let's not worry about that just yet."

"No, ma'am, that wasn't the deal." There was a dignity and maturity about the boy that many a grown man would envy. "I aim to pay for me and Cissy's keep. If you don't have work for me, I'll find work elsewhere so I can pay you what's owed."

Mitch held his breath, hoping Cora Beth would understand the boy needed this.

And of course she did.

"Very well. First thing tomorrow morning you can get to work in the garden. There's a row of squash that needs weeding and then you can check the tomatoes and pick the ripe ones for me to pickle."

Cora Beth's answer seemed to satisfy the boy. "I'll go back now and stay with Cissy till then."

Ethan moved toward the hall door, paused and turned back to Mitch. "You gonna come in and see Cissy? She asked for you when she woke up a while ago."

It seemed he and Ethan had formed a truce of sorts. Mitch patted his shirt pocket. "Yep. I have her lemon drops right here. I just want to have a word with Mrs. Collins first."

As soon as they were alone, Cora Beth stood and started pacing. "I'm so angry I could spit nails. How could anyone treat kids that way? Mitch, that man should be locked up."

Mitch agreed. Too bad he couldn't do much about it. "I'm not sure there are any charges we can legally bring against Titus, but I promise you that he will *not* get his hands on those two kids again." That sorry excuse for a man would have to come through him to get to them.

She paused and her face seemed to crumple. "Oh, Mitch, what those kids have been through. It near breaks my heart."

He stood and put a comforting hand on her shoulder. "I know. It's hard to believe even Titus could be that cruel to a couple of kids."

She stepped closer. Almost of its own accord his hand slipped around her back until he was holding her in a one-armed embrace. She needed comforting. He was just being a friend, he told himself—that was all.

"I feel as if I let them down," she was saying as she kneaded her left hand with her right, "as if I should have done something to help them before it got this far. At the very least I should have tried harder to befriend their mother."

He gave her shoulder a light squeeze and was unaccountably pleased when she leaned back into his arm. "This is *not* your fault," he said. "If you want to start passing blame around, dump a load of it at my door. As sheriff I should have been more vigilant in checking what was going on out there." He caught a whiff of cinnamon and honey, a sweet and spicy mix that seemed to be a part of her. He fought not to let it distract him. It wasn't easy—Cora Beth was truly a lovely woman, inside and out.

"No, don't—" She suddenly went still and then eased herself out of his hold. "I'm sorry." Her cheeks were prettily stained with pink. "You must think I'm being a goose."

"Not at all." His arm still tingled where she'd pressed against him, felt bereft without its sweet weight to support. "Hearing Ethan's story would upset anyone with a heart."

"Hand wringing doesn't do anyone any good. Those kids need more than my sympathy."

One thing about Cora Beth, her emotions always led to action. "You're already doing your part to help them. And even though we may not be able to change what's past, sure as night follows day we can make sure it doesn't happen again." Not on his watch at any rate.

"My biggest concern right now is what's going to become of them." She raised a hand, palm forward. "And don't you dare mention that orphanage again. They deserve something better than that."

This time he agreed. "I know. I'm just not sure what we can do about it." He felt strongly that he needed to do something to make amends for his inaction. Sending them off to an orphanage hardly qualified.

"How much time do we have to figure something out?" she asked.

"We can put off doing anything official until Cissy is fully recovered—maybe a week or so. And then there's the matter of having them declared wards of the state. The paperwork on that could take a bit more time."

She sat down again. "That's something. I'll be praying that the Good Lord shows me the answer."

Mitch had a pretty good idea how this was going to end up. But she was right—leave it in God's hands for now.

She gave him a sympathetic look. "I'll also be praying that things go as they should with your meeting with Titus tomorrow. I certainly don't envy you that encounter."

Despite the worry in her eyes, Mitch found his thoughts focused more on how sweet it had felt to hold

Cora Beth than on what his meeting with Titus would be like.

He'd held her before. Whenever there was a town dance, he always made a point of claiming Cora Beth as his partner for several dances. But this had been different. This time she'd come to him. This time she'd drawn comfort from him.

This time she'd *needed* him.

Courting her was out of the question, of course. He wouldn't take the risk of hurting her the way he knew he could.

But maybe, as long as he kept firm control of his own treacherous feelings, he could be the friend she leaned on when she needed comfort or support.

Surely there was nothing wrong with that.

Cora Beth rubbed her upper arms, wondering what Mitch had thought of the way she'd leaned on him. Had she shocked him? Or was he thinking she was one of those women who let their emotions get the better of them?

At any rate, she wasn't at all sorry it had happened. Phillip had been gone five years now, and it had felt nice to have a man's arms around her again, regardless of the reason. She refused to feel any guilt over it.

And was it just wishful thinking on her part or had he enjoyed the moment just the tiniest bit himself?

Chapter Eight

Mitch halted his horse in front of Titus's house. The place was ramshackle, unkempt. Before he could dismount, though, the door opened and Titus stepped out, adjusting his suspenders.

Mitch laid an arm across his pommel, fighting the urge to get down from his horse and light into the man. "Morning, Titus."

"I done told you before, Sheriff, I don't need no checking up on. I'm just fine and I like my privacy. And I ain't got time to mess with trespassers."

"Well, you're going to have to make time. I'm here on official business."

Titus's expression turned guarded, wary. "What kind of official business?"

"I came across Ethan and Cissy the other day."

Titus hooked his thumbs in his suspenders and rocked back on his heels. "Found my runaways, did you? So why didn't you bring those two little varmints with you? I don't have a whole day to waste going back to town to fetch them."

Mitch's fist clenched around the reins. "That's just as well since, if I find you within twenty yards of either one of them, I'll haul your sorry carcass to jail, lock you up and throw away the key."

Titus's eyes narrowed. "I don't know what them two's been saying about me but you can't believe anything they say. They're a pair of mealy mouthed liars."

Mitch didn't bother to hide his sneer. "Unlike the fine, upstanding citizen you are."

"You ain't got no call to talk to me like that. And another thing. Them two are thieves to boot. They took my mule and a whole bunch of supplies and tools."

No more than they were entitled to as far as Mitch was concerned. "Tell me what happened to their mother."

Titus spat on the ground in front of him. "She was a puny, sniveling excuse for a wife. Always mewling about her kids. Then she up and died on me. Marrying that one was a waste of time and money."

Just concentrate on getting the information you need. "How'd she die?"

"How should I know? I ain't no doctor."

Mitch fought to keep his voice even. "I'll ask you again—how did she die?"

Titus let out a string of oaths. "That woman was always whining and complaining about some ailment or other. One day she took to her bed and refused to get up. Next thing I know she's stone-cold dead."

"Did you even once consider calling for Doc Whitman to look in on her?"

"Like I said, I didn't figure it was anything more serious than what she'd had before. Besides, doctors cost money."

With Titus, it always came down to what was best for Titus.

"I want them kids back." Titus glared belligerently. "You can't keep them from me, I'm their stepdad."

"Forget it, Titus. Unless you can produce adoption papers you have no legal claim to them. They're wards of the state now."

"Those kids owe me. They stole my mule and a hatchet and a bunch more of my stuff. It's only right they come back here and work it off."

Over his dead body. "You got a right to press charges if that's what you want to do." He kept his tone conversational but didn't bother trying to hide his contempt. "Come by my office whenever you get ready to file the paperwork. And when you do, we'll also talk about what charges might be filed against you on Cissy and Ethan's behalf."

A look of something akin to fear crossed Titus's expression, quickly followed by a chest-out posture that was pure bluster. "They got no claim against me."

"Don't they? The state of Texas looks harshly on folks who abuse kids."

"I never abused those kids. Just had 'em working for their keep is all, same as any real pa would do."

"Shall we put it to the test?"

Their gazes locked for several long moments. Titus was the first to look away. He crossed his arms over his chest. "Keep 'em then. They weren't much use to me anyway."

But Mitch wasn't quite through with him yet. "Ethan mentioned a locket that belonged to his mother. She promised it to Cissy, but it appears to have gone missing after she died."

"I sold it." The belligerence was back. "And don't you go telling me I had no right. I needed some way to pay for taking care of those two. Them and their mangy cur ate more in vittles than they worked off in chores."

Mitch seriously doubted that, but arguing wouldn't do any good. "Who'd you sell it to?"

"Danvers over at the mercantile." Titus spat on the ground again "Now if you're done asking me all these fool questions, I got chores to do. It's lots of work taking care of a place like this when you ain't got no help."

Mitch didn't waste words or time responding to that, simply turned his horse and rode away. Too bad he couldn't find some excuse to arrest the man. If ever a body needed locking up, it was Titus Brown.

Thirty minutes later he marched into the mercantile. He was relieved to see Horace Danvers didn't have any customers at the moment—he'd just as soon not have an audience for this little bit of business.

Horace leaned on the counter near his till. "What can I do for you today, Sheriff?"

"Titus came in here a while back and sold off a locket. You remember the piece?"

"Yep. Matter of fact, I still have it. It's right over here in the display case." Horace bent down and retrieved the keepsake. He laid it on the counter for Mitch's viewing. "Pretty little bauble, isn't it? I wondered how Titus came to have such a thing but he assured me it was his to sell."

No point debating that now. "How much do you want for it?

Horace's lips turned up in an arch smile. "You going courting, are you, Sheriff?"

"No," Mitch said, firmly repressing the sudden image of placing the locket around Cora Beth's neck, "and don't you go spreading any rumors to the contrary." Danvers had a marriageable-aged daughter and a matchmaking wife who loved to talk. The last thing he needed was a rumor flying around town.

Horace raised a hand in protest. "You know me, Sheriff, the soul of discretion."

Mitch decided to let it go at that and reached for his wallet.

Twenty minutes later he was seated in Cora Beth's kitchen, sipping on a cup of coffee. He seemed to be spending a lot of time there lately. "How's Cissy doing?"

"She had a rough night last night, poor darling. But her fever finally broke this morning and she's sleeping much easier now. Dr. Whitman stopped by to check on her and he thinks she's past the worst of it."

"Good to hear. And how about Ethan?"

"He never left her side last night. But bright and early this morning he headed out to the garden and spent the biggest part of it hard at work. That young man has a strong sense of duty. And more than his share of stubborn pride."

Mitch understood that. The boy probably felt pride was all he had left, that Titus had taken everything else. He'd learn in time that, with Cora Beth in his corner, he didn't have to constantly prove himself.

Cora Beth sighed. "I don't know what I'm going to do with him. He needs to be in school with the other children. Neither he nor Cissy have been to school since they moved to Knotty Pine. I only hope his mother was able to teach them at home."

Mitch imagined Titus had kept them much too busy to allow time for that.

"I saw Titus this morning."

Cora Beth stilled, apprehension drawing her jaw tight. "And?"

"I don't think he'll be bothering the children again."

Some of the tension slid from her shoulders. "Thank the good Lord for that." She smiled. "And thank you, too."

He shrugged. "Just doing my job." Better late than never.

She plopped her elbows on the table. "You can't fool me, Mitchell Hammond. I know it's much more than that."

The last thing he needed was for her to try to label him a hero. Especially considering he'd failed so tragically in this case. "I owed it to those kids."

He carried his coffee cup to the sink. "There's still the matter of all those items Ethan stole." He held up a hand to stop her protest. "I know he didn't think he had any other choice, though I still don't know why he thought he needed Nelda's blamed plant, but the fact of the matter is, in the eyes of the town, he's a thief."

To his surprise, she nodded. "You're right. And I think he feels bad about doing it."

"Feeling bad is a start, but it's not enough."

"What do you suggest?"

"You're the parent. If it was one of your girls or Danny who did that, what sort of punishment would you dole out?"

She stared at him for a minute and he could see her mind working to formulate an answer. Finally she sighed. "I'd make them face the consequences of their actions."

"I thought so."

"When do you want to talk to him?"

"No point putting it off."

She nodded. "He'll be in from the garden soon."

Mitch reached into his pocket and pulled out the wrapped packet he'd picked up at the mercantile. "When you have a moment, give him and Cissy this."

She stepped closer to have a look. "What is it?

He unwrapped the tiny parcel. "It's the locket that belonged to their mother."

"Oh, Mitch, I know how much this is going to mean to them. How in the world did you manage to talk Titus out of it?"

"Titus sold it to Danvers over at the mercantile a few weeks ago. Luckily, Danvers still had it."

Rather than taking the locket from him, she closed his fist around it. "I think it would be more appropriate if *you* gave it to them."

They stood there with her small hand closed over his, gazes locked. Mitch felt unable to move or look away. There was such warmth in her touch, such tenderness in her eyes. He didn't think anyone had ever made him feel so special before.

He wasn't sure how long they stood like that. The spell was finally broken by the sound of the back door opening. As Ethan stepped inside, Cora Beth quickly turned back to the sink and began rinsing out Mitch's coffee cup.

But not before he saw the color rise in her cheeks.

He could tell already that his plan to keep things between them on a friendship basis was going to be sorely tried.

Cora Beth vigorously scrubbed at the hapless coffee cup. She hoped neither Mitch nor Ethan had noticed the warmth blossoming in her cheeks. Goodness, what must Mitch think of her, holding on to his hand like some schoolgirl with an inappropriate case of puppy love? And this on top of the way she'd acted just yesterday. Goodness only knew how long she would have held on to his hand if Ethan hadn't walked in.

She heard Ethan acknowledge Mitch's presence with a quick hello, and she turned back around, hoping she looked sufficiently composed.

"I've got the row of tomatoes and cucumbers weeded. Looks like there'll be some ready to pick in the next day or so."

"Thank you." She nodded toward the hall door. "You can clean up over in the washroom, then come back in here. Sheriff Hammond and I need to speak to you."

Ethan looked from one to the other of them, a worried frown on his face. But he merely nodded and left the room without another word.

While they waited, Cora Beth dried the cup and set it carefully back in the cupboard. Neither she nor Mitch said a word. Was he thinking about what he had to say to Ethan? Or about what had just passed between them?

When Ethan returned, they all took seats at the table.

Mitch cleared his throat. "First, you should know, I went out to Titus's place today."

She saw Ethan's face pale. "You told him where we were?"

Mitch shook his head. "No, but I did tell him I'd found you two." He leaned forward, his expression open and earnest. "I made it quite clear that in the eyes of the law he had no claim to you or Cissy and that you two were under my protection for the time being. He shouldn't be bothering either of you again."

"Good to hear."

Cora Beth looked pointedly at Mitch. "I think you have something for Ethan and Cissy."

Something unreadable flickered in his expression. Then he reached back into his pocket. "That's right. I almost forgot."

Ethan craned his neck. "What is it?"

Mitch held the necklace by its chain, letting the locket dangle at Ethan's eye level. "I came across this over at the mercantile. Thought it might be the one you mentioned yesterday."

It was just like Mitch to downplay his efforts.

Ethan didn't make a move to take the locket, just stared at it as if he were a starving man and it was a steak. "That's my ma's locket." He finally looked up, meeting Mitch's glance. "I'll pay you back whatever it cost just as soon as I'm able."

There was a long pause and Cora Beth tried to send a mental message to Mitch. *Please don't dismiss Ethan's offer. He needs to know you take him seriously.*

Finally Mitch leaned back. "All right. I figure you can spend an hour sweeping and taking care of some other chores over at my office every day for the next two weeks. That ought to just about cover it."

Two weeks—good. That meant Mitch wasn't planning to send them away any time soon.

Ethan nodded. "Yes, sir. I reckon that sounds fair."

He extended his hand. "Well then, go ahead and take it."

But Ethan moved his hands to his lap. "No, sir. You hold on to it until I've worked it off. Won't feel right otherwise."

Cora Beth couldn't have been prouder of the boy if he'd been her own son. She exchanged a quick glance with Mitch and his lips turned up for just a moment in a smile of understanding.

"I tell you what," he said to Ethan. "Why don't we ask Mrs. Collins here to hold it for us until you're ready to claim it? If she doesn't mind, that is."

"I'll be glad to." Cora Beth accepted the locket and set it on the table in front of her. "As soon as we're done here I'll place it in my jewelry box along with my mama's wedding band and my cameo brooch."

Deciding it wouldn't be right to make Mitch deliver the bad news, Cora Beth took a deep breath and stared directly into Ethan's eyes. "Speaking of paying off debts, Ethan, there's something else we need to discuss with you."

"Yes, ma'am. Do you have some more chores for me to do?"

"That's not it. We wanted to talk to you about those things you took from the folks around town."

The boy shifted, looking suddenly eleven years old again. "That was wrong I know, but I didn't know what else to do."

"I understand. But I think there are some folks that you at least owe an apology to."

His face paled, but he swallowed hard and nodded. "Yes, ma'am. As soon as Cissy gets—"

"I think today would be better," she said firmly. "No point putting off something like this. My Grammy Alma used to say, if you're dreading something you know you have to do, do it quick and be done with it. If you put it off, it'll just keep clawing at your insides and make you plumb miserable. Do you understand what she meant?"

Ethan had hung his head and was no longer meeting her gaze. "I suppose so."

Cora Beth looked at Mitch and he nodded, then leaned forward. "Okay, Ethan, we already know you took a shirt and sheet from Mrs. Johnson's clothesline, a pie from Mrs. Evans's windowsill and a potted plant from Mrs. Oglesby's greenhouse. Was there anything else?"

Ethan nodded and began to enumerate his thefts. "I took a few pieces of scrap lumber from somebody's woodpile, and I grabbed a couple more from an old shed that was falling down. I took a small pail and a handful of loose nails from someone else's back porch. I took two eggs from a chicken coop. Oh and I found almost a whole roll of twine out behind the mercantile and I took a broken board and a scoop of corn from a feed sack over at the livery."

Construction materials for his shelter and food for him and Cissy. But there were a few items Cora Beth couldn't figure out a purpose for. "I understand why you took most of these things," she said, "but can I ask why you took a plant from Mrs. Oglesby's greenhouse? I mean, it wasn't as if it were edible or useful."

"I know. But it was Cissy's birthday and I wanted to make the day special for her, like Ma used to do back when we lived in Howerton. That's why I took that cherry pie, too. After I took the pie I got to thinking that a fancy place like that big ole glass shed with the plants inside might have some special fruits or something. But it was just flowers."

His voice dripped with a young boy's disgust for such girly things. "Since I'd already broke in and Cissy liked pretty things, I reckoned that maybe nobody would miss it if I took just one. I mean there were so many and all, and I was careful to pick a small one. A raccoon followed me in, though. I caught just a glimpse of it and next thing I knew pots were falling over and there was a big old mess."

"I see." So much for Nelda's malicious prankster.

"And you're sure it wasn't you who knocked those plants over by accident?"

"Yes, sir. I was real careful."

Mitch believed him. "Do you think you can remember what houses you took all those things from?

"Yes, sir." He stared at Mitch as if prepared for the worst. "Are you going to put me in jail?"

"If you own up to what you did and offer to make restitution, I don't think that'll be necessary." He gave the boy one of those stern lawman looks he coul do so well. "If you ever do anything like that again, t it'll be a whole different story. Understand?"

"Yes, sir. It won't happen again."

"Good. Then I think you and I need to make visits this afternoon."

Cora Beth stood. "Mind if I come along?" She ured it might be good if the townsfolk saw that Et had her support as well as Mitch's.

Mitch gave her a considering look. "That might nice, Mrs. Collins. For Ethan," he added.

Cora Beth smiled. "I'll ask Uncle Grover or Mr Plunkett to sit with Cissy after lunch and then the thre of us can make some house calls."

Chapter Nine

"Well, hello, Sheriff, Cora Beth. Is there something I can do for you?" Rita Evans stepped out on her front porch to greet them, a surprised but welcoming look on her face.

Cora Beth returned her smile, but decided to let Mitch do the talking.

"Hello, Rita." Mitch touched the brim of his hat in greeting. "We just wanted to talk to you for a few minutes if you've got the time."

"Certainly." Rita patted her soft white hair and stepped to one side. "Y'all come on inside and let me fix you up a glass of lemonade."

"No need for refreshments, this'll only take a few minutes."

"Well, suit yourself then." She allowed the screen door to close and looked from one to the other of them. "What can I do for you?" she asked again.

Cora Beth nudged Ethan to the forefront. "This is Ethan Prentiss. He and his sister Cecelia are staying over at the boardinghouse for a while. And he has something to say to you."

Rita gave him a friendly, grandmotherly smile.

"Hello, young man. What was it you were wanting to tell me?"

Ethan's posture was fence-post stiff and his expression rigidly controlled. But he held up his head. "It was me who took your pie the other day, ma'am. I'm truly sorry and I'd like to make it right with you."

"Oh. I see." Rita looked from the boy to the adults, her smile fading to uncertainty. "I suppose you must have had a good reason."

"My reason don't matter none, ma'am. Stealing is stealing and it ain't right no matter what."

Cora Beth was proud that the boy wasn't making excuses for himself. It was a good sign that he truly regretted what he'd done.

"Well, of course but—"

"Perhaps you have some chores that Ethan could take care of for you," Cora Beth prompted.

"Oh. Why yes." Rita took her cue and her flustered expression changed to something more businesslike. "As a matter of fact, I've been after Alfred to whitewash our front fence for a month now but he's just been so busy lately."

Ethan nodded. "I'll be glad to take care of it for you, ma'am. And don't you worry, I promise to do an extra special job. I can do it tomorrow morning if you like."

"Tomorrow will be fine. I already have the whitewash and brushes."

As they stepped back onto the sidewalk a few minutes later, Cora Beth gave Ethan an encouraging smile. "You did just fine. Are you ready for the next name on our list?"

Within two hours they had visited just about every one of Ethan's "victims." Most had taken it as well as

Rita—a few were a bit more huffy—but all agreed to let Ethan repay them with chores, which meant he had quite enough to keep him busy for the next two weeks. Cora Beth had made careful note of each obligation.

"There's just one more stop we need to make," Mitch said.

Ethan shook his head. "Don't you mean two more? The livery owner and the lady with the glass plant house."

Cora Beth smiled. "I'm the livery owner. At least my family is."

The boy halted midstep, pausing for a heartbeat before continuing on. "Oh."

"I think an hour or so mucking out the horse stalls should more than cover the cost of one board and a scoop of corn."

"Yes, ma'am. So I guess now we go visit the lady with the plant house."

Mitch exchanged a look with Cora Beth. "That's right. Mrs. Oglesby. Before we knock on her door, though, you need to understand that she feels very strongly about her greenhouse and the plants she grows there. And apparently the plant you took was one of her favorites."

Ethan nodded gloomily. "You're trying to say she's going to be angry with me."

"Very likely."

Cora Beth gave him a sympathetic look. "Mrs. Oglesby tends to get a bit dramatic over things like this."

"You think she's going to yell at me?"

Cora Beth shook her head. "Oh, no, I doubt she'll actually yell." Though Ethan might prefer she had when it was all said and done.

Ethan squared his shoulders. "Well, I suppose I deserve whatever she wants to throw at me. Everyone else has been so nice, there was bound to be at least one person who wanted to give me what for." He gave them both a weak smile. "Like your Grammy Alma said, best to get it over and done with instead of worrying over it."

A few minutes later, they stood on Nelda's front porch, waiting for her to answer Mitch's knock.

When she opened the door her brows went up, but she offered them a neighborly smile. "Sheriff, Cora Beth, to what do I owe this unexpected visit?"

Cora Beth decided to take the lead on this one. "Mind if we speak to you for a few minutes, Nelda?"

"Of course." Nelda moved to let them in. Then she eyed Ethan suspiciously and stepped outside instead. "So, who is your young friend here?"

Cora Beth placed her hand at Ethan's back, not certain if she was offering support to Ethan or herself. "This is Ethan Prentiss. He has something to say to you."

"Does he, now." Nelda drew herself up to her full height. "Well, young man, out with it. What do you have to say to me?"

"I—" Ethan faltered, then straightened. "I'm the one who stole the plant from your glass shed."

Her eyes narrowed. "So you're the little thief, are you?" She turned to Mitch. "Well, Sheriff, I'm glad to see you've finally captured this criminal. What do you plan to do with him?"

Mitch crossed his arms. "Now, Nelda, hear him out. Ethan is here to make amends."

"Make amends? How can he possibly make amends

for what he did?" She glared at Ethan. "And just what did you do with my prize orchid?"

"I gave it to my sister for her birthday."

"And did you tell her that you stole it? Is that how you honor your sister on her special day, with ill-gotten goods?"

"Please, ma'am. I'm awful sorry." Ethan sounded desperate. "If there's anything at all I can do—"

Nelda cut him off midsentence. "Where are your parents? They should be here with you, not Cora Beth."

"Ethan's parents are no longer with us," Cora Beth explained. "He and his sister are staying with me for the time being."

"Staying with you? This boy should be under lock and key so he doesn't prey on any more innocent folk while they sleep."

"Oh for goodness' sake, Nelda, he's just a boy." Cora Beth tried to hold on to her temper but the woman had perfected the art of making mountains out of molehills. "And he's trying to make things right."

"The bible tells us to 'withhold not correction from the child.' The only way for a wicked child like him to learn is to make sure he faces the consequences for his crimes."

How dare she call Ethan wicked? Cora Beth tilted her chin up. "It also tells us to forgive others as the Father forgave us."

Nelda drew herself up. "Of course I forgive him. I know my Christian duty as well as you do, Cora Beth Collins. But discipline is part of training up a child."

This was getting them nowhere.

Fortunately, Mitch stepped in. "What is it you want us to do?"

Nelda waved a hand. "He's outright confessed to being a thief. What does the *law* say you should do?"

Mitch stared her down. "I'm *not* going to lock up an eleven-year-old boy for stealing a plant to give to his seven-year-old sister for her birthday. Especially when he's willing to make restitution. Now, what do you think is a fair exchange? He can do chores around here if you like."

"I most certainly do *not* like." She stared at Ethan as if he were a hardened criminal. "I will not subject my daughters to his regrettable influence. Odine and Loretta are such delicate flowers themselves—"

"Very well, then, we'll find a way for him to earn some money. What is the replacement cost for that plant?"

Bless Mitch for keeping a level head.

"I'm not certain I can find another just like it. I labored over it for so long, took such care—"

"Nelda." Mitch's tone said he was reaching the limit of his patience.

"Oh, very well." She tossed her head majestically. "I suppose fifteen dollars would cover it."

Cora Beth blinked. "Fifteen dollars? For a *plant?*"

"It's a very special plant. You asked me my price and that is it."

"Agreed." Mitch put a hand at Ethan's back. "Now, if you'll excuse us, we'll be going."

None of them spoke as they strode down the walk to Nelda's front gate. Finally, as they stepped onto the sidewalk, Ethan broke the silence. "She sure was powerful angry."

"That she was." Mitch's tone was agreeable but firm. "But you *did* steal her plant."

Abashed, Ethan was quiet for several minutes. Then

he kicked at a pebble. "It'll take me a long time to earn fifteen dollars, if I can even find a paying job. Do you think she's willing to wait?"

Mitch didn't turn his head. "I'll loan you the money. You can pay me back a little at a time."

Cora Beth smiled. Much as he tried to deny it, Mitch had a soft spot for these kids. "I'll hire you to help out at the stable," she added. Then she tapped the list. "Once you take care of all these other chores, that is."

There was another short silence, then Ethan looked from one to the other of them. "Why are you both being so nice to Cissy and me?"

Cora Beth found his question heartbreakingly sad. Had they really encountered so little kindness that he'd find this remarkable? "Ethan, I know you were treated poorly by Titus, but most folks around here aren't like that. They try to help others out when they can. Sheriff Hammond and I are glad to help you this way. And it's not like it's charity. You're paying for your keep by doing chores for me. And you're the one making things right with the folks around here. The sheriff and I just tagged along."

She placed a hand on his shoulder. "I'm very proud of how you handled yourself today. And more importantly, I know your mother would be very proud, as well."

Ethan's expression lightened and he stood a bit taller at that.

As they approached the boardinghouse, Cora Beth quickened her steps. "It's just about time for school to let out. I need to start working on supper." She turned to Mitch. "You're welcome to join us for our meal this evening if you like."

"That's mighty tempting but I think I'll pass. I have some things that need my attention at the office and I have evening rounds to make. But I'd like to come by and check on Cissy a little later if that's okay."

The idea that his only reason for coming to visit was to check on the kids pricked at her pride. But she managed a smile. "You don't need to ask. You're welcome to stop in for a visit anytime."

With a touch of his hat brim, he took his leave.

As Cora Beth watched him walk away, she wondered what he would say if he knew that she sometimes daydreamed about having him court her. For a fleeting moment she toyed with the idea that she should borrow from Mrs. Plunkett's example and let her feeling show more.

But she quickly pushed that notion aside. After all, any number of other ladies—much more suitable than her—had done just that. If Mitch wasn't swayed by their efforts, what would make her think he'd be swayed by hers?

Still, as long as she kept her daydreams to herself, they would cause no harm.

Mitch walked down the hall of the boardinghouse, not sure why he felt slightly off balance this evening. He'd found Cora Beth on the front porch swing, taking care of some mending in the fading evening light. Rather than pausing to chat with him as he'd expected, though, she'd smiled, waved him on with a quick *you know the way* and gone back to her sewing.

Shaking off the vaguely dissatisfied feeling, he entered Cissy's room to find not one but four little girls there, playing with a set of rag dolls.

Dealing with one little girl was one thing, but four—

Audrey spied him first. "Oh, hello, Sheriff Hammond."

"Hi, Audrey, ladies. Don't you girls look as bright as a springtime garden." He turned to Cissy. "Glad to see you're feeling well enough to play today, Buttercup."

Cissy sat up straighter when she spotted Mitch. "I'm all better now but Audrey's mom says I have to stay in bed a little longer."

"That's right. We want to make sure you have all your strength back before you start running around with these two-legged whirlwinds."

"Why'd you call her 'Buttercup'?" Audrey asked. "Her name is Cissy."

"I know. But with her yellow hair and pink cheeks she reminds me of a buttercup."

"Oh." Audrey thought about that for a second. "Do I remind you of a flower?"

"You sure do. I think of you as a sweet pea. Pert and sassy."

Audrey turned to her sisters, preening. "Did you hear that? Sheriff Hammond thinks I'm like a sweet pea."

"What about us?" one of the twins asked.

Mitch had to think fast. He couldn't tell which twin was which and he didn't want to slight either of them. "Well, you," he said pointing to the one who'd spoke up, "remind me of a daisy because of how sweet and bright you are. And you," he said turning to the other twin, "remind me of a morning glory because you're quieter but your eyes are always sparkling like morning dew."

"Hear that, Pippa? I'm a morning glory."

Okay, he'd have to remember that—Pippa, daisy; Lottie, morning glory.

"Do you want to play with us?" Cissy asked. "We'll share our dolls."

"Thank you for the invitation but I'm afraid I can't stay long. I did bring you all something, though."

Cissy's eyes lit up. "What?"

"Lemon drops." He pulled the candy wrapped in wax paper from his pocket. "I have just enough here for you to each have a piece."

That earned him a chorus of "yes, please's" and "thank you's."

Once he'd handed out the last piece, he straightened. "Well, I'll leave you ladies to your dolls now. But I'll be back tomorrow to check on you again."

"Before you go," Cissy asked, "would you sing me that song again?"

Mitch felt his smile freeze. Singing out of desperation to a sick, fretful child in the middle of nowhere was one thing. But singing to four alert little girls was something else entirely. "But that's a lullaby and it's not time to go to sleep yet. I'm sure Audrey and her sisters would rather play with the dolls than hear me sing."

Her eyes widened like a forlorn puppy's. "Please?"

"We want to hear it, too," Audrey added.

The twins nodded. Mitch found himself the target of four pairs of pleading little-girl eyes and discovered he would rather face down a hardened criminal on a rampage. At least with someone like that he'd have a fighting chance.

"All right, you win." Taking a deep breath, he began to sing. *"Good night, happy dreams, my sweet little one. Close your eyes..."*

Cora Beth paused with her hand on the kitchen door and smiled as she heard the faint sounds of Mitch's singing coming from Cissy's room. The girls would be enjoying such special attention from him, she was sure.

She stood there in the hall, letting the words wash over her, as well.

Mitch definitely had a way with the ladies, even the very young ones like the quartet he was with now. Part of his charm was that he made a lady feel special, worth looking out for. And he did it effortlessly, naturally and without being overbearing. More than likely, if you were to ask him, he'd deny he was doing anything out of the ordinary. Which made it all the more charming.

But it also meant any attention he was showing her was not to be taken too much to heart. Mitch was just being Mitch. He wasn't trying to single her out or make her feel in any way special.

Suddenly she wasn't quite so charmed. Truth be told, she *wanted* Mitch to see her as special. Was that wrong of her? And more to the point, was there any chance it would ever happen?

Chapter Ten

The next morning, Dr. Whitman arrived right after breakfast. Once he completed his examination of Cissy, Cora Beth stepped into the hall with him. "So, how is she?"

Before the physician could answer, Ethan popped into the hall from the kitchen. "Is she all better now?"

Dr. Whitman smiled reassuringly at the boy. "She's doing just fine." Then he turned back to Cora Beth. "In fact, if you'd like, you can let her get up for a while today. A bit of exercise will be good for her—just as long as you make certain she takes it easy and doesn't overdo it for the next few days."

"That's good to hear." Cora Beth turned to Ethan. "You can go back inside and check on her if you like."

With a nod he disappeared into Cissy's room.

"She'll be glad to hear the good news," she said. "I think she was getting tired of staring at those same four walls."

"Like I said, it's important that she takes it easy for the next day or two, and she'll be just fine. If anything comes up, though, you know where to find me."

"Are you sure I can't get you a cup of coffee and slice of pecan pie before you leave?"

"That's mighty tempting but no, thank you. I promised Mrs. Addison I'd check in on Billy this morning. Poor kid sprained his ankle when he fell out of a tree yesterday."

"Well, give Willa my best. And thank you again."

After she'd escorted the doctor to the front door, Cora Beth returned to Cissy's room to find the girl sitting up, her eyes sparkling with excitement. "Ethan says it's okay for me to get out of bed today."

"That's right. But you have to agree to go slowly and not tire yourself out. Can you do that?"

"Oh yes, ma'am."

"Good. Then I think a bath will be our first order of business this morning."

Cissy wrinkled her nose. "Do I have to?"

"Only if you want to get out of bed."

As Cora Beth escorted Cissy to the washroom she took note of the child's limp. "Does your leg heart you, sweetheart?"

"No, ma'am. I mean, sometimes, when the weather's damp or really cold or I been playing hard, it'll hurt some. But mostly it just doesn't work as good as my other leg."

"I see. Well, no doubt a nice warm bath will do it and you a load of good."

Once she'd taken her bath, Cissy was ready to explore the rest of the house. The child was self-conscious of her limp at first, but Cora Beth had already told the other members of her household what to expect, so it wasn't long before the four girls had their heads together, chattering and giggling over little-girl things.

For a while Ethan hovered over his sister like a biddy

hen protecting its chick, but after a bit, when he realized no one was going to make her feel uncomfortable,
he relaxed. By midmorning he headed off to the Evans
place to whitewash their fence. After that he was headed
to the sheriff's office to start working off the money for
the locket.

Danny worked at the livery on Saturday mornings so
he was already gone. And Uncle Grover and Mrs. Plunkett had gone out on another field trip.

That left her and the four girls on their own.

"All right, girls, it's Saturday, and you know what
that means."

"Baking day," her daughters said in unison.

"That's right, so get your aprons and head for the
kitchen." Cora Beth usually got her daughters involved
in helping her with her baking on Saturdays. It served
to not only teach them skills they would need later in
life, but gave her additional time to spend with them.

"Can I help, too?" Cissy asked.

"Are you sure you wouldn't rather just watch?"

"I'm sure. My ma taught me how to make stews
and boil vegetables, but I never learned much about
baking."

The reminder of what the child had been through
caused Cora Beth to swallow hard and work to maintain her smile. "Well, come along then. I have an extra
apron you can use."

Once everyone was gathered in the kitchen and Cora
Beth had gotten out the basic supplies, the girls all stood
around the table.

"All right, before we get started," Cora Beth said,
"we need to explain to Cissy how this works."

Audrey raised her hand. "Can I do it?"

Cora Beth nodded her permission.

"We usually make nine pies," Audrey explained, "one for each day of the week and a couple of extras, just in case."

Cissy's eyes grew wide. "That's a lot of pies."

"We have a lot of people who live here." Audrey said this as if she were personally responsible. "Anyway, Mama lets each of us pick one kind of pie to make, and then we help her roll out the dough and put the filling in."

Audrey turned to Cora Beth. "Can Cissy pick a pie, too?"

"Of course."

"What's your favorite kind of pie?" Pippa asked.

"Apple."

"Mine, too," Lottie announced. "But I want to add in some blueberries."

"Mine is buttermilk," Audrey said with conviction. "At least this week it is."

"And I want a pecan," Pippa said. "Mixed with walnuts."

Sometimes her girls liked to get creative. "All right then. It sounds like we have an order for one apple pie, one apple pie with blueberries, one buttermilk pie and one pecan pie with walnuts. And how about we add two peach pies, two custard pies and a plain pecan pie to round out the week? What do you think?"

There were enthusiastic nods of approval all around.

Ten minutes later, each girl had an assigned task and, depending on her abilities, was sifting flour, whisking eggs, gathering filling ingredients or laying out pie tins. Cora Beth crossed the room to check on the oven temperature and glanced out the window as she passed by, the same as she'd done a half-dozen times this morning.

Somehow she'd gotten used to Mitch paying visits every morning and every evening. But so far no sign of him yet today.

Just as she was turning around to the girls, though, she spotted a movement from the corner of her eye. Sure enough, Mitch was headed toward the back porch.

And suddenly her whole morning seemed just a tiny bit brighter.

Mitch stood in the doorway, surveying the kitchen full of females. "Well, well, looks like Miss Cissy is feeling lots better today."

Cissy stepped down from her stool and gave Mitch a hug around his knees. "Hi, Sheriff." Then she looked up at him, her flour-dusted face beaming. "I'm helping make pies."

Mitch was caught off guard by the demonstrative gesture. Uncertain how to react, he glanced up at Cora Beth for some hint.

When all he got was an amused smile, he looked back down at Cissy and gave her an awkward pat. "Good for you."

"We're all making pies," Audrey added. "I'm wishing the eggs."

"Whisking," Cora Beth corrected. She turned back to Mitch, that smile still teasing at her mouth. "Is there something we can do for you this morning?"

Cissy had returned to her task and Mitch cleared his throat, hoping to clear his head at the same time. "Just checking in to see how things are going. I saw Ethan over at the Evans place. Rita was plying him with lemonade."

She nodded. "I'm sure he's doing a good job for her.

He also plans to spend some time over at your office today."

"Good. I'll be ready for him." Ethan's prickliness he could handle much more easily than Cissy's adoration, or the smile it brought to Cora Beth's face.

"Do you want to help us make pies?" Cissy asked.

"I'm afraid I'm not much of a baker."

"You can share mine when it's done. I picked apple."

"Well now, that's mighty generous of you, but I'm sure Mrs. Collins here is planning to serve these with her fine suppers this week."

"Then you can come to supper, too." She turned to Cora Beth. "That would be okay, wouldn't it?"

He saw Cora Beth swallow a smile as she solemnly nodded her head. "That sounds like a fine idea."

"We'll see." Mitch stuffed his hat back on his head. It wouldn't do for him to start feeling like one of the family. "I gotta be going. Bye, ladies."

Cora Beth followed him out to the back porch. "It seems Cissy has a bad case of hero worship."

Mitch rubbed the back of his neck. "What do I do about it?"

"Enjoy it. And treat her affection with respect."

"But I'm nobody's hero." In fact he was far from it. If they only knew.

"You are a hero to her. She probably sees you as an adult version of her big brother." Cora Beth touched his sleeve. "It's a blessing you're the first man she came in contact with after what she experienced with Titus. You're exactly what she needs in her life right now."

Those words scared him worse than a charging stampede. "That's one heck of a responsibility."

"Which is why God gave it to you—the perfect man for the job."

As Mitch headed away, he mulled over her words. Him a hero? Ridiculous. Only a scarred little girl like Cissy could see him that way.

What about Cora Beth, though? Not that she really needed a hero. She was a strong woman—self-reliant, full of heart and solid as that huge oak that shaded her side lawn.

Just exactly the kind of woman that a man would slay dragons for.

At least *this* man would.

Mitch looked up from his desk when the door opened.

Ethan stood there, a closed-off expression on his face. "I'm here to start working for what I owe you for the locket."

"Good. There's a broom over there in the corner. You can start by sweeping out the place."

With a nod, Ethan went straight to work.

Mitch leaned back in his chair, tipping the front legs up slightly, and watched the boy work. For a while, the only sound was the swishing of the broom.

"I stopped by the boardinghouse earlier. Your sister's up and looking well."

"The doc says she's a lot better."

Another long silence. The boy sure wasn't much of a talker. "How are you liking it over at the boarding-house?"

Ethan shrugged. "It's okay. Mrs. Collins is a nice lady. And she treats us good."

Did the kid realize how lucky he was that he'd landed on her doorstep and not someone else's?

Ethan paused for a moment. "You reckon she'll let us stay there until I get everyone paid back? I mean, I can make it camping okay, but Cissy ain't as strong as I am."

"I don't think that'll be a problem. In fact, I believe she's counting on it."

Ethan nodded and went back to pushing the broom.

"I saw you over at the Evans place earlier. You been there this whole time?"

Ethan nodded. "Wanted to get it finished up today so I can move on to something else on Monday. The faster I get all these chores done, the faster I can get back to earning some traveling money for me and Cissy."

The kid still thought he was going to take Cissy and head out, just the two of them. "Ethan, I meant it when I said you have nothing to fear from Titus anymore. There's no need for you to keep running."

"Folks around here think I'm a thief and maybe worse. They're not going to give me a chance to prove different. Especially that Mrs. Oglesby—and I found out today she's the mayor's wife. I just think we'll be better off settling somewhere else."

"Not everyone feels that way. Mrs. Collins, for instance, told me how proud she is of the way you faced up to what you did. And I'm proud of the way you look out for your sister. There's others around here who'd be willing to give you the benefit of the doubt and let you prove yourself to them."

Ethan shrugged. "Still and all, starting over with a clean slate, with folks who don't already think the worst of me, just sounds like it would be better."

"And what if you run into folks in the next town who get the wrong idea about you? Are you going to move on again? Or if Cissy gets sick or hurt again—are you sure there'll be someone around who'll care as much about her as Mrs. Collins does?"

His chin jutted out. "We'll be okay."

"Ethan, at some point you have to put down roots and stand up for who you are and who you want to be. And you need to give Cissy a real home. That some-place could be right here." He'd pushed hard enough—time to back off. "Think on it anyway."

"I will. But I ain't making any promises."

What would happen when the boy realized the decision was not going to be his to make? Would he feel resigned? Relieved? Or betrayed?

Cora Beth sat on her front porch swing, an open book in her lap but her gaze was directed toward some unseen point past their front gate rather than at the pages. She absently reached down and scratched Scout's head and his tail thumped the porch floor in appreciation. She and the dog had become good friends these past few days.

It was Sunday afternoon, and they'd passed yet another hurdle with Ethan and Cissy—the pair had accompanied her family to church service that morning.

Cissy had walked in between her and Ethan and had held tightly to her hand as they walked down the aisle to their pew. But that was the only sign she gave of being self-conscious about her limp. And after the service Audrey had introduced her to several of her friends, including Loretta Oglesby. From what Cora Beth could see, Nelda's reservations didn't seem to be shared by her youngest daughter.

She'd noticed that Ethan stood off to the side by himself, hands stuffed in his pockets, a glower on his face and his gaze glued to Cissy. How long would it be before the boy learned to let down his guard and *be* a boy again?

After church they all had lunch at Sadie and Eli's house. Josie, Ry and Viola were there, as well. It was an opportunity for Ethan and Cissy to meet the rest of the family and for the adults to catch up with each other. Cora Beth surreptitiously kept an eye on the children, and she was dismayed to see Ethan again holding himself apart.

She had hoped that Danny would have been happy to have another boy by his side in the midst of all the girls, but he seemed to still distrust Ethan for some reason. She'd have to get to the bottom of that soon.

Very soon.

Because sometime between leaving Sadie's and their arrival back at the boardinghouse, Cora Beth had decided she was going to take in Ethan and Cissy on a permanent basis, and make them an official part of her family.

It was something she'd spent the last few days praying about, making sure this was the right choice for everyone—the two orphans, her own children, Danny, herself.

It wasn't just that she couldn't bear the idea of sending them to an orphanage anymore. Even if they had another place to go, another family who wanted to take them in, it would break her heart to lose them. Ethan and Cissy already felt as dear to her as her own children. So there was really no reason not to make the arrangement a permanent one. Sure, there were a few things that would need to be resolved, some issues to address, but with a bit of time and effort it would work out.

As soon as she'd made that decision a sweet peace had filled her. It wasn't going to be smooth sailing, she knew that, but it was the right choice. Already she couldn't imagine the household without them.

Would Ethan and Cissy be pleased? She was fairly certain Cissy would, but with Ethan it was hard to tell. He was so fiercely independent, so walled off. But, given his other choices, surely he would see this as his best option.

Her first thought was to tell Mitch, to discuss it with him and see what he thought. Not only was his advice down to earth and sound, she knew he would also offer her comfort and support.

But that was foolish, selfish, wholly inappropriate. She should tell her family first.

Heavenly Father, thank You for sending these children to me. Help me to be the kind of mother they need me to be, to make this a true home for them, to help them forget the terrible things that have happened to them. And most of all, give me the right words to say to them and to my family when I inform them of this decision. Open Ethan's and Danny's hearts especially to the rightness of this plan.

Scout barked, as if to add an amen to her prayer.

Chapter Eleven

"I have something I want to discuss with you."

Ethan and Cissy looked at her with equally solemn faces. But their expressions were quite different. Cissy just seemed puzzled. Ethan on the other hand looked braced for something terrible.

How sad that he always expected the worst. She would have to do her best to see that he learned to expect good from others.

Ethan looked at her straight on. "You've decided what you're going to do with us now that Cissy's better, haven't you?"

She smiled. "Let's just say I've decided what I'd like for us to do."

His hands were balled in a fist. "We're not going to any old orphanage if that's what you have in mind. They split up the boys and girls and I wouldn't be able to watch over Cissy."

Cissy, her expression suddenly stricken, snaked a hand out to capture her brother's, and her lower lip began to tremble.

So he'd thought through the possibilities already. "Oh, no, Ethan. That's not what I had in mind at all."

His shoulders drew back. "Then you're going to let us go on our way?"

But Cissy didn't seem as pleased as her brother with that plan. "Does that mean we have to sleep in the woods again, Ethan?"

Cora Beth didn't let the boy answer that one. "Oh, no, sweetheart, I have a much better idea." Cora Beth looked from one to the other of them. "I would like for you to both stay here with me and be part of our family."

"You would?" Cissy straightened, her smile splitting into that endearing gap-toothed grin.

"More than just about anything in the world."

The little girl turned to her brother. "Oh, please, can we, Ethan? I really like it here."

Rather than answering, Ethan turned to Cora Beth, his suspicion still very much in evidence. "What would we have to do in return? I can work hard at whatever chores you set me, but I won't have Cissy turned into a servant again."

"You don't understand, Ethan. I said you would be part of the *family*, not servants. What you'd be expected to do is to accept the responsibilities that go along with that. While I know I'd never be able to take the place of your real mother in your heart, you'd offer me the respect and obedience the same as you would her. And you'd have chores to do, just like Danny and the girls. And you'd be expected to go to school regularly and do your best to learn what Mr. Saddler and Miss Honoria try to teach you."

"That's all?"

"Other than being respectful and supportive of the others, just as they will be to you, and accepting our love and friendship, yes, that's all."

"I won't be able to start school right away," Ethan said. "Not until I work off all my debts to everyone."

"Schooling is important and you've already missed too much. I think we should just plan on you taking up most of your Saturdays getting those chores done."

"But I promised the sheriff I'd work for him for two weeks."

"I believe an hour a day *after* school should cover it."

He didn't seem happy with that answer, but he nodded. "Yes, ma'am."

"Would Sheriff Hammond be part of our family, too?" Cissy asked.

It would be wonderful to be able to say yes. "No. But he would be a very good friend."

"Because he has another family?"

"No, I'm afraid Sheriff Hammond doesn't have any other family. He has his own house to live in, though, and his own work to do. But you'll still be able to see him often."

"Okay."

Cora Beth stood and held out a hand to each of them. "Now, let's go tell the others, shall we?"

Ten minutes later the three of them stood in the parlor with the rest of the family gathered around them. Audrey, Pippa and Lottie had plopped down on the settee, while Uncle Grover and Danny each claimed an armchair.

"I have something exciting to tell you," Cora Beth began. "I've just invited Ethan and Cissy to stay here with us permanently, and they've agreed. As of today, they are officially part of our family."

Everyone, with the exception of Danny, popped out of their seats immediately and came rushing over.

Uncle Grover shook Ethan's hand and patted Cissy on the shoulder. "Wonderful news! Welcome to the family. The more the merrier, I always say."

Audrey gave Cissy an enthusiastic hug. "We can be twins, just like Pippa and Lottie," she said excitedly. Then she turned to Ethan. "Do you want to be twins with Danny?"

"Don't be silly," Danny interjected gruffly. "You can't be twins with someone unless you're born that way."

"Can too," Audrey insisted. "Can't we, Mama?"

Cora Beth frowned at her brother, then turned to Audrey. "Danny's right, you won't be twins by birth. But you can be twins of the spirit if you want to be." Why was Danny still so begrudging and suspicious of Ethan?

Satisfied, Audrey linked arms with Cissy. "Well, we want to be, don't we?"

Cissy nodded.

Once the initial hubbub had quieted down, Cora Beth waved everyone back to their seats. "All right, I know we're excited, but we should talk over what this means. Just like with any change, we're going to need to make a few adjustments to make this work. First off, the sleeping arrangements. Pippa and Lottie, I think you girls are big enough now to have a room all to yourselves. Audrey, we're going to move you to one of the extra guest rooms and you'll be sharing it with Cissy." She'd given that some thought because of Cissy's limp, but the girl had already tackled the stairs earlier when Audrey had taken her up to her room. Other than being a bit more deliberate in her steps and holding onto the banister, she hadn't seemed to have any problems. And Cora

Beth had a hunch she'd rather be upstairs than isolated on the first floor.

Audrey gave Cissy's arm a squeeze. "See, just like twins."

Cora Beth turned to Danny, knowing he was not going to like this next part. "We'll put an extra bed in your room and Ethan can share it with you."

As she'd expected, Danny didn't look any too happy with that idea, but Cora Beth shot him a warning look and he kept his complaints to himself. A quick glance Ethan's way told her he was well aware that Danny was not going to be laying out the welcome mat.

"We're also going to redo the chore assignments. Cissy and Ethan, I expect you to lend a hand with getting the table cleared and dishes washed after every meal. And I also expect you to do your part to keep your rooms and the rest of the house neat and tidy."

She turned to Cissy. "You can help me and the girls with the household chores."

"Including the Saturday baking?"

"That's right." Then she turned to Ethan. "You can help with getting the firewood taken care of and the lamps filled and wicks trimmed. You can also lend a hand at the livery when needed—Danny can show you the ropes over there." Maybe getting them to work together would help ease some of the tension between them.

"I can handle what needs doing at the livery," Danny said.

"Be that as it may," Cora Beth said firmly, "I want Ethan to learn how to manage things there, too."

Danny didn't say anything else, but his eyes spoke volumes.

"All right, we'll figure the rest of this out as we go.

For now, let's get the rooms rearranged so we can all get a good night's sleep tonight."

She waved her hands. "Boys, you help the girls move their furniture around, please. I'll be up to check on things in a little bit. I need to talk to our resident school-teachers for just a minute—Ethan and Cissy start school with you tomorrow morning."

As they started to disperse, she caught her brother's eye. "Danny, stay behind just a minute, please. I'd like to discuss something with you."

With a reluctant nod, Danny plopped down on the settee. After everyone else had gone, Cora Beth took a seat across from him. "Please tell me why you can't seem to get along with Ethan. Has he done something to deserve your distrust?"

"I just don't have much use for thieves and liars is all."

His tone, as much as his words, were full of anger. "Daniel Edward Atkins, I'm surprised at you."

"It's true, isn't it? I mean, he stole from half the families in town and everyone knows it. He even admitted it. How do you think it looks to my friends that we're treating him like he hasn't done anything wrong? And now I'm supposed to share a room with him?"

Cora Beth felt a stab of disappointment. "Danny, we can't control what others think, and we also can't let it control *us*. Yes, Ethan stole some things, but he was trying to provide for his little sister. It was the wrong way to go about it and he knows that now, but you can't fault him for *why* he did what he did. You also can't say that you've never done anything wrong yourself."

Danny's mouth was set in a stubborn line. "Stealing is stealing. I hear he lived with old Titus Brown for a while, and that he's turning out just like him."

Cora Beth felt her temper rise at that. "Whoever said that doesn't know what they're talking about." She held up a hand when he started to protest. "I mean they don't know the whole story. If they did, they'd probably think of him as a hero."

"Hero?"

She had tried to shield the children from the truth of what had happened, but perhaps that had been the wrong thing to do. "Titus treated both Ethan and Cissy very cruelly when they were with him. He never let them go to church or school. In fact, he never let them leave his farm. Titus stole the few items they had that were worth anything and sold them for whiskey. He forced them both to work from sunup to sundown, and he shackled Cissy with a leg iron so she and Ethan wouldn't run away. And still Ethan managed to get his sister safely away and keep them both alive for nearly two weeks out in the woods."

She held his gaze. "Now you tell me, what would you have done if it had been you and you had Audrey or one of the twins to protect?"

Danny swallowed hard. Then he rallied. "He could have just asked folks for help," he said defensively.

"True. But he wasn't used to folks being particularly kind to him. And he didn't want to take the chance of someone handing him and Cissy back over to Titus."

Danny didn't respond to that. He sat there, his posture and expression still defensive.

It was obvious he wasn't ready to listen to reason on this just yet. Did his friends' opinions mean that much to him? "Well, promise me you'll think about what I just said. And whether you like it or not, he's family now. I can't make you like him, but I do expect you to be civil to him. Understood?"

"Yes, ma'am."

Amazing how much displeasure and resistance he was able to pack into those two words.

She sighed. "All right, run along and help the others with setting up the rooms. I'll be up shortly."

As she went in search of the schoolteachers, she wished she could talk to Mitch, as well. Not only did she want to tell him about her decision to keep the children, but she would dearly love to get his opinion on how to handle this situation with Danny. Sometimes it was really hard to be both the father and the mother. Children, especially boys, needed a man in their lives. And she couldn't think of a better candidate than Mitchell Hammond.

Too bad he didn't seem interested in the job. Too bad for the boys—and too bad for her, as well.

Cora Beth had decided a long time ago that Monday was her least favorite day of the week. Of course, that was mainly because doing laundry was her least favorite chore.

It wasn't quite so bad in the summertime. Although the summer heat made the back-breaking work even more hot and sticky than usual, she at least had the children around to both lend a hand and make it a more sociable activity in the process. When school was in session, she was completely on her own.

As she hung the final pillowcase on the clothesline, though, she realized that she'd barely stopped humming all morning. Yesterday evening's decision to take in Cissy and Ethan still felt so right, so meant-to-be.

They'd headed off with the other children for school this morning, if not enthusiastically at least willingly. Ethan would be in Mr. Saddler's group of older children and Cissy would be in Honoria's younger group. Both teachers had assured Cora Beth last night that they'd keep an eye on their new students and do their best to help them fit in.

And to top things off, Danny had seemed just a tad less belligerent this morning. Maybe their little talk last night had had more of an impact than she'd thought.

She'd asked the children to keep an eye out for when Josie dropped Viola off, and to ask her to come by the boardinghouse before heading back to her place.

When she'd told Josie about her plans to make Ethan and Cissy part of the family, her sister had let out a whoop and given her a big hug. Then she laughed and said she'd already told Ry she figured there'd be two extra places set at the table from now on.

Cora Beth still hadn't seen Mitch since church service yesterday. Not that that was at all unusual. Up until Ethan burst into her life, Mitch had had no reason to stop by her place on any kind of regular basis. It was just that she'd gotten used to his twice-a-day visits this past week. She'd known it was only natural that things would go back to their normal routine in time—she just hadn't figured on it being this soon.

Cissy, of course, would miss seeing him every day.

Perhaps she'd stop by the sheriff's office later. After all, he seemed to feel he had as big a stake in securing a good future for Ethan and Cissy as she did. It was only right that she let him know about this turn of events.

A little corner of her mind hoped that her news became the cause for another of those hugs. She felt her face color at the thought, but so be it. Two friends could celebrate such a momentous decision without it meaning anything special, couldn't they?

* * *

Mitch approached the boardinghouse, wishing himself anywhere *but* here. At least when it came to this particular errand. He didn't like the idea of having to bring troubles to Cora Beth's doorstep.

He rounded the corner to the back of the boardinghouse and found Cora Beth approaching from the side yard with an empty laundry basket. Her face broke into a large, welcoming smile as soon as she saw him. Too bad that would disappear once he stated his business.

Sometimes he just didn't like this job.

"Why, hello," she said as the distance between them closed. "I was hoping you'd stop by this morning."

Any other day that would have been music to his ears. He noticed the becoming touch of pink in her cheeks—too much sun? "Were you now?" *Coward— just get to it.*

"Uh-huh. I have some wonderful news I wanted to share."

"Let me guess. You've decided to take Ethan and Cissy into your family permanently."

"You heard." She pursed her lips in a mock pout that somehow didn't detract from her sweet appearance.

He took the basket from her and let her precede him up the porch steps. "Audrey was proclaiming it to anyone who would listen on her way to school this morning."

Cora Beth's smile turned rueful. "That's my girl."

He reached past her and pulled open the screen door.

She turned, her face close enough that he could count the freckles on her nose. "Can I fix you a cup of coffee?"

He cleared his throat. "Uh, no, thank you."

She must have finally noticed something in his tone or expression. Her gaze sharpened. "What's wrong?"

"Nelda came to see me this morning."

She scrunched her nose. "That doesn't bode well for somebody. And since you're here, I assume that that somebody is me. What did I supposedly do?" She seemed more amused than worried.

"It's Ethan, actually."

That wiped the smile from her face. "Surely she's not still upset about that plant Ethan took? He's apologized and it's been paid for. I don't know what else he can do."

"No, it's something new. Someone broke into her greenhouse again last night and made quite a mess in there."

Cora Beth sat down with a plop. "And Nelda thinks Ethan had something to do with it?"

"She does."

Cora Beth folded her hands on the table. "He wouldn't do that. I mean, the first time he was just trying to make his sister's birthday into something special. He'd have no reason—"

He held up a hand. "You don't need to convince me. I said that's what Nelda believes, not that I believed it." He took a seat next to her. "The thing is, nothing was taken as far as Nelda could see. Someone just went in and knocked over some of her pots."

"Then Ethan definitely had nothing to do with it. He's not malicious." She tucked a strand of hair back behind her ear. "So what happens now?"

"I'll talk to Ethan when he gets out of school this afternoon. I assume he's still planning to work off that money I loaned him."

She nodded. "And when he says he had nothing to do with it—then what?"

"I'm confident I'll be able to tell whether or not he's telling the truth." Mitch shrugged. "After that, it'll be her word against his. There's nothing to point to Ethan other than Nelda's suspicions."

"I just hate to have this air of distrust and suspicion hanging over him." Her eyes clouded. "He already feels so beaten down. I wish you didn't have to say anything to him about it."

"But I do have to. It's my job. And better he hear it from me than from someone else."

"I know. It's just that this is not going to help his self-confidence any, or make him feel as welcome in Knotty Pine as I'd hope he would."

Mitch placed a hand over hers, stilling her nervous fluttering. "Give it time. Once folks around here get to know him better, they'll learn to trust him. And making him a part of your family is definitely going to up his standing in the community."

"As I told Mrs. Plunkett the other day," she said dryly, "patience has never been my strong suit."

He gave her hand a last squeeze and then stood. "Trust me, we'll weather this just fine."

Ethan walked into the sheriff's office that afternoon and with a quick nod headed for the corner where the broom was kept.

"The sweeping can wait," Mitch said. "Have a seat, I want to talk to you."

Ethan eyed him warily, but did as he was told.

"I hear Mrs. Collins offered to take you and Cissy in. How do you feel about that?"

The boy nodded. "All right I guess. She's treated

me and Cissy real nice these past few days. And Cissy needs a good place to stay and someone to treat her good."

"What about you? What do you need?"

"I don't need much. Just to be left alone."

"That sounds a mite lonely."

Ethan only shrugged.

The boy's walls were solid as granite. But if anyone could breach them it was Cora Beth.

Time to get down to that unpleasant bit of business. "Mrs. Oglesby came to see me today."

"The lady with the glass plant shed?"

"That's the one." He was watching Ethan closely but saw no sign of guilt or unease.

"Did she change her mind about me working for her? Because that's okay, I'll do whatever she thinks is fair."

"That's not it. It seems somebody broke into her greenhouse last night and made a mess of the place."

That got a rise out of him. "It wasn't me. I promise I didn't leave the boardinghouse at all after supper. You can check with Danny—we share a room now."

"I believe you. But I think you can understand why Mrs. Oglesby might think you had something to do with it."

Ethan looked down at his shoes. "Yes, sir. You gonna arrest me?"

"No. For now it's just her word against yours, so unless I get some proof convincing me otherwise, I'll assume you're innocent."

Ethan nodded, then glanced up and met his gaze. "Do you have to tell Mrs. Collins about this?"

He understood the boy's distress. He'd hate to disappoint Cora Beth, too. "Sorry, Ethan, she already knows. But don't worry—she doesn't think you did it. She jumped to your defense right away."

Ethan looked glumly down at the floor again. "I suppose everyone in town knows about it, too."

"I can't say for sure, but Mrs. Oglesby's not one to keep her grievances to herself." He couldn't leave it at that. The boy needed some encouragement. "Just hold your head up and don't give folks a reason to distrust you. You may not realize it but by confessing and working off your debts, you're making some friends here."

Ethan didn't look up. "If you say so. Can I get back to work now?"

"Just one more thing. You know Mrs. Collins is a special lady, don't you? The kind of person who always tries to see the best in folks."

That earned him an emphatic nod. "Yes, sir. I ain't never met anyone quite like her."

"I sure would hate to see someone, especially someone she cares a great deal for, betray that trust."

"I wouldn't do that, Sheriff, not even if somebody held a gun to my head."

Mitch hid a smile at the boy's dramatic assurances. "I believe you. Now, I've got work to do and you've got floors to sweep."

He hoped he'd handled that right. Had he been too easy on the boy? Too tough? How would Cora Beth have handled it? And how in the world did she manage to deal with these kinds of crises, day in and day out, with four youngsters—make that six youngsters now?

His considerable respect for her went up another notch. God had definitely handed those kids to the right woman.

He leaned back in his chair and stared absently at the ceiling. The right woman in so many ways. Amazing that she'd never remarried after Phillip passed. He would have thought some lucky man would have snatched her up by now. Sure, she came with a lot of family and other responsibilities, but if he were a marrying kind of man he wouldn't have let that hold him back. No sirree. The men in this town must be blind and lacking in common sense to have left such a fine woman unattached.

And for reasons he didn't care to explore, he was happy they had.

Cora Beth was in the front yard, weeding her flower beds while Scout lay at her heels, when the four girls came up the walkway, chattering like magpies. She was so pleased to see how quickly Cissy had become like a sister to her daughters. If only Danny and Ethan got along as well.

Scout offered slobbery greetings all around, eliciting giggles and mock protests that were music to her ears.

"Hello, girls, where's Danny?"

"He stayed behind to talk to some of his friends," Audrey said. "I think Charlie had a penny and was going to treat them to licorice whips over at the mercantile." She scrunched her nose indignantly. "He said no little kids allowed."

Cora Beth laughed. "Don't worry, you're going to grow up fast enough. So, Cissy, how was your first day at school?"

"Miss Honoria is nice."

"Yes, she is."

"Did you know Cissy is a good draw-er?" Audrey asked. "She drew a little bird that looked just like the sparrow outside our classroom window."

"Did she now? How wonderful." Before she could say more, she caught sight of Danny marching quickly up the sidewalk, a thunderous expression on his face. What was wrong now?

He stopped in front of Cora Beth, his posture broomstick stiff. "I need to talk to you."

Cora Beth turned to the girls. "There's a cookie for each of you in the kitchen. Help yourselves and then get to work on your lessons."

After they'd departed Cora Beth climbed the porch steps and took a seat on the swing. She patted the spot next to her, but Danny remained standing. Not a good sign. "So, what do we need to talk about?"

"I was in the mercantile and I heard a couple of ladies talking about Ethan. Did you know he broke into Mrs. Oglesby's plant house again?"

She'd been afraid it had something to do with that. "It wasn't Ethan."

"How do you know? Just cause he denied it don't mean—"

"I haven't talked to him yet. But this wasn't a theft, it was an act of pure destruction, and I know he wouldn't do such a thing, any more than you would."

"Those ladies sure seem to think he was guilty."

"They don't know Ethan as well as we do. And Mrs. Oglesby's understandably upset by what happened and is ready to blame someone, whether she has proof or not."

She touched his arm briefly. "Danny, we talked about this last night. Ethan's not a bad kid. You need to give him the benefit of the doubt."

"Maybe he had a good reason for what he did before, but there's no excuse this time."

This was getting exasperating. "You're not listening to me. Ethan didn't do it."

"They always say where there's smoke there's fire

and I sure see a lot of smoke circling around that Ethan. He's nothing but trouble."

"If so, then he's *our* trouble."

Danny folded his arms over his chest, stopping just short of huffing at her. "You're just too trusting."

"And you're not trusting enough." *Heavenly Father, please help me to get through to him.*

She took a deep breath. "Danny, we can't keep having this argument. If you won't trust Ethan, then trust me." She eyed him steadily. "At least promise me you'll pray about it."

"All right. But while I'm at it, I'm also gonna pray that God finds him another place to live." And after that shocking rejoinder, he spun around and headed inside.

Cora Beth found herself in a subdued mood the rest of the afternoon. The conversation with Danny kept playing over and over in her mind and she couldn't shake the feeling that she'd somehow failed him. Still, there had to be something more to his distrust of Ethan than what she could see on the surface.

When Ethan came home, she could tell Mitch had talked to him. The boy would hardly meet her gaze. She let him know that she hadn't believed Nelda's accusations for even a moment, but still Ethan remained quiet and aloof.

After supper, while she was seated in the family parlor working on a bit of mending, Ethan knocked on the door.

"Mrs. Collins, can I talk to you for a minute?"

Pleased that he was initiating a conversation, she lowered her mending to her lap and smiled a welcome. "Sure. Have a seat."

He remained standing and stuffed his hands in his

pockets. "I hope you don't mind, but I went exploring up in your attic this afternoon."

"I don't mind at all. It's just filled with old bits of furniture and castoffs anyway. Did you see something you'd like to have?"

"Actually, I was looking at all the space you have up there. Almost half of the room has a high enough ceiling for a man to stand upright in and if you did a little rearranging, there'd be plenty of empty space."

"I suppose." Where was he going with this?

"I was wondering if, I mean, would it be all right, if I…" His words trailed off as if he wasn't quite sure he should continue.

"If you what, Ethan?"

He took a deep breath. "If I cleared me off a corner up there to turn into my own room?"

Oh dear. Had it come to this between him and Danny? "Mind if I ask why you don't want to stay in the room you're in now?"

"It's a fine room," he said a little too quickly, "and I sure do appreciate you fixing up an extra bed in there and all, but I kinda like the idea of having a place to myself. I won't take up much of your attic space, I promise, and I'll do all the rearranging myself."

Perhaps the two boys *did* need their own space. "I see. Well, if you're really certain that's what you want, you don't need to move into the attic. You could have the extra room at the end of the hall. It's kind of small, but—"

"No, ma'am. I know that's for when you have extra boarders and I wouldn't want to get in the way of that."

"You wouldn't be. We're used to doubling up when we have temporary guests—Danny moves in with Uncle

Grover, or the girls move in with me. It gets a bit snug but we manage."

"Still, I'd feel better if you just let me fix up a place in the attic."

She could see he felt strongly about that. "All right. And help yourself to any of the furnishings you find there to set it up."

"Thank you. I'll get right to it."

"Would you like my help?"

"No, ma'am, I can handle it."

Once Ethan had rushed off to set up his room, Cora Beth slowly picked up her sewing and set back to work. Had she done the right thing by letting him have his way? Or would it have been better for her to make him stay in the room with Danny and hope the forced proximity would help them to eventually work out their differences?

More and more lately, as Danny moved into that shadow land between adolescence and manhood, her thoughts turned to Mitch. She wished she could discuss these things with him, to work through her fears and hopes and dreams—for the kids and, selfishly, for herself, as well. But she couldn't ask him to be any more involved than he already was.

Heavenly Father, please help me to make the right decisions regarding these children. And, if You could see Your way to helping me figure out what's got Danny so stirred up, I'd sure appreciate that, too.

Chapter Twelve

Alice Danvers, the hostess for this week's Wednesday afternoon meeting of the Ladies' Auxiliary, handed Cora Beth a cup of tea. "The little girl you had with you at church service—Cissy, was it? I noticed she walked with a limp. Did she injure herself?"

Cora Beth smiled as she took the cup. Thank goodness the meeting had been relatively short today. She really wanted to get back to her sewing. Both Cissy and Ethan were in desperate need of new clothing. "I'm afraid it's a permanent injury. Ethan says it happened when she was just a baby."

Alice's face softened in sympathy. "Oh, that poor little angel. Does it pain her much?"

"According to her, only when the weather is damp or she's been overexerting herself."

"Well I suppose that's a blessing of sorts."

Ida Van Halsen joined them. "Is it true those two are Titus Brown's stepkids?"

"Not anymore," Cora Beth said firmly. "Once their mother passed on, his claim to them ended."

"I'm sorry to hear about their mother passing, but it was unfortunate that she brought two children to live under that man's roof in the first place." She gave Cora Beth an approving smile. "It's good of you to give them a more wholesome place to stay while the little girl gets better."

"Actually, Ethan and Cissy will be staying with me permanently."

Ida looked taken aback and even Alice paused in the process of pouring another cup of tea. Both women cast quick glances Nelda's way.

Ida cleared her throat and fiddled with the handle of her teacup. "Do you think that's wise? I mean, you don't *really* know anything about these children, do you? Maybe they have other kinfolk."

"Actually, Sheriff Hammond looked into that and it doesn't appear that they have anyone else." She sensed rather than saw Nelda walk up behind her. "As far as what I know about them, I know that they're good kids, that they've had to deal with a lot of tragedy and hard times in their short lives, and I know that I care for them a great deal."

Nelda moved forward to join the conversation. "You always did have a soft heart. But sometimes it's best to let your mind take precedence over your emotions. Otherwise you might be in for disappointment and heartache."

Did Nelda truly believe that? If so, Cora Beth felt sorry for her. "Some things are worth taking that risk over."

Mrs. Plunkett strolled up and served herself a tea cake. "Cora Beth, did everyone get off on the train okay this morning?"

Cora Beth turned to her with a smile, sending her boarder a silent thank-you for the timely interruption. "Yes, but not without a lot of last minute scurrying.

They're all very excited about visiting Hawk's Creek again." She gave the group of ladies a smile-with-me shake of her head. "If the looks on their faces were any indication, I'd guess the adults were looking forward to the trip every bit as much as the kids, if not more so."

Mrs. Plunkett lifted her cup. "Ah, the sign of a happy childhood is the eagerness to return to our home place once we grow older."

Cora Beth nodded, moving with her across the room as she did so. "From all indications, then, Ry and Sadie had a very happy childhood." And she intended to see that Ethan and Cissy built equally fond memories during what was left of theirs.

She found herself thinking of Mitch and wondering what kind of childhood memories he had. Like Ethan and Cissy, he'd been very young when he lost both parents—in fact, he'd already been orphaned and living with his grandmother when she'd started school and first got to know him.

Did he remember his parents? Had his grandmother been good to him despite what rumor said she was like on the outside?

Suddenly, she wanted answers to those questions. Would it be considered snooping for her to try to find out? Or merely the gentle probing of a friend who cared—deeply?

The next day, Cora Beth strolled up the walk to the boardinghouse, humming. She'd just finished her marketing and not even the strange, speculative looks she'd received from Alice Danvers had dampened her mood. If folks were talking about her, let them. It was a gloriously lovely day, Ethan and Cissy seemed to be settling in well now that Ethan had moved into his attic room, and Mitch was still stopping by every day to check on how things were going.

She refused to think about why the idea of Mitch's visits added so much to her good mood—better just to savor the pleasant feelings while they lasted.

Scout ran up to meet her as she turned onto her front walk. "Hi, boy." She lifted the nearly overflowing basket she carried. "Sorry I can't pet you right now—hands full."

Scout seemed willing to forgive her for the slight, and trotted happily at her heels.

As she approached the house, she studied the honeysuckle vine growing on the trellis guarding one end of the front porch. It was getting too thick and raggedy looking. Trimming it back would give her a great excuse to spend more time out in the fresh air this afternoon.

Just as she reached the steps, Scout barked a greeting to someone behind her. She turned to find Mitch approaching. The day seemed suddenly brighter than before.

"Mitch, hi, I'm just back from doing my marketing. Come on in and I'll fix you a cup of coffee."

"Thanks, but I'll have to pass." He reached out and took the basket from her.

Her pleasure at seeing him quickly turned to concern. His usual easygoing demeanor was missing—instead, his expression was somber, controlled. Had Nelda filed another complaint? "What is it?"

"I need you to come with me to the mayor's office. Right now."

That sounded ominous. She bent down to stroke Scout's head with hands that shook slightly. "Why?"

"Nelda has called a meeting of the town council." His grim tone matched his expression.

The town council? "About what?" She caught her breath as a possible reason occurred to her. "Mitch, does she want to force you to arrest Ethan?"

She saw the muscles in his jaw tighten. "No. This goes deeper. She wants to discuss the suitability of your taking in Ethan and Cissy."

Cora Beth felt the blood drain from her face. "What do you mean? What business is it of hers or the town council?"

"You know Nelda—*everything* is her business."

Cora Beth, her mind spinning with all sorts of scary possibilities, was already heading for the front door. "If you don't mind, set that basket in the kitchen for me while I tell Uncle Grover where I'm going."

Please God, don't let them take those children from me. They are so precious to me. To send them to an orphanage would be heartbreaking for all of us. I promised to give them a home—they need me. And I need them.

Chapter Thirteen

The town council was composed of Archibald Oglesby, who was both the mayor and Nelda's husband; Horace Danvers from the mercantile; Hamilton Melton, who ran the hotel; and Alfred Evans, the town barber. She tried to guess how each would view Nelda's complaint.

Mayor Oglesby's leanings were pretty clear. Chances were high that he would side with his wife.

Alfred Evans was a bit harder to predict. Ethan had spent some time working at his place so hopefully that had given the barber an idea of what a hard worker the boy was. On the other hand, Ethan *had* been responsible for taking his birthday pie so that could still rankle with him a bit.

Horace Danvers was usually a fair man, but his wife Alice was a good friend of Nelda's and it was hard to say how much influence that would have over him.

As for Hamilton, she had no idea what he'd heard or how he felt about the whole matter.

By the time Cora Beth and Mitch arrived at the mayor's office she was a jangle of fears, nervous energy and determination. She and Mitch walked into the inner office to find the mayor and all three members of the town council seated along the wall behind the desk, facing the door. Nelda was there as well, seated in a chair facing the council. There was an empty chair beside her.

The men stood as she entered, and the mayor waved her to the empty chair. "Thank you for coming here on such short notice, Mrs. Collins. Please take a seat."

Cora Beth, mustering what composure she could, gave her most regal nod, and sat in the vacant chair. She sensed Mitch behind her, leaning against the wall near the door. He seemed a far distance away at the moment.

Once everyone had taken their seats, Cora Beth deliberately met each councilman's gaze in turn, holding it for a few heartbeats before moving to the next. Finally she asked, "Just what have I been summoned here for?"

Mayor Oglesby tugged on his lapels. "You're here because Nelda has raised some legitimate concerns about your plans to take in those two orphan kids. Since I'm certain we all agree that the welfare of such children is a matter not to be taken lightly, we thought it only fair that the town council listen to her concerns. And of course we also want to afford you the opportunity to respond to whatever she has to say."

He cleared his throat. "Since I could be deemed to have some bias in this matter, being as I am married to the complainant, I will merely be an observer to this discussion, not a participant." He nodded to the councilman to his right. "Mr. Danvers here will take the lead in my place."

Cora Beth clasped her hands in her lap, mostly to still their trembling. "I'm not certain I understand what concern it is of any of you just who I decide to take into my home, but I am prepared to listen."

Mr. Danvers frowned at that, then waved a hand. "Nelda, you have the floor."

"Thank you." She turned to Cora Beth with a smile that was sugary sweet. "First off, I want to say that it is very commendable of you to want to take in those two orphans. Your family has a history of taking in those less fortunates who seem to have no place else to go. No one here is questioning the purity of your motives."

Cora Beth gave a short nod to acknowledge the compliments, if that's what they were. She had no illusions, however, that there wouldn't be a "but" coming next.

"But, my dear, you already have so many responsibilities." Nelda began to enumerate them on her fingers. "You have three children of your own, a younger brother and elderly uncle who both look to you for support, you almost single-handedly run the boardinghouse, and since Josie got married and moved outside of town, you've taken on more responsibility for the livery, as well."

Cora Beth was determined to hold her temper. "I feel that I've been managing things quite well. As far as I know there haven't been any complaints from either livery customers or from my boarders."

Nelda waved a hand dismissively. "Be that as it may, you must admit that all of those responsibilities keep you quite busy. Even if these were two normal children, I don't see how you could manage the extra work involved." Her nostrils constricted as if she'd smelled something unpleasant. "But, as we all know, these are *not* normal children. The boy has troublesome behavioral issues that, if left unchecked, could prove detrimental to the community. And while we've yet to learn

whether his sister has any of these unfortunate tendencies, the poor child is a cripple and that alone means
she'll need more attention from whomever cares for
her."

How dare she talk about Ethan and Cissy in those
terms!

"I ask you," Nelda continued, "as a mother yourself,
don't you think those two orphans deserve to be under
the care of someone who'll be less distracted by other
responsibilities and have the time to focus more closely
on them and their needs?"

Cora Beth forced herself to speak deliberately. "First
of all, I do not agree with your assessment of those
children. Yes, Ethan did some things he shouldn't have
before I took him in, but he was desperate. He's since
apologized and he's doing his best to make amends. And
he's given me his word he won't do such things again."
She ignored Nelda's huff of disbelief. "And Cissy is a
sweet child who doesn't demand or expect any special
treatment."

Nelda raised her chin. "There's some in this town
who are not as convinced as you that the boy has
changed his criminal ways."

Mitch spoke up from the back of the room. "No one
has come forward with any proof to the contrary."

Cora Beth shot him a quick smile, grateful for his
support.

Nelda, however, seemed less than pleased.

Before the woman could say anything else, Cora Beth
continued with her line of reasoning. "But all of that
aside, is there someone else, someone with fewer *distractions,* who has stepped forward to take them in?
If so, I'd like to speak to them." What would she do if
Nelda said yes?

"It's my understanding that the orphanage at Cason-ville has already agreed to take them in. It seems the ideal solution on a number of levels."

This time the look Cora Beth shot Mitch had an ac-cusing edge. Had he told Nelda about the orphanage? But he shook his head and she quickly turned back to Nelda, cutting her off before she could start listing the so-called advantages. "Surely none of you here honestly believes that those children would be better off in an or-phanage than they would with me. No matter how good the caretakers there are, there is no way they'd have any more time to give the children individual attention than I would, regardless of my other responsibilities."

Again Nelda flashed that superior smile that made Cora Beth want to scream. "I know you have a soft spot for these orphans, my dear. But sometimes we only see the things we want to. The folks who operate the orphanage have experience in dealing with such chil-dren and undoubtedly have a love for what they do. One would assume they would do their best to find them good homes, homes with couples who would love them every bit as much as you do, perhaps more so if they are childless, and who would also have the advantage of being able to provide both a mother and a father to those children. Something, regrettably, you cannot do."

That last bit hit home. Cora Beth *couldn't* provide them with a father. But as far as anyone else loving them as much—

"Besides, you mustn't be selfish." Nelda clutched the handbag on her lap a little tighter. "This decision doesn't just affect you. I'm concerned, of course, about how a boy of such questionable character will fit into our com-munity. It could have a tragic effect on our own dear children if they are allowed to associate freely with him.

After all, he lived with Titus Brown for over a year. One can only guess what kind of regrettable influence that horrid, unprincipled man had on him."

"Actually, Ethan found Titus's lifestyle as repugnant as you do, perhaps more so since he experienced it first-hand."

"Of course he would *say* that. And yes, the boy may seem fine to you now that things are easier for him. But how will he handle any troubles or frustrations that will come his way? Will he revert back to his criminal ways? No, as good as your intentions are, a boy like that needs the strong influence of a father, something you can't offer him."

Apparently, now that Nelda had found her weak spot she planned to keeping poking at it.

Cora Beth turned to the town council. "And what about all of you? Do you doubt my ability to raise these children?"

Horace Danvers spoke up. "It's not that we doubt you would give it your all, Cora Beth. But what Nelda is saying makes a lot of sense. And for you to take on such a responsibility might even affect the time you could devote to your own children."

This was getting more frustrating and insulting by the second. "I disagree. It is exactly *because* I have such a large family that this will work. They will have built-in playmates and peers to interact with. Uncle Grover will provide a grandfatherly influence. Living at the boardinghouse will provide them with a comfortable, loving home, as well as duties to help them grow into responsible adults."

Nelda shook her head. "That sounds all well and good, but that little crippled girl is going to require more than playmates—she's going to need some individual attention."

Cora Beth bit back an angry retort. How *dare* Nelda use that tone when speaking about Cissy?

Mitch had been doing his best to hold his tongue throughout this farce of a meeting, but he'd finally had enough. "Her name is Cissy," he said through clinched teeth.

Nelda cast a startled glance his way, obviously surprised by the interruption. "Yes, of course." She turned back to Cora Beth. "*Cissy* will need special attention. But the boy is another matter altogether. I shudder to think what might happen if his more reprehensible tendencies erupt. As I said, it might be different if there were a strong father figure, a man who could not only provide an upstanding example, but who had a firm hand when it came to—"

Mitch cut across her words again, tired of hearing her hammer Cora Beth with the same arguments over and over. "So your main objection is not some uncharitable grudge against the children?"

The mayor's wife drew herself up sharply. "Why I never! Of course not. I am definitely *not* the sort of person to bear grudges. I only—"

"Then it's that you don't think Mrs. Collins can handle this on her own, that the children need a firmer hand and a person with fewer distractions to watch over them. Do I have that right?"

"Exactly." Nelda's bearing spoke of righteous indignation. "Why, I feel for those poor orphaned children as much as the next person. I'm concerned for their welfare every bit as much as I am for the town's."

Mitch felt the stirrings of an idea. A totally outrageous idea. "Quite admirable. So if, say, a married couple could be found here in Knotty Pine who would be willing to take them in, and see that they were raised to be God-fearing and responsible, you'd have no objection?"

Cora Beth sat up straighter. What was Mitch doing? "But—"

He gave her a warning look, cutting off the rest of her protest. It stung to see the hurt in her gaze, but he'd explain later.

Nelda eyed him suspiciously. "I suppose. But it would need to be someone of strong character who understood exactly the gravity of the situation."

"Of course. Someone just like Mrs. Collins here, only married and with fewer encumbrances."

"Exactly. But as there is no one like that coming forth to volunteer, I'm afraid our next best option remains the orphanage."

That outrageous plan was taking clearer shape. It seemed doable. But he needed time to turn it over in his mind, look at it from all angles, run it by Cora Beth.

Mitch turned to the councilmen. "Gentlemen, I'm sure Mrs. Collins is understandably overwhelmed by what she's been put through here this morning. I think it only fair to give her a bit of time to reflect on it and try to come to terms with the situation before we make any hasty decisions."

The mayor frowned. "Sheriff, we're all busy men with other matters to attend to."

"Of course you are. But don't you reckon that when we're talking about splitting up a family, even one that's newly formed, it's worth a couple of hours' reflection before a firm decision is made?"

The men had the grace to look abashed at that.

But Nelda was staring at him with growing suspicion. "Sheriff, surely you don't think that in so short a time you can talk someone else into taking in those children. I assure you—"

"Mrs. Oglesby, surely *you* don't begrudge Mrs. Collins a few hours of time to gather her thoughts and try to come up with an alternate solution that will be acceptable to everyone, do you?"

"Of course not."

He turned to Cora Beth, eager to get her out of the room before she said something to sabotage his plan before he could even propose it. He needed to think. Was his far-fetched idea really worth pursuing? Would she buy into it? "Then, Mrs. Collins, might I suggest you take your leave now."

"But—"

Mitch grasped for whatever straw he could find to get her moving. "Perhaps a visit with Reverend Ludlow would help you settle things in your own mind. I'd be pleased to escort you there."

"Excellent idea," Mayor Oglesby said. "I'm sure the reverend would be able to offer you some sound counsel on this matter."

Mitch tried to communicate a mental *trust me* to her. "Then allow me to escort you to the parsonage. Gentlemen, Nelda, since it's nearly lunchtime, let's say we meet back up here at half past one."

Without waiting for a response, he took a firm hold of Cora Beth's elbow and led her from the room. He refused to meet her gaze until they were on the sidewalk. Once in the fresh air again he let out a long breath.

Cora Beth stopped dead in her tracks, forcing him to stop with her. "Mitchell Hammond, I'm not sure exactly what that was all about in there, but—"

"I can explain, but not here in the middle of the public sidewalk." He gave her arm a gentle tug and she started walking again.

"I will have you know that, much as I respect Reverend Ludlow, nothing he has to say is going to change my mind. And I don't care what your duty to that badge tells you that you have to do, I am not giving up those children without a fight."

He smiled. "I'd expect nothing less."

She looked at him with a surprised expression and some of the fight seemed to leave her. In its place was a worried frown. "How will I be able to face Ethan and Cissy with this news after I promised them that they were part of the family now? You don't just break up families this way."

"I thought you weren't going to give up without a fight." He was itching to explain everything to her but not here.

"Can they legally take those children from me and put them in an orphanage?"

He winced. She wasn't going to like his answer. "The children are technically wards of the state. Theoretically, the council can lodge a complaint with the circuit judge that you are unable to care for them properly and the state would have no choice but to investigate. But I'm hoping it won't come to that."

"So what's this plan you have?"

"We're almost there."

She looked around and frowned. "I thought you were going to drag me to the parsonage. We're going the wrong way."

"We may want to speak to Reverend Ludlow later, but for right now, you and I need to talk. Alone."

"I agree. So where are you taking me?"

"I thought the church might be a good place to talk. There's usually not anyone there this time of day."

They didn't say another word until Mitch escorted her inside the church. He seated her in one of the pews, but remained standing himself. And suddenly, he wasn't sure he could go through with this.

He had to be crazy. Marriage. After all these years of denial and restraint, was it possible that this was his answer? But would Cora Beth go for it? He wasn't even sure he wanted her to. No, that was a lie. He suddenly wanted this more than anything.

God, I know I made a vow not to ever marry, but I hope You'll grant me this exception. I made that vow because I didn't want to make any promises to a woman that I couldn't keep. But, if Cora Beth agrees to my proposition, this will be a different kind of marriage. I plan to make good and certain Cora Beth knows I'm only offering friendship and support, not any romantic fairy tales. If I don't give her any promises of a forever-after love then I can't disappoint her if my feelings change once things are settled between us.

"Well, are you going to stand there fiddling with your hat brim or are you going to tell me what this plan of yours is?"

Mitch rubbed his jaw, trying to pull his thoughts together. "I have an idea to run by you."

"An idea for how I can hold on to the children?"

"Yes."

"Then let's hear it."

Again he hesitated.

"Don't worry," she said. "Whatever it is, I promise not to bite your head off. I know you're trying to help and I'm sorry I got so upset earlier." She swallowed, then lifted her chin. "Is it that you have another couple in mind to take them in? I plan to fight to keep them, but if it comes down to a choice between an orphanage and another family, then—"

"No, that's not my idea." He took a deep breath. "I'm still trying to work all this out in my own mind. I mean, it's going to sound crazy, but just hear me out."

"I'm listening."

"What if you could find a way to resolve all of Nelda's objections, to erase the reasons she gave the council to prove you unsuitable?"

"How would I do that? Short of getting married I mean." Then her eyes widened. She was suddenly very still, her expression guarded. "Please explain."

He took another deep breath and plunged ahead. "I guess what I'm saying is, what if you and I got married?"

Her face lit up in a brilliant smile. "You're proposing to me?"

He nodded, glad to see she was as taken with the plan as he was. "I know this is not the most traditional of proposals, but there's no time to do this proper."

"I don't care about traditional. But are you sure? I mean, it wouldn't be fair to force your hand if you don't really want to—"

"I'm most definitely sure. In fact, this is perfect for me. I've been resigned for some time to the fact that marriage wasn't for me. But I've been thinking lately that it might be nice to be part of a real family. This way, I get the family without all the romantic entanglements."

Like blowing out a lamp, the sparkle in her eyes dimmed. "Oh, I see. So this would be strictly for the kids' sake."

Had she thought—

Mitch mentally berated himself for not explaining this more clearly from the get-go. He wasn't handling this well at all. "That's right. One of them in-name-only sorts." He rubbed the back of his neck, struggling to get the words right. "I mean the two of us suit well enough—at least I think we do. And I want those children to have a good home as much as you do, so we have a shared purpose. Even if we don't love each other, there's still plenty there to base a marriage on."

He decided, for both their sakes, he needed to be really clear on that point. "I want to be up front with you. I consider you a friend, one I respect a great deal, but I don't love you, at least not in the, uh, romance—or rather, romantic sense. And I can't promise that I ever will." Was he being completely honest with her? With himself? He wasn't sure anymore. Something about what he'd just said felt wrong.

Why didn't she say something?

"It's a generous offer," she finally said, "but I can't accept."

Mitch felt his chest constrict. He hadn't realized how badly he'd wanted her to accept until just this moment. "Mind if I ask why?"

She waved a hand then dropped it back into her lap. "Don't you see? This just wouldn't be fair to you. I mean, that 'romantic' kind of love you dismiss so easily is something very precious and not something to forego lightly. I had my taste of it with Phillip, but you, well, you need to hold out for it."

He ignored the stab of jealousy he felt at the mention of her former husband. "Cora Beth, you don't understand. I don't really think I'm capable of that kind of love. In fact, like I said, I was already resigned to the idea of never getting married. So you see, I won't be giving up on anything."

"Is it because of Dinah?" she asked softly. "Because of the depth of your feelings for her?"

"Yes." *But not in the way you think.* "I promise you, if you agree to this proposal, I will honor you and respect you and never give you any cause to regret marrying me."

He had to give it one last try. "I know it sounds crazy, but think of what this would mean to Ethan and Cissy. What it will mean if we *don't* go through with it. They've gotten under my skin and I don't like the idea of sending them to an orphanage any more than you do. If we got hitched, Nelda couldn't say they wouldn't have a father, and I could help lighten some of your load at the boardinghouse so it would give you more time to spend with the kids—*all* of the kids."

Her expression remained closed, unreadable. "*If* I accepted your offer," she finally said, "how exactly do you see this working?"

He felt hope flare up again. At least she was considering it now. "I suppose if I was going to be a proper father to the kids, I'd need to move into the boardinghouse. But, don't worry, we would maintain separate rooms." He saw her cheeks redden at that. A bit indelicate to speak of such things he supposed, but best to get it all out in the open as quickly and clearly as possible. That was the only way he could reconcile this plan with his vow. "What I'm saying is that you need have no fears that I'll impose on you in any manner that would make you uncomfortable."

"I see."

He wished he could figure out what she was thinking. Had he shocked her? Insulted her? Or did she understand he was truly trying to help? Her face, normally so open and readable, was a complete blank at the moment.

Mitch had the distinct sense that he was doing this wrong. Completely wrong.

Cora Beth hoped her face didn't reflect the chaos her thoughts and emotions were in right now. Truth to tell, she wasn't quite sure *what* she was feeling at the moment. What Mitch was proposing was the answer to her problems, possibly a God-directed solution that she'd been praying for since she first learned what the council meeting was all about. This plan should certainly satisfy all of Nelda's *stated* concerns.

And it had been so gallant and generous of him to make the offer. A lady couldn't ask for a more noble knight-errant to rescue her. But marriage! And one that both was and wasn't a true marriage. To a man who declared in no uncertain terms that he wouldn't—couldn't—offer her anything deeper than friendship.

The prideful part of her shrank from the knowledge that, if she agreed, everyone in town would know exactly why they were marrying—that it was purely a response to Nelda's attempt to wrest the children from her. Would they think this had been her idea? That she'd somehow twisted Mitch's arm into helping her?

And how dare he just assume she didn't want to hold out for a man who would love and cherish her the way a husband should? Did he think she was past such dreams and desires?

But it was true that neither her pride nor personal yearnings were the most important thing here today. If doing this meant Ethan and Cissy could stay with her uncontested, then she would go through with it, pride be hanged.

She just wished—No! No point thinking that way.

She bowed her head and closed her eyes. *Heavenly Father, help me to be thankful for the blessings You send me, no matter what guise they wear. It's not what I'd hoped for when I'd dared to dream for a closer relationship with Mitch, but I also know You can take any situation and use it to carry out Your will in this world. And I just have to believe that it can't be Your will for Ethan and Cissy to go to that orphanage. So please bless what Mitch and I are about to do. And help me to do my best to make sure that he never, ever regrets making this offer.*

Finally she looked up and met Mitch's waiting gaze. "Very well, I accept."

She saw the flare of joy blaze in his eyes and felt a sharp pang that that joy was not a result of his love for her, but for the children.

What had she just gotten herself in to?

Forty-five minutes later, Cora Beth took the same seat she'd vacated nearly two hours earlier, but this time Mitch didn't hang back. He stood beside her, his presence offering silent support.

The time between her acceptance of his proposal and their arrival back here had passed in a bit of a fog. Mitch had escorted her back to the boardinghouse where she'd fixed them both a cold lunch. There'd been very little discussion between them—as Mitch had said when they left the church, there was no point in discussing any plans until they heard what the council had to say. Which Cora Beth understood to mean if Nelda or the council found a hole in their plan, then he saw no point going through with the wedding. She didn't even want to imagine what that outcome would do to her pride.

As they were leaving the boardinghouse, he'd given her a searching look. "You're mighty quiet. Having second thoughts?"

Oh yes, she had plenty of those. But she was committed now, and she couldn't let the children, or Mitch, down. "Just a little anxious about facing the council again."

He gave her that smile that could melt her fears. "Just leave them to me. If it's all right with you, I'd like to do most of the talking."

How could she not feel something for a man like that?

"Well then." Horace Danvers' words brought her thoughts back to the present, "Let's get back down to business again. Mrs. Collins, now that you've had some time for reflection, do you have anything else to add to what was said earlier?"

"I believe Mrs. Collins and I have found a solution to the serious concerns that were raised this morning."

The group's gazes shifted from Cora Beth to Mitch, displaying various levels of surprise.

Horace turned back to her. "Mrs. Collins, is Sheriff Hammond speaking on your behalf?"

She held her stiff-backed pose, refusing to fidget. "Yes, he is."

Horace waved an impatient hand. "Then let's get on with it."

Mitch nodded. "If I remember correctly, Mrs. Oglesby's primary concern was that these children be put in the care of someone with a firm hand to deal with any disciplinary problems that might come up, someone with the time to care for their needs properly, and ideally someone with a home that includes both a mother and a father."

Nelda nodded. "That's correct. I only want what's best for both the children and the town."

Mitch raised a brow. "That's what we *all* want. And we have found the ideal solution." He smiled down at Cora Beth. "I'm pleased to announce that Mrs. Collins has agreed to do me the great honor of becoming my wife and to allow me to shoulder a portion of her responsibilities. We plan to get married in short order."

Cora Beth wondered what he meant by "short order." Surely they would wait at least until Josie and the others returned from Hawk's Creek. Pushing that thought aside as inconsequential for the moment, she glanced at the others in the room. Most of the men were leaning back in their seats, mouths agape, looking as stunned as if Mitch had announced he was going to the moon.

Nelda, on the other hand, had turned an alarming shade of red and looked ready to spit. "Are you mocking us, Sheriff?"

Mitch placed a hand on Cora Beth's shoulder and she could feel his warmth seep through the fabric of her dress. "I assure you that we are quite serious. I hope you all will agree that as her husband I am quite capable of providing the strong hand and fatherly influence you feel these children need."

"This is preposterous." Nelda looked from Mitch to Cora Beth, her eyes wide with disbelief. "Cora Beth, you can't get married just to keep from sending those kids—"

Mitch cut her off. "Mrs. Oglesby, I hope you're not presuming to now tell Mrs. Collins who she can marry and for what reasons."

Nelda straightened at that, getting herself back under control. "No, of course not, it's just—"

Mitch turned, dismissing her and facing the council. "Then, if you gentlemen have no further concerns on the matter of the disposition of Ethan and Cissy, I hope you will excuse Mrs. Collins and me. We have a lot of plans to make."

Cora Beth stood, more than ready to make her exit.

"Of course." Mayor Oglesby offered them both a relieved smile. No doubt he was glad to have the matter settled. "You have my congratulations," he said. "And we wish you both well with this new family you're building." He gave his wife a pointed look. "Don't we, Nelda?"

Nelda stood. "Yes. Of course. Congratulations to you both. Now, if you will excuse me, I have other matters to attend to." And with a swish of her skirts, she exited the room.

Cora Beth imagined Nelda scurrying off down the street to spread the word of their sudden engagement and the reason behind it. There was no telling what sort of light she would paint it in.

Dear Lord, forgive me for my not very charitable thoughts. I know I shouldn't judge and that everyone has their own struggles and faults, myself included. But there are times when I just want to give that woman a good shake.

When they stepped back on the sidewalk for the second time today, Cora Beth took a deep breath and turned to Mitch, feeling suddenly shy and awkward. What did they do now?

"I think that went about as well as could be expected," Mitch said, his voice perhaps a little too hearty.

"The children are safe, and that's what matters." She managed a weak smile. "I won't forget that I have you to thank for that. In case I didn't say it earlier, I am more grateful than I can ever say for what you're doing. I know this is a sacrifice for you." And that was the part that truly stung—the feeling that his hand had been forced by circumstances.

But his smile seemed free of regrets. "Not a sacrifice at all. I figure I'm getting the better end of this bargain and you're the one who had to bear the brunt of their inquisition."

Was it her imagination, or were the glances being cast their way on the sly side?

Mitch seemed to feel it, too. "I need to get back to work, but why don't I come by your place this evening and we can talk about what comes next?"

She nodded, and with a tip of his hat, Mitch headed down the sidewalk toward his office, his gait easy and unhurried.

As Cora Beth made her way back to the boarding-house, she couldn't shake the feeling that she was being watched from every doorway and window. Ridiculous, since Nelda hadn't had time to tell more than one or two folks. Still, she kept her chin up and her eyes focused straight ahead, and did her best to seem at ease while fighting the urge to lift her skirts and run.

Chapter Fourteen

Cora Beth stepped into her kitchen and looked around as if she'd never seen it before. Everything seemed suddenly different, foreign. But, regardless of how her whole world had just tipped on its axis, her day-to-day life had not changed—at least not yet. She still had responsibilities to her household. If she didn't get something on the stove soon, there'd be a lot of hungry folks at her table come suppertime.

She moved to the pantry and stood staring at the contents without really seeing anything. The children would be home soon. She'd tell them the news right away, of course. They should hear it from her before someone else told them. Would they be happy? She knew they liked Mitch, but how would they feel about him becoming part of the family, moving into the boardinghouse, taking on the role of father?

They'd already faced so many changes these past few days, would another one just be taken as a matter of course? Or be the final straw that got everyone up in arms?

Cora Beth moved to the table and sat down, her meal still unplanned. She'd need to choose her words carefully when she told them, paint this in the most positive light possible. The last thing she wanted was to make Ethan or Cissy feel they'd forced her and Mitch into this marriage.

She just hoped this wouldn't give Danny yet another excuse to lay a black mark at Ethan's door.

At least Cissy would be happy—it seems her wish to have Mitch be a part of their family was going to come true after all.

She felt a bubble of hysteria rise in her throat— whether it would erupt as laughter or a wail she wasn't quite sure, and she didn't want to find out. She swallowed hard, fighting to get herself back under control. What was wrong with her? This was a *good* thing.

Wasn't it?

She heard the door open behind her and straightened, trying to school her features into some semblance of normalcy. She didn't turn around but the sound of skirts swishing and the faint scent of lavender water told her it was Mrs. Plunkett.

Her heart sank—that woman saw way too much.

"There you are," Mrs. Plunkett said. "I looked for you earlier. I wanted to ask you something."

Cora Beth threw a smile over her shoulder, then moved toward the sink. "I'm sorry, I had some unexpected business to attend to."

Mrs. Plunkett quickly closed the distance between them. "My dear, what's the matter?"

So much for her abilities as an actor. She turned and leaned back against the counter, bracing her hands against it for support. "Was there something in particular you needed me for?"

"That can wait. You look as if you've just been given

a dose of bad news. Now sit yourself down here and tell me what's wrong."

Cora Beth slowly walked back to the table and took a seat. "Nothing's wrong. In fact you should congratulate me." She gave the woman a smile that she knew didn't ring true. "I'm getting married."

"I see. Isn't this rather sudden?"

"Aren't you going to ask me who I'm marrying?"

"I assume it's Sheriff Hammond, of course."

"You assume—"

"My dear, it's obvious you two were meant for each other. What I want to know is what finally brought him to his senses and why do you look like you've just received a death sentence?"

"It's not like that. I mean, this isn't, isn't a love match."

"Balderdash!"

"Truly." It seemed of utmost importance that she convince Mrs. Plunkett of the truth. "He only proposed to me to keep the town council from taking Ethan and Cissy from me."

"What nonsense is this? Why would the council want to—" She put up a hand. "No, don't tell me. Nelda Oglesby was behind this, wasn't she?"

"She was concerned that a widow with my responsibilities wouldn't be able to give them the attention they deserved," Cora Beth said, choosing her words carefully. "That's why Sheriff Hammond made the offer. It's a business arrangement, really, for the sake of the children."

Mrs. Plunkett studied her thoughtfully. "And that is how Sheriff Hammond couched his proposal?"

"Of course." Cora Beth reached in her pocket for a handkerchief. "As I said, this isn't a love match. We're both sensible adults who have a shared interest in seeing that Ethan and Cissy are well cared for."

"Well, I must say, you two have come up with a very practical solution to your dilemma." Mrs. Plunkett touched the brooch pinned to her bodice, a thoughtful expression on her face. "So when is this wedding to take place?"

Cora Beth wiped her nose, feigning a sneeze while she tried to pull herself together. "Everything happened so fast that we haven't worked out the details yet. Sheriff Hammond is coming by this evening so we can begin planning."

Mrs. Plunkett stood, giving her a probing look. "Well, you just let me know if there is anything I can do to help with the arrangements or the planning. I so enjoy a good wedding."

"Yes, of course. That's very kind of you to offer." Cora Beth stood as well, stuffing the handkerchief back in her pocket.

Before she could say anything else, the door opened and Uncle Grover stepped in. "I understand congratulations are in order," he said with a smile.

"You heard the news."

"Yes. Horace told me when I stopped by the mercantile to see if he had gotten in the new display case I ordered." He took her hands. "Are you happy, my dear?"

That was a good question. She wasn't *un*happy. "I am absolutely positive this is the right thing to do," she temporized.

He frowned. "Mitch is a good man—you couldn't ask for a finer husband. But if this is not what you want…"

Cora Beth gave his hands a squeeze. "Really, Uncle

Grover, Mitch and I will get along wonderfully." What was it Mitch had said, that they would "suit well enough"?

She freed her hands from his and turned to Mrs. Plunkett. "Oh, I almost forgot. What was it you wanted to see me about?"

The woman waved a hand dismissively. "Don't worry about that. It can wait for another time. As a matter of fact—" she turned to Uncle Grover "—perhaps *you* could help me with something."

Uncle Grover looked startled for a moment, then his gentlemanly instincts came to the fore. "Of course. What can I do for you?"

Mrs. Plunkett moved to the door. "Let's leave your niece to her work. We can discuss this in the parlor."

As the two moved into the hall, Cora Beth smiled. Mrs. Plunkett was definitely not letting any grass grow under her feet. Would there be another marriage in the family soon?

If so, she hoped it would have more going for it than being a "good business arrangement."

Mitch looked at the clock, alternately thinking that the hands were moving too slow and then too fast. School should have let out a few minutes ago. He'd been waiting for Ethan to arrive, wondering what he would say to the boy. He didn't have any illusions that Ethan wouldn't have already heard the news. Apparently everyone in town now knew that he and Cora Beth were planning to get hitched.

There'd been more traffic through his office this afternoon than in the entire month preceding. Some came by with pretenses of business, others out and out professing their curiosity. He certainly hoped they'd left

Cora Beth alone. She'd seemed okay on the surface when he'd left her, but something about her smile had hinted at a certain fragility of spirit that had him a little worried.

The door opened, interrupting his thoughts, and Ethan stepped inside. As soon as Mitch saw his face he knew the boy had heard.

He tried to read Ethan's expression to gauge how he'd reacted, but Ethan headed directly for the corner where the broom was stored, never looking at Mitch.

"How was school today?" Mitch asked.

Ethan shrugged, pushing the broom with a bit more force than usual.

Okay, better get right to it. "I suppose you heard the big news."

A quick glance, a nod, and then back to sweeping.

"Well, what do you think?"

"They say neither one of you really wanted to get married but that you're having to do it because of me and Cissy. They say it's a shame you had to be saddled with so many unwanted burdens."

Mitch's temper rose at that. He wasn't getting *saddled* with anything he didn't want to take on. And it was nobody's business but his anyway. "I don't know who *they* are, but no one is making either one of us do anything."

The look Ethan shot him said he wasn't buying it.

Mitch reined in his temper and tried again. "Look, I like Mrs. Collins. And I like all of you kids. Getting to be part of a big family is going to be a new experience for me and it's one I'm looking forward to. So don't go thinking I'm making a big sacrifice here, because I'm not."

Ethan kept right on sweeping. "You sound just like

my ma before she married Titus. She did it 'cause of me and Cissy and look how that turned out."

So that's what had him so upset. "Ethan, Mrs. Collins and I are not your ma and Titus. We've known each other a long time and we know each other pretty well. We also know just what we're doing and why we're doing it." Or at least he hoped that was true. "This is a good thing—you'll see."

"Doesn't matter. Seems like whenever anybody does something 'for my own good,' it turns out bad."

The boy definitely had a problem seeing the bright side of anything. "Ethan, look at me."

Ethan stopped sweeping and did as he was told.

"You like Mrs. Collins, don't you?"

His expression immediately softened. "She's one of the nicest ladies I ever met. I'd do anything for her."

"I thought so. One thing you need to understand about Mrs. Collins is that she has a very strong spirit. As you've already learned, if she believes in you, she'll stand up for you against anything and anyone."

He leaned forward. "But she also has a very soft, tender heart. Granted this marriage plan of ours is a little unusual, but it's very important to her. That's because *you and Cissy* are important to her. So, don't make this difficult for her, okay?"

Ethan thought about it for a minute, then slowly nodded. "I still think it's a bad idea but I won't let Mrs. Collins know."

Mitch nodded approvingly. "I knew I could count on you."

Ethan went back to sweeping. "There's something you probably ought to know, though."

"What's that."

"Danny didn't look none too happy when he heard the news. And he took off like a shot for the boarding-house."

Cora Beth took a deep breath when she heard the front door open. The kids were home from school—time to tell them the news.

Danny came bursting through the kitchen door. "Is it true?" he demanded. "Are you and Sheriff Hammond getting married?"

Cora Beth mentally cringed. Why was he so upset? "Yes, it's true. Though I was hoping to be the one to break the news to you all."

"It's all over town—it's all anyone is talking about."

She sincerely hoped he was exaggerating. And it was clear from his tone he did *not* think the marriage—or the gossip—was a good thing. "Well, it's nice that our neighbors take such an interest in us," she said mildly.

"You're doing this because of them, aren't you? Ethan and his sister, I mean. If they hadn't come here you wouldn't be having to do this."

"Daniel Edward Atkins, I'm getting really tired of hearing that kind of talk from you. Ethan and Cissy are part of our family now and you will treat them that way."

Danny set his lips in that rebellious thin line she was learning to hate.

She took a deep breath, tried to remember the sweet little boy he'd been not too long ago, and placed a hand on his shoulder. "Danny, I'm getting married. And whether you believe it or not, I *want* this. Can't you be happy for me?"

She could see the internal struggle play out in his changing expression. Before either one of them could say anything more, though, the girls came rushing in. At least *they* hadn't abandoned the slower-moving Cissy.

"Mom, Danny wouldn't wait for us," Audrey complained.

"I was in a hurry, squirt." He shrugged off her hand but his tone and smile toward the girls was back to big-brother teasing. At least he didn't let his anger spill over to his sisters. Without a backward glance for Cora Beth, he left the room.

"Is it true?" Audrey asked, claiming Cora Beth's attention.

"If you mean am I going to marry Sheriff Hammond, then yes, it's true."

"That means he's going to be part of our family, doesn't it?" Cissy seemed pretty pleased by that idea.

"Yes, it does. Won't that be nice?"

"Is he going to live here?" Pippa asked.

"Yes, he is." She wasn't ready for them to start digging any deeper than that and quickly changed the subject. "All right, that's enough questions for now. There's a cookie for each of you on the counter and then you need to get to your lessons and afternoon chores."

Danny avoided her for the rest of the day.

Later that evening, Cora Beth opened the front door to find Mitch standing there, hat in hand.

"I hope I'm not interrupting anything."

"No, of course not. Supper's over and the evening chores are done. Come on in."

"I thought maybe we could talk out here on the porch. It's a nice evening."

"Of course. But first come in and say hello." She pushed the door wider. "You're going to have to face them all eventually, and as Grammy Alma used to say—"

"Get it over with sooner rather than later." He gave her a stern look. "And just for the record, I'm a lawman. I've had to deal with thieves, bullies and drunken cowboys. I was *not* dreading facing these folks."

She didn't say anything, merely raised a brow in disbelief.

He grimaced good-naturedly. "All right, I wasn't dreading it *much*."

As Cora Beth had expected, Mitch had barely stepped across the threshold before nearly every member of her household came out to greet him. Only Ethan and Danny were absent. They'd both disappeared to their respective rooms once evening chores were done.

The four girls held back while the adults spoke, though Cora Beth could see they were barely containing themselves.

Mr. Saddler stepped forward first, pushing his spectacles up with his left hand while sticking out his right. "Let me offer my most sincere congratulations on your happy news, Sheriff. You're a very lucky man to have garnered the favor of so fine a woman as Mrs. Collins."

"Thank you. And I heartily agree."

Honoria merely smiled shyly and offered a soft congratulations to the mix.

Her mother was not so reticent. "Well, Sheriff," Mrs. Plunkett said, "I must say your news came as a most pleasant surprise. It's about time our Cora Beth here found a man worthy of her."

Not quite sure how to respond to that, Mitch merely smiled.

Uncle Grover gave him a surprisingly focused,

assessing look. "Just see that you don't hurt our girl and you'll fit in here just fine."

Mitch nodded deferentially. "Yes, sir, you have my word."

The older man smiled, his expression returning to the jovial, slightly bemused look he normally wore. "In that case, welcome to the family."

Cissy tugged on Mitch's pant leg, apparently unable to remain quiet any longer. "Mrs. Collins says you're going to come live here with us. Are you really?"

He smiled down at her. "Mrs. Collins wouldn't lie to you, Buttercup."

"When are you going to move in?"

"Soon. Mrs. Collins and I are going to talk about that in a little bit."

Lottie tilted her head and clasped her hands behind her back. "What room are you gonna take?"

Time to break this up before the girls got too personal with their questions. "Enough with all these questions. Sheriff Hammond and I are going out on the front porch to talk."

"Can we come, too?" The question came from Audrey, naturally.

"No, right now we need to do some grown-up talking."

Uncle Grover stepped in. "Actually, Mrs. Plunkett was telling me just this afternoon about some new slides she got for her stereopticon. Why don't we see if she'll show them to us?"

"What's a steri-op-con?" Cissy asked, puzzled.

Mrs. Plunkett's brows rose and she placed a hand on her bosom. "You've never seen a stereopticon? Oh my dear, then we must get the slides out and show you how wonderful they are."

While Uncle Grover and Mrs. Plunkett herded all the children toward the main parlor, Cora Beth and Mitch made their escape to the front porch.

As Mitch pulled the door closed behind them, Cora Beth moved to the porch rail and looked out over the front lawn. Twilight was settling in and she could hear frogs harumphing in the distance. She rubbed her upper arms, not sure what to expect out of this meeting. Would they be awkward together now? She most desperately hoped not.

Pasting a smile on her face, she turned and took a seat on the porch swing. Mitch took her place at the rail, leaning a hip against it as he turned to face her.

He was the first to break the silence. "I guess we need to decide on a date for the wedding."

She nodded. "I hate to say this, but I won't feel the children are completely safe until we're married. I definitely want to wait until Josie and the others get back from Hawk's Creek, but I don't want to wait much longer than that."

"Of course. They'll be back on Saturday, right?"

Cora Beth nodded.

"Then how about a week from Saturday?"

Cora Beth's heart fluttered as she nodded. In a little over a week she'd be a married lady once more.

Mitch smiled. "That's settled then. We can go by and talk to Reverend Ludlow in the morning."

Trying to match his businesslike approach, Cora Beth lifted her chin. "Now, as for you moving in here, I've been trying to figure out the best way to make that work fairly for everyone. I mean, I know you're used to having a whole place to yourself, but space is at a premium here."

"Don't worry, I don't need a lot of space."

"Oh, I didn't mean I wanted to give your needs short shrift. Surely you need more than just a place to sleep. There's a small room we call the family parlor on the first floor. It's not as big as the parlor the boarders and guests use, but it's got plenty of windows to let in the light and it's a pleasant enough space. The family tends to congregate in the kitchen anyway, so it's hardly used at all. We could easily turn it into a study or office for you. If you had a desk or favorite chair you want to bring with you—"

"Cora Beth."

"Yes?"

"It's okay. Like I said, I don't need a lot of space. And other than a few personal items that'll fit in my bed-chamber, I'm not attached to any of the furnishings in my old place. I plan to leave them there for whomever decides to buy the place."

"You're really selling your house?" It was the place he'd acquired when he got engaged to Dinah.

He shrugged. "Don't see any point in my holding on to it. Do you?"

"No, of course. I just—" Aware she was babbling, she took a deep breath and moved on. "As for sleeping accommodations, we've rearranged things a bit to make room for Ethan and Cissy, but there's still one vacant room upstairs and of course there's the downstairs bed-chamber. You can look at them—"

"No need. I'll take the one downstairs."

"Don't you even want to take a look at the one up-stairs?"

"I meant it when I said I don't need much space. And since my job as sheriff sometimes requires me to work late or have people calling on me at all hours, it'll be less disruptive if I'm on the first floor."

"If you're sure that's what you want, then that's fine. The downstairs room is probably larger anyway." She brushed an invisible speck of dust from her skirt. "About the wedding itself, under the circumstances I thought we'd keep it very simple."

"I'll leave that up to you, but simple is fine with me. If you need me to do anything, just let me know. Otherwise, you plan it and I'll show up and do my part."

Apparently the ceremony itself was not important to him. Why should it be? They were pledging their troth to each other, not their love. She wished that didn't sting quite so much, that she could be more pragmatic about it.

"I want you to know," Mitch said, "that even though this is going to be a name-only kind of marriage, I plan to pull my weight around here."

She smiled. "I have no doubt of that. I think being a father to six children is going to require more out of you than you imagine right now."

He grimaced. "I hope I'm up to that. But I was talking about the actual operations of the boardinghouse."

She frowned. This was her domain. "You already have a job—being sheriff. I've managed just fine all these years and I can continue taking care of things." Though, with her mother gone and Josie married and moved out, it had been a mite lonelier and more burdensome lately.

"I don't doubt your capabilities, and I don't claim to know anything about operating a boardinghouse, so you don't have to worry about me coming in and getting in your way. But I've been thinking that maybe there was just a kernel of truth in something Nelda said today."

She felt a little prick of defensiveness. "What was that?"

"She said that with all your responsibilities, you wouldn't have time to give the kids the attention they need."

How dare he! "But I—"

He raised a hand to cut off her protest. "I'm not saying the kids are being neglected. Far from it. You're a great mom to those kids. They don't lack for anything important, they've been raised to be respectful and God-fearing, and it's obvious they love you back. And it's plain that they know that you love them and you'd do just about anything for them, which is real important to a kid."

The way he said that made her wonder again what his life had been like in his grandmother's home.

"But you gotta admit that running this place is a lot of work," he continued. "It keeps you busy from cock's crow to owl's hoot."

Being busy wasn't a crime. "I enjoy running this place."

He gave her a skeptical look. "I'm sure you enjoy some parts of it, but you can't tell me you actually enjoy all the day-to-day work that goes into it. The cooking, cleaning, laundry—ah-ha!" He pointed a finger at her. "I saw that grimace. So laundry is your sore spot."

She laughed. "All right, so I'm not fond of doing laundry, but I can't let you—"

He quirked a brow. "Can't let me what? Take on the role of man of the house?"

"Somehow, I don't normally think of the man-of-the-house role as one that includes doing the wash." She had trouble picturing him wielding a paddle to stir a wash-tub full of wet laundry.

"You misunderstand me—I'm not being *that* noble.

What I would like to do is hire someone to help out around here."

"Hire someone? Oh, Mitch, I don't know. That doesn't seem like a good use of money."

"And what else do I have to spend my money on? I mostly spend my sheriff's salary on groceries, stabling my horse and the little bit of upkeep my place needs. Moving in here is going to take care of most of that, which isn't going to do much for my standing as family breadwinner. If this marriage is going to work, I need to feel like I'm contributing to the household in a real way."

Ah, the male's need to be the provider. "I suppose I *could* use some help on laundry day." Actually, not having to tackle that wretched job alone was something she could quite happily get used to.

"Oh come now. I'm sure if you thought hard enough you could find tasks to keep a helper busy every day of the week."

"Then what would I do? Besides, there's not many folks available for full-time work of this sort."

"I have no doubt that you'd find plenty to keep you busy. And you'd be surprised who's available. In fact, Benny Thatcher's oldest kids, Hannah and Paul, have been trying to find odd jobs around town for several weeks now. I'm thinking Hannah might be a good one to talk to about the job."

Now he wasn't playing fair. The Thatcher family had fallen on hard times this past year and were having trouble making ends meet. The Ladies' Auxiliary had put together several food baskets for them. If she turned her back on this opportunity to help them she'd feel like a wretch—and Mitch knew it. "I still plan to do most of the cooking," she said huffily.

He held up both palms. "You won't get any argument from me. I don't think there's a finer cook in the county and I'm looking forward to a steady diet of your meals after the wedding."

"Actually," Cora Beth said, "it might be a good idea if you start taking some of your meals here before the wedding. It'll give you a chance to ease into the routine around here, and it'll give the family and the boarders a chance to get to know you better before you actually move in."

"I reckon I can live with that." He grinned. "So, are you saying yes to hiring Hannah full-time?"

He was going to make her say it, was he? She let out a melodramatic sigh. "Yes, I suppose, for the sake of your fragile, manly pride, I will let you talk me into this."

Mitch repressed a smile at her saucy response and shook his head dolefully. "I can tell I'm going to have to keep on my toes around you."

She laughed, then quickly sobered. "By the way, thank you for whatever it was you said to Ethan this afternoon. By the time he made it home he seemed very accepting of the notion that we were getting married."

He decided against telling her about Ethan's first reaction—comparing their upcoming wedding to his mother's marriage to Titus. "He's a reasonable kid. A few words about it being what we both wanted was all it took." He gave her a probing look. "But I hear Danny didn't take it so well."

She shook her head. "Goodness, there really aren't any secrets in this town. Who'd you hear that from?"

"From Ethan."

"Oh." She nibbled on her lip for a moment, and he could tell something was worrying her.

Impulsively he moved to the swing and sat beside her. "Anything I can help with?"

"I don't know. Maybe. It's just, Danny hasn't been acting like himself lately and I can't figure out what's wrong with him."

"Tell me about it."

"He seems to have it in for Ethan. He believes every little word whispered against him, he seems to value his friends' opinions above mine and he wears a log-size chip on his shoulder whenever he and Ethan are forced together."

She waved a hand. "He's never been like this before. I mean, he's certainly no angel, but he's always been fair-minded and considerate of others."

"Danny's growing up. He's not a man yet but he's not a little boy anymore, either. That can really turn a kid on his ear sometimes."

"I understand that. I mean, I think I do. I don't have a lot of experience with adolescent boys. It was just me and Jo growing up for the most part. Danny didn't come into our lives until I was fifteen and I got married and moved out three and a half years later."

She frowned. "And that's another thing that has me confused about his attitude. Because of what happened to him, he of all the people in this household should have some sympathy for Ethan and Cissy's situation. It just seems like there's something going on with him that I'm missing."

How much did she know about Danny's life outside the boardinghouse? "I reckon this might have something to do with the fact that he's sweet on Odine Oglesby."

The stunned look on her face confirmed that she'd had no idea.

"Nelda's daughter? What—I mean, how— I mean, are you sure?"

"If you're wondering if anyone told me outright, no. But as sheriff I hear things. I also have a good view of the schoolyard from my office."

She sat back, a thoughtful look on her face. "So, what Odine's mother thinks has a big influence on Odine. And what Odine thinks—"

"—has a big influence on Danny," Mitch finished for her. Then he shrugged. "As far as what you do about it, sorry, that's outside my area of expertise."

"Don't apologize, this is quite helpful. At least now I know why he's acting the way he is."

There now, he liked it much better when she was wearing that soft smile rather than a worried frown. Before he could stop himself, he reached out to touch her arm.

For a second, he savored her soft skin, her warmth and her sweetness.

Their gazes locked and he saw her pupils widen and heard a little catch of breath. Was it his imagination or had she moved closer? What would she do if he leaned in to kiss her? A quick, best-friend kind of kiss, of course. They were engaged now after all. Tied to each other in a till-death-us-do-part partnership.

Wasn't that the kind of deal usually sealed with a kiss?

Chapter Fifteen

Cora Beth held her breath, waiting. Would he kiss her? If he was looking for permission, surely he would read it in her eyes.

They were isolated here. Even if the honeysuckle trellis hadn't screened them from the casual passerby, twilight had deepened to dusk while they'd talked and the moon was not yet up. The pool of diffused light coming from behind the dining-room curtain was enough light to see by, but it stopped short of spotlighting them.

Slowly, as if she were a bird that could be startled by a sudden movement, he reached up and caressed her cheek. She closed her eyes and leaned into the warmth of his hand—his large, rough, achingly gentle hand.

"Cora Honey." The whispered endearment was husky.

Cora Honey. So much nicer than Cora Beth.

"I think I'm gonna kiss you now."

Did he think she'd protest? Not a chance. She lifted her face, eager to meet him halfway.

And kiss her he did. Gentle at first, gentle and chaste. But just when she was feeling a stab of disappointment, it changed. His arm snaked around her back and he pulled her closer, deepening the kiss, making her heart race and her thoughts scatter. Being held in his arms like this felt wonderful, felt *right*.

When he finally pulled away, he looked as dazed as she felt. "That wasn't supposed to happen," he said bemusedly.

A smile tugged at her lips. "But it did."

He straightened and his expression turned to one of consternation, as if he were only just now aware that he'd spoken aloud. He popped up from the swing as if prodded from below and rubbed the back of his neck. "I'm sorry. I need to go. We'll talk some more tomorrow."

Was he apologizing for the kiss or because he had to leave? "Of course. And don't forget, I expect you to start taking your supper meals here."

"Yes, looking forward to it. Good night."

And with that he headed off, taking long, quick strides as if he couldn't get away fast enough.

Cora Beth moved to the porch rail and stared out into the night, a satisfied smile on her face.

She'd like to believe that if Mitch was upset it was because his own feelings had caught him unaware. There *had* been feelings behind that kiss, no matter how much he wanted to pretend there weren't. And knowing that gave her hope.

He might still have strong feelings about Dinah, and she might never take her place in his heart, but now she could believe that he just might have room there for both of them.

What in the world had he just done? Mitch raked his hand through his hair as he marched through town, wishing he had something he could vent his frustration on. Woe to any rowdy townsman who dared kick up a ruckus tonight.

He should have never given her that kiss, never allowed himself to enjoy it so much. It had been selfish and dangerous. He could only go through with this marriage if she went into it without looking for or expecting more than a purely business arrangement. If he let her believe he loved her, let her grow to love him and count on his love in return, it would only result in heartache and eventually bitterness.

And he couldn't, *wouldn't* do that to Cora Beth.

No, friendship was what he'd planned to settle for and it was what she needed to settle for, as well.

But, oh, how could he go back to thinking of her as just a friend after that kiss—that sweet, heart-stopping kiss that tasted of joy and sunshine and the spirit that was uniquely Cora Beth?

With a groan, Mitch picked up his pace knowing he'd keep himself out patrolling for quite some time tonight.

Chapter Sixteen

"Put away your mop and apron, we've got shopping to do."

Cora Beth, who'd been pleasantly daydreaming about her tête-à-tête with Mitch yesterday evening, looked up to find Mrs. Plunkett staring down at her with a frown. Had she mentioned shopping?

"I'm sorry, I did my shopping yesterday, before…" Before her whole world got turned on its head. "Well, before I met with the town council."

Which was just as well. Cora Beth wasn't particularly looking forward to her next visit to the mercantile. There's no telling exactly what Nelda had reported after the town council meeting yesterday, but she was sure it hadn't painted her in the most flattering of lights.

"We're not going shopping for you," Mrs. Plunkett said with exaggerated patience, "we're going shopping for *me*. I've decided I need a new dress for your wedding, and I want you to help me pick out the fabric."

Now why would she want her opinion on fashion? She'd never asked for it before. "Oh, you don't need me for that. Besides, I have all this cleaning to do—"

"It'll keep. I insist you accompany me."

This conversation was truly odd. What was going on? Cora Beth brushed the hair off her forehead with the back of her hand. "I'm sorry—" she strove for an equally firm tone "—but as I said, I'm in the middle of mopping my floors."

"Cora Beth Collins, you disappoint me. I've never before considered you a coward."

A coward? "I don't under—"

"You have to face everyone sooner or later. It won't get any easier by putting it off."

Cora Beth winced as she took in Mrs. Plunkett's version of her Grammy Alma's advice. And, much as she hated to admit it, it was still good advice. She'd been avoiding the moment when she'd have to face everyone, have to smile and accept their congratulations while wondering what they were thinking behind their smiles.

"Besides," Mrs. Plunkett added, "I'd think a woman who was newly engaged to one of the most sought-after bachelors in town would want to flaunt it a bit, no matter what the circumstances surrounding that engagement."

Cora Beth leaned on her mop as she thought about that for a moment. Mrs. Plunkett was right. There was no way she was going to give anyone the impression she was embarrassed to be marrying Mitch, regardless of the circumstances.

She propped the mop against the corner and untied her apron. So what if Mitch's proposal had lacked a more traditional romantic element? He'd come to her rescue when she had needed him most, just like a true storybook hero, and that was romantic enough for her.

"As a matter of fact," she said as she placed her apron back on its peg, "I think I'll see if I can find a nice bolt of fabric to make myself a new dress, too." She gave Mrs. Plunkett an apologetic look. "Would you mind terribly if I went alone? I think it will be better that way."

Mrs. Plunkett beamed approvingly. "Good for you. My shopping can quite easily wait until this afternoon.

Fifteen minutes later, Cora Beth stepped into the mercantile to find Alice Danvers assisting two other ladies with their purchases. Smiling a greeting, she nodded and moved unhurriedly toward the bolts of fabric near the rear of the store.

Before long, Alice came bustling up to offer assistance, just as she'd expected.

Taking a deep breath, she turned to the mercantile owner's wife with a smile. "Hi, Alice. I'm looking for some fabric for my wedding dress."

Mitch was feeling grumpy and out of sorts this morning. He hadn't slept well last night—in fact, he hadn't slept much at all. And today hadn't started off much better. He'd not only managed to burn his breakfast, but he'd nicked himself shaving, too—something he hadn't done since he was a knob-kneed adolescent just learning to wield a razor. Then he'd got to the office and found Jonas Pickering waiting for him, all set on lodging yet another complaint against one of his neighbors. This time he'd supposedly spotted the Lawton kid cutting across his property to get to the next farm over instead of using the road.

He hated dealing with bickering neighbors, especially when the complaints seemed so petty. But the law was the law and upholding it was his job.

With a sigh Mitch unfolded himself from his chair

and grabbed his hat. He'd make the rounds here in town and then ride out to the Lawton place and deliver a lecture on the ramifications of trespassing.

When he passed by the mercantile, though, he paused. Was that Cora Beth inside? He propped up his boot on a nearby bench, pretending to clean something off his heel with a pocketknife while he gave himself a moment to think.

He'd planned to keep his distance today, to make sure that their next encounter had a businesslike feel to it so that what had passed between them last night could fade into the background where it belonged.

But he was very aware of the kind of speculations that had been circulating since their engagement became the talk of the town yesterday. It was one thing for some of the more brash townsfolk to make gibes to him, disguised as good-natured jesting, of course, but he didn't like the idea of Cora Beth facing that alone.

He wavered a moment, then, swallowing an oath, headed inside. Hopefully Cora Beth would take what he was about to do in the spirit with which it was intended.

As soon as he stepped inside, conversations stopped and he became the focus of every pair of eyes there. To be more precise, *they* became the focus of every pair of eyes there as the others looked from him to Cora Beth and back again. But he'd expected as much and made sure his smile didn't waver and that his glance never left Cora Beth. "There you are, sweetheart," he said as he approached. "Thought I saw you duck in here." He placed an arm around her shoulder and gave her a squeeze before stepping back.

She never blinked, just met his smile with one of her

own. "I thought I'd treat myself to a new dress for the wedding."

"Sounds like a fine idea. But you're going to make a beautiful bride no matter what you're wearing."

Cora Beth laughed and gave his arm a playful pat. "Flatterer." Then she put her hands on two different bolts of fabric. "Now be serious. I can't decide between these two. This yellow is pretty the way it's sprinkled with those little blue flowers, but this green is such a rich color."

"Definitely the green," he said without hesitation. "It matches your eyes."

"The green it is then." She pulled out the bolt and handed it to Alice Danvers. "Would you cut me four yards, please?" After a moment she pulled out the yellow, as well. "Actually, I think I'll take some of this one, too, to make new dresses for the girls."

Then she turned to Mitch. "Was there a particular reason you tracked me down?"

Her eyes were dancing. The little minx, she was enjoying this bit of playacting. Why hadn't he seen this side of her before? "As a matter of fact, there was. I forgot to ask you last night what time you want me over for supper this evening."

"We eat promptly at six-thirty. But you're welcome to come early if you like."

"You can expect me around six then." He smiled and then threw in a wink for good measure. He had the satisfaction of watching her have to swallow a laugh. "I need to get back to work. See you this evening." He turned back to face the others in the store and tipped his hat. "Good day, folks. By the way, hope you can all make it to the wedding next Saturday."

He stepped out on the sidewalk and decided today wasn't such a bad day after all.

Cora Beth watched him go, a smile playing around the corners of her lips. If the townsfolk wanted to see how she was taking this wedding plan, they were going to get an eyeful right now.

As Alice cut the fabric and chattered on about what a pretty bride Cora Beth was going to make, and how the sheriff had certainly become rather *demonstrative* lately, Cora Beth was very glad she'd decided to take Mrs. Plunkett's advice.

She'd made her appearance and come out the better for it. The worst was now behind her and she could face the rest of the town with a smile on her lips. Let them talk behind her back if they wanted to, but no one would be able to say she was moping or dragging about.

And who would have guessed Mitch could get into the spirit of putting on a show so thoroughly? The man was a ham at heart!

And most definitely her hero.

Chapter Seventeen

By Saturday morning, the novelty of Mitch and Cora Beth's engagement had begun to wear off and things were getting back to normal, at least as far as the towns-folk were concerned.

For Cora Beth, however, things were anything *but* normal. She was working hard to get the boardinghouse ready for Mitch's arrival. She'd cleared the downstairs bedchamber—which tended to get treated like a store-room most of the time—of any clutter, and scrubbed and polished every visible surface until the room fairly sparkled. Then she made new curtains for the windows and placed one of her best quilts on the bed.

First thing next week, between her regular chores, she planned to tackle the parlor and turn it into Mitch's office.

But it was more than just the preparations that had her feeling a bit on edge. She couldn't get that kiss, and what it might mean for the two of them, out of her mind. To her disappointment, Mitch had avoided all mention of it. And while he'd been very good about making cer-tain everyone knew he was happy about the upcoming nuptials when they were in public, when they were alone he'd been equally careful to keep their interactions brief and to the point. Even when he'd joined them for meals at the boardinghouse, he'd spent more time interacting with the children and Uncle Grover than with her.

But Cora Beth was not ready to give up. Now that she'd seen the signs of a spark in his heart, she was determined to do her part to help that spark grow. More than likely he was just feeling a touch of guilt at an imagined disloyalty to Dinah's memory. There was a time after Phillip's death that she'd felt the same. But, as much as she'd loved him, she'd grown to realize that God didn't want His people living in the past. He wanted them to move forward, to be happy and fulfilled and whole again. It was up to her to show Mitch that that was true for him as well, that it wasn't an either-or proposition. He could cherish the memories of his lost love and still find room in his heart for a new love.

It would take time, but in this particular instance, she wouldn't try to hurry things along. She would be patient and wait on God's timing.

And this morning, the two of them were headed to the train depot to meet the returning Reynolds and Lassiter families. She'd wanted to be certain Josie and the others heard the news from her before anyone else told them, and the only way to ensure that was to be there when they stepped off the train. And it had only seemed right for Mitch to be there, as well.

Assuming his role of proud fiancé, Mitch had tucked her hand in the crook of his arm. It felt good to have him act so solicitous, so protective. In fact, Cora Beth decided, if this was the only way she could get him to drop the businesslike attitude, she'd have to come up with more excuses for them to be seen together in public.

They arrived at the depot just as the train whistle sounded in the distance. Before long, the train was coming to a noisy, soot-filled stop in front of the depot.

Josie was the first of the group to disembark and she hurried up to give Cora Beth a hug as soon as she spotted her.

"Hi! It's great to see you but you didn't have to come out here to meet us. I was planning to stop by your place before we headed out to the ranch."

Then she spotted Mitch and her expression sobered. "What is it? Has something happened? Are all the kids okay?"

"Relax, it's nothing like that." By this time the others had congregated around them and greetings were hastily exchanged.

Josie allowed them only a few minutes of chatter before she waved a hand impatiently. "Well then, if everyone's okay, to what do we owe the honor of this little welcome-home reception?"

Cora Beth could feel her cheeks warm. "Mitch and I have an announcement to make and we wanted you all to hear it from us first." As she spoke, Mitch moved up closer beside her, placing her hand on his arm and putting his over it.

Before she could say more, Josie's face broke into a broad smile and Sadie let out a little squeal of excitement.

Mitch grinned. "As you ladies seem to have guessed, Cora Beth here has done me the honor of agreeing to be my wife."

There were more squeals as Sadie and Josie vied with each other to hug Cora Beth. Ry and Eli resorted to thumping Mitch on the back and pumping his hand.

Penny and Viola stared at the adults as if they thought they'd gone a bit mad.

Finally Cora Beth straightened. "There's more we need to discuss with you, but why don't we do our talking at the boardinghouse instead of standing out here on the platform."

Ry looked at Eli with mock resignation. "We might as well. There's no way we're going to pry our wives away from Cora Beth anytime soon."

Cora Beth smiled her best bride-to-be smile.

As soon as they reached the boardinghouse, Penny and Viola went in search of the other children, which left Mitch and Cora Beth free to explain what had led to their sudden engagement.

"So you see," Cora Beth said once the story was out, "Mitch and I are entering into this arrangement as a purely business proposition, for the sake of the children. I wanted to give you the whole story because, unfortunately, the way events unfolded, it's been the subject of a lot of talk around town."

Sadie patted her hand. "I'm so sorry we weren't here to support you when this all came up. It must have been a difficult meeting to sit through."

"It was. But, thanks to Mitch's quick thinking, everything worked out for the best."

"I'm sure there are some legal ways to fight this," Ry said, "without you two having to go through with a marriage you don't want. Legal adoption for one. If you want me to look into filing the papers—"

Cora Beth held up a hand to stop him. "Thank you, but something like that could take time, and there's no guarantee the judge who reviews the case would grant my request. No, I think this is the best plan. That is—"

suddenly realizing it wasn't entirely her decision, she turned to Mitch "—unless you want to try that approach first?"

Mitch shook his head. "I'm fine with holding to the current plan. As I said at the time, I like those kids and like the idea of being part of their lives." He turned back to Ry. "But it might not hurt to look into filing for adoption after the wedding."

Pleasantly surprised, Cora Beth touched his arm briefly. "What a wonderful idea."

Ry nodded. "Good. I'll brush up on what'll be required so I'll be ready to help whenever you say the word."

Josie gave Mitch a broad smile. "Well, whatever the circumstances, welcome to our family." Then she looked around the table. "A lawyer, a banker and now a lawman—who would've guessed a year ago that today I'd find myself so well connected."

Ry stood. "Well, as much as I've enjoyed this visit, I need to check on how things are going at the stables. Ladybird was due to foal when we left." He bent down to take Josie's elbow and help her up. "And you've had a long day already. We need to get you home so you can rest."

"Well we don't have quite so dramatic a reason, but we need to get back home, as well," Eli said as he also stood. "I'm sure Sadie is also ready for some rest."

Josie and Sadie looked at each other and rolled their eyes. "Men."

Then Josie smiled at Sadie while she reached for Ry's hand. "We might as well let Mitch in on our news. He's practically family now anyway."

"I agree," Sadie said as she, too, reached for her husband's hand. "Besides, now that the girls know it won't be a secret much longer."

Josie turned to Mitch. "Both Sadie and I are in the family way."

Mitch's face split in a wide grin. "Well now, don't that beat all. Congratulations, folks." He rose and pumped first Ry's hand and then Eli's hand. "Looks like cause for celebration all the way around."

Josie nodded. "This family's sure enough growing by leaps and bounds.

Sadie stood, and Eli's arm snaked around her petite frame. "We do have to head home," she said, "but we hope you'll all come by our place for lunch after church service tomorrow. That includes you, too, Mitch."

"I'd be honored."

Once the others had gone, Cora Beth led Mitch back to the kitchen. "Thank you for helping me break the news to them."

"It was my news, too."

"And come next Saturday, they'll be your family, too." She waved a hand. "Well, technically Eli and Sadie aren't family, but they're as close as no never mind to it."

He shook his head, a crooked smile tugging at his lips. "It's going to be strange to be part of such a large family. You're used to it so I guess it's nothing remarkable in your books. But for all those years it was just me and Granny Todd. Then, after she passed, it was just me."

She smiled. "From desert to flood, I guess. You may find yourself in the midst of more family than you can stand." Not that she'd trade off any one of them for all of King Solomon's gold. But would he find their numbers overwhelming?

* * *

Monday morning, just as Cora Beth was finishing up with the breakfast dishes, she heard someone on the back porch. Looking through the screen door, she saw Hannah Thatcher raise her hand to knock.

"Come on in," Cora Beth said as she dried her hands on her apron.

The girl stepped across the threshold, then stopped, as if unsure of her welcome. "Good morning, Mrs. Collins. I hope I'm not interrupting anything."

"No, no, come on in."

"Sheriff Hammond, he said I should come talk to you. He said you might have some work for me."

Cora Beth studied the girl, taking in her thin frame and well-worn dress. For all of that, though, she was neat and clean. Her straw-colored hair was pulled back in a tidy braid and her clothing was spotless.

"Have a seat and let's talk for a bit. Can I fix you a cup of coffee?"

"No thank you, ma'am." She sat but she didn't relax. She perched primly on the edge of her chair, as if ready to take off at the first sign of trouble.

"So then, tell me, what sort of work are you looking for?"

"I can do just about any chores you set me to, ma'am. I can clean and cook and do laundry. I can do mending and scrub floors and—"

Cora Beth smiled and held up a hand. "So you're willing to do whatever is required." She gave the girl a sympathetic smile. "Tell me, how are things at home?"

Hannah lifted her chin. "My folks are doing the best they can, ma'am, but it's been hard this year. What with Pa hurting his leg right at planting time and those wild pigs getting into the vegetable garden and making a terrible mess of things and then our milk cow up and dying a'sudden like, it's been just one thing after the other. Pa says if we can just make it through this winter, things'll be better come spring." She finally paused to take a breath. "Folks have been real nice, but Pa don't like taking no charity."

It was worse than she'd heard. The family really did need help.

Hannah apparently mistook her silence for hesitation. "There's no need to pay me with cash money," the girl said. "I can work for vittles to bring home for the table, if you rather."

Cora Beth wondered just how sparse the meals had been at the Thatcher place. There were seven other children in that family, ranging from three years old to Hannah here at sixteen.

"I'll tell you what," she said. "Today is laundry day. Why don't you work with me here today and then we'll see whether we want to make it a permanent arrangement or not."

Hannah sprang from her chair as if given a reprieve. "Yes, ma'am. I promise I'll do you a fine job."

The girl was as good as her word. She was a hard worker, taking direction well and never complaining. She was also surprisingly good company. After she got over her initial shyness, she chatted away about everything from the weather to the antics of her siblings.

She made friends with Scout, professing to like animals of all sorts. She tossed him the occasional stick but never let it get in the way of her work.

Once the last piece was hung on the line, Cora Beth led the way back into the kitchen. "Well, now that you've got a taste for how much work is involved in the upkeep of a boardinghouse, are you still interested in working here?"

"Oh yes, ma'am." She grinned. "That's not a whole lot more laundry than we have at my house on wash day."

"Well then, here is my proposal. I would like to have you work here five days a week. You'll be in charge of getting most of the laundry and cleaning done—I'll continue to handle the shopping and most of the cooking."

"Thank you, ma'am. I promise I'll do you a good job."

"I'm sure you will. But I'm not finished with my proposal. Your family's place is a fair piece out of town. To make things easier on both of us, I think it would be best if you take over one of the upstairs rooms and sleep here. You could, of course, go back to your home place on Friday evenings and return on Monday mornings if you like—that would be up to you since Saturdays and Sundays would be yours to do with as you please. Of course, you would take your meals with us whenever you were here. Oh, and we'll figure out a weekly wage that will be fair to both of us." She sat back and looked at Hannah expectantly. "How does all that sound?"

"It sounds mighty generous." She leaned forward, her expression hopeful. "But excuse me, did you say I could have a room here?"

"Yes. Though I'm afraid the room I have in mind isn't very big, but it's clean and well lighted."

"Oh, Mrs. Collins, with four sisters I ain't never had a room all to myself before. That sounds downright wonderful."

Cora Beth laughed. "I'm glad. But don't give me your answer just yet. I want you to go home and talk to your parents and pray about it, and we'll talk again tomorrow. And for the work you did today, would a slab of bacon and a couple of jars of peach preserves work?"

"Oh, my goodness, that's much too generous."

"Nonsense. You worked hard today, and we'll consider it a good faith offering for your folks."

"They'll be right pleased to have it."

"Now, there are a few rules we need to discuss. My boarders here expect to have their privacy respected. For that matter my family does, as well. You don't go into any of the bedchambers without knocking first. And I don't hold with gossips. You are not to speak of anything that goes on in this household to outsiders—not even your own family. Is that understood?"

She nodded hard enough to make her braid fly. "Oh yes, ma'am, Mrs. Collins. I wouldn't ever go doing anything like that, I promise."

"Good. Now then, do you have a way to get back home?"

"Pauly is doing some work for Mr. Ivers today and he has the wagon so I can ride home with him."

Cora Beth stood, intending to gather up the foodstuffs she'd promised Hannah. Before she'd crossed the room, though, Mitch appeared at the back door. He gave Scout a friendly scratch behind the ears, then came on inside. "Hi, ladies. Y'all work everything out?"

Hannah gave him a broad smile. "Oh yes, sir." Then she clasped her hands in front of her as if to contain her joy. "Mrs. Collins is going to let me have a room here all to myself."

"Is that right?"

Cora Beth smiled. "Nothing's settled yet. Hannah is going to talk to her parents tonight and get back with me in the morning."

"I'll be here bright and early."

Cora Beth laughed. "Wait until daylight." She handed the girl a sack with the bacon and produce. "And if your parents want to speak to me about our arrangements before making a decision, they are more than welcome to come by in the morning, as well."

"Yes, ma'am, I'll be sure to tell them that."

With a wave and a decided spring to her step, Hannah exited the kitchen.

"Well, what do you think? Today was laundry day, wasn't it?"

She laughed. "Okay, you were right, it was nice to have some help with that."

"So you think she'll work out? If not, you can look for someone more to your liking."

"Mitchell Hammond, you knew good and well that once I spoke to Hannah, I wouldn't be able to turn her down."

He grinned. "That thought did occur to me."

She rolled her eyes. But she was pleased—quite pleased—at how well her husband-to-be seemed to know her heart.

Chapter Eighteen

Mitch liked the way Cora Beth's eyes sparkled this morning. He was happy that his idea to hire Hannah seemed to be working out so well. Perhaps this marriage arrangement could benefit her in other ways besides allowing her to hold on to Ethan and Cissy. He liked the idea of lightening her load and making her happy.

"So, did you stop by just to check on how Hannah and I were getting along?" she asked.

"Uh, no. There was something I wanted to talk to you about. I was taking stock last night of what I needed to clear out of my place, and there's a couple of pieces I might want to bring with me."

"Of course. You're more than welcome to bring whatever you like from your place. What kind of pieces are they?"

"One is a hall stand. It's nothing fancy, but my pa made it for my mother and I kind of like it." He felt a little foolish for being sentimental over such a thing.

But Cora Beth wasn't looking at him as if she thought him foolish. "Well, of course you do. We can put it right next to the hall tree I already have in the entryway."

He tried to wave aside that idea. "Like I said, it's not

very fancy—Pa wasn't much of a woodsmith, so it's okay if we just set it here by the back door or in a corner somewhere."

She shook her head indignantly. "Absolutely not." Then she grinned. "Besides, the way this family is growing, I have a feeling a second hall tree will come in handy."

Deciding not to argue further, he moved on. "The second piece is my mother's hope chest. It's a fine piece, made out of cedar and rosewood." He rubbed the back of his neck, wondering what she'd think of his idea. "I know you probably already have one of your own but I figure maybe someday one of the girls might like to have it."

Her expression softened and she touched his arm. "Oh, Mitch, what a lovely idea. I already promised my mother's to Audrey, so it would be a lovely gift for Cissy. In fact, we can bring Mother's down from the attic when you bring yours over and place them both in the girls' new room. But I warn you, we'll probably have to deal with a little jealous pouting from Pippa and Lottie."

He definitely didn't want to be responsible for something like that. "If it's gonna cause problems for you, I can—"

She laughed. "You're going to have to learn to deal with a lot worse than that if you're going to help me raise those kids." His face must have shown his momentary panic, because she sobered and smiled reassuringly. "Mitch, just because one of the kids gets to pouting is no reason to withhold something from one of the others. As these little squabbles come up we deal with them, treat them as learning opportunities, and move on. That's how kids learn to deal with the big disappointments later in life—by learning to deal with the smaller ones when they're young."

Was he really up for playing the role of father? "Sounds like there are going to be a lot of 'learning opportunities' in my future."

She patted his arm. "Don't worry, I think you'll get the hang of it soon enough." Then she crooked her finger. "Now if you have a minute, I'd like to show you how I plan to rearrange the parlor to make it into your office."

Talk about your stubborn women. "I told you that wasn't necessary. I don't need—"

"Nonsense. Every man needs a sanctuary of some sort. Consider it my wedding gift to you." She moved toward the hall, giving him no option but to follow.

As he went with her to the room in question, Mitch found himself understanding that there was a lot more to this complex woman than even he had realized.

And wouldn't it be a grand adventure getting to learn it all?

Tuesday morning, Hannah showed up right after breakfast, accompanied by her father. Once Cora Beth assured Mr. Thatcher that she had in fact offered Hannah a permanent job and a place to stay, he gave his blessing, admonished Hannah to be a good girl and work hard, then promised to return on Friday evening to pick her up and took his leave.

With Hannah on hand to do most of the chores, Cora Beth was free to work on other things.

Tuesday afternoon, she took advantage of her new-found freedom to catch up on her sewing. She already had a good start on her new dress, but finishing that and making four little-girl dresses before Saturday was a lot to tackle in a short period of time.

Deciding to take advantage of the pretty day and outdoor light, Cora Beth carried her sewing basket to the front porch and took a seat in the porch swing. Remembering the kiss she'd shared with Mitch in this very spot brought a smile to her lips and a longing to her heart. If she had her way, there'd be many more of those in her future.

She'd barely had time to make her first stitch when the front door opened and Mrs. Plunkett stepped out. "Mind if I join you?"

"Not at all. I'd enjoy the company."

Mrs. Plunkett sat in a nearby rocking chair, then eyed the yellow fabric in Cora Beth's lap. "I'm glad to see you finally had the good sense to hire someone to help you around here. The Thatcher girl seems to be a hard worker."

Cora Beth smiled. "Yes, she is. But actually, hiring her was Mitch's idea."

"Good for him. He's making a positive difference in your life already."

"Do you mind if I ask you something?" Cora Beth said impulsively.

"Not at all."

Cora Beth paused a moment, wondering if she should have acted on that impulse. Well, she'd already opened the door, might as well go through it. "Did you know Mitch's grandmother very well?"

"Opal Todd? I knew her, though I'm not sure I'd say I knew her well. It was hard to get to know that one, especially in her later years."

"Can you tell me about her?" She met the woman's gaze head-on. "I promise I'm not just indulging in idle gossip. I'd like to learn a little more about the woman who raised Mitch."

Mrs. Plunkett nodded. "Opal was about six years older than me so we didn't spend a lot of time together growing up—six years difference can seem a pretty wide gap at that age. But I do remember her wedding. She married Jasper Todd, one of the handsomest men around at that time." She smiled at Cora Beth. "Mitch favors him a bit."

Then she turned serious again. "Anyway, I'm afraid things didn't work out well for them. Rumor had it that Opal was jealous more than was warranted and that Jasper was not the most understanding of men. Whatever the case, by the time Mitch's mama was nearing school age, Jasper decided to head out and try his luck in the California gold fields. He promised to send for Opal and little Rebecca when he was settled in, but that never happened."

"Did she ever find out what happened to him?"

"Not that I know of."

"How awful. That must have been very hard on her."

"It turned her into a bitter old woman. She cut off ties with just about everyone and kept to herself mostly. Just came into town to do her marketing and to attend church services. It's a wonder Rebecca and Mitch turned out as well as they did."

Poor Mitch. It was no wonder he didn't believe he could love someone—it seemed he'd grown up in a home where very little love existed.

Well, somehow Dinah had gotten through to him.

And, God willing, she would, too.

The rest of the week passed in a blur. Josie popped in every morning after dropping off Viola at school. She helped with the sewing, handling the simple but time-consuming things like hemming, and leaving the more complex construction to her sister. She also informed Cora Beth that she planned to arrive bright and early on Saturday morning to help her get ready because "that's what sisters do."

On Wednesday, Cora Beth considered skipping the Ladies' Auxiliary meeting, but decided at the last minute not to, especially since Sadie was hosting this week.

On Thursday, it rained, and she saw Uncle Grover and Mrs. Plunkett bent over a chessboard in the parlor. Apparently they had found a common interest that they could indulge indoors.

And every evening she had Mitch's visits to look forward to. He usually arrived thirty minutes before suppertime and stayed until the dishes were done. He'd started moving some of his things into the house, as well. She went into the downstairs bedroom Thursday morning to add a starched cloth to the top of his dresser and paused on the threshold. It felt strange going inside now, almost as if she were intruding on him.

She looked around as she arranged the cloth, noting the little touches he'd added here and there. A trunk now guarded the foot of the bed. An old wooden chair with a leather seat sat in a corner, a pair of boots against the wall nearby. A leather-bound bible sat on the bedside table.

Nothing fancy, just serviceable, sturdy, honed furnishings. Like the man himself.

Mitch was a little late arriving at his office Friday morning. Not that he'd overslept. He'd moved the last of things, barring a few personal items, to the boardinghouse bright and early and stayed to have breakfast. Hard to believe that starting tomorrow that would be his home full-time.

Whistling, he locked up his desk and prepared to make his morning rounds. But before he could make his escape, the door opened and in walked Nelda Oglesby. And she didn't look happy.

"Sheriff Hammond," she said without preamble, "I demand that you do something about that boy."

Mitch swallowed a groan. Nelda's complaints were getting to be routine, which was not a good thing. "What seems to be the problem?"

She drew herself up. "My greenhouse has been ransacked again. It is an utter mess in there."

Again? Why in the world would anyone keep breaking into that place? Unless it was just to torment Nelda. "Was anything taken?"

"Not that I could tell, but that's not the point. And this is after I padlocked the door."

Padlock? Mitch remembered something Ethan had said about the time he slipped in and took the orchid for Cissy. Could it be… "Was the padlock broken?" he asked.

Nelda seemed unprepared for the question. "Why, no, I don't believe it was."

He reached for his hat. "If you don't mind, I'd like to have a look around the place."

She gave an approving nod. "Of course. I'm glad to see you're finally taking this seriously. Perhaps the sight of all that destruction will convince you of the severity of the crime."

Mitch kept his thoughts on *that* topic to himself. He merely opened the door and let her precede him out to the sidewalk.

Fifteen minutes later he was stooped down, examining the rich black soil that had spilled on the greenhouse floor.

"Do you see what I mean?" Nelda demanded. "This is pure spite and meanness."

Mitch didn't bother to look up. "I'm not so certain of that. It may just be clumsiness."

"Clumsiness? Sheriff, if you're not going to take this seriously after all—"

"Oh, I assure you I'm taking it very seriously." He stood and slowly made his way across the loam-scented building, keeping his eyes on the tracks in the debris.

"Whatever are you doing?"

"Trying to figure out where your late-night visitor entered from since he didn't come in the locked door."

"Oh." She seemed to think about that a moment. "Do you think he broke one of the glass panels?"

"Possibly, but more than likely he took advantage of a hole that was already there." He reached the far wall where a low table containing a number of pots and garden implements stood. He stooped and smiled. "There it is, the hole your intruder used to get in."

Nelda bent over and frowned. "But that's not big enough for a toddler to get through. Surely you're not trying to suggest a mere tot did this?"

"Of course not. Your intruder is a raccoon." He hated to admit it but he took some pleasure in making that announcement.

"A raccoon! But—"

"See these tracks here in the soil? They were made by a raccoon—a fairly large one, by the looks of it. And I remember Ethan mentioning he saw one in here the morning he took your orchid. He figured the critter followed him in but I'm guessing it was already inside

when he arrived. No doubt that animal has been for-
aging around for any tasty bulbs and other morsels he
could find."

She looked around fearfully. "Do you think he's still
in here?"

"I doubt it. But you might want to ask the mayor to
patch up that hole as soon as possible. Once that's taken
care of, I don't think you'll need to worry about this sort
of problem again." He dusted the dirt from his hands.
"Now if you'll excuse me, I have rounds to make."

He tipped his hat and left, amused to see Nelda scurrying quickly after him. As soon as she was outside she
slammed the door shut and replaced the padlock.

It would be interesting to see if Nelda shared the information about the raccoon as widely as she had the
accusations against Ethan.

He would make certain, though, that everyone at
the boardinghouse knew the whole story. Perhaps it
would help ease some of the tension between Danny
and Ethan. And even if it didn't, they were his family
and they deserved to know.

His family—that had a nice ring to it.

Cora Beth sat on the porch swing, sewing. She just
had a little more work to do on Pippa's dress and then
everything would be ready for tomorrow.

Tomorrow. Her wedding day.

A smile crossed her lips every time she thought of
it.

A welcoming bark from Scout let her know she had
visitors. Looking up she saw Mitch and Ethan heading
up the walk, with Mitch carrying a toolbox.

"Well, hello, you two. What are you up to?"

"Today is Ethan's last day of work for me, so I

thought, rather than sweeping out my office again, I get him to doing something more meaningful."

"Such as?"

"Such as seeing what we could do about those porch rails you mentioned."

Goodness, he remembered that casual reference she'd made two weeks ago. "It's those three slats over near the end," she said pointing. "They're pretty loose and I think at least one of them is rotted off near the bottom."

"We'll have a look. I was thinking maybe Danny could lend a hand, too. You know where he might be?"

She nodded. "He's in the kitchen, working on his lessons. Want me to fetch him?"

"No need. I know the way." He turned to Ethan. "I'll be right back."

After he'd stepped inside, Cora Beth went back to stitching. "So your two weeks are up, are they?"

"Yes, ma'am."

"You going to miss working at the sheriff's office?"

He shrugged. "Sheriff Hammond was a fair boss."

"You know what else this means, don't you?"

"Ma'am?"

Had he forgotten why he was working for Mitch? "Now that you've worked the two weeks, that locket of your mother's is yours, free and clear. Do you think Cissy would like to wear it to the wedding tomorrow?"

He gave her a broad grin—for once, there were no tinges of shadow. "Yes, ma'am, I think she'd be right proud to."

"Good. Then I'll fetch it for you to give to her as soon as you finish your work here."

The door opened and Mitch stepped out, followed by Danny. As soon as Danny caught sight of Ethan, he paused and his expression closed off. If Mitch noticed, he chose to ignore it.

"Okay, boys," he said, "while I take a look at these three slats, why don't you check out the rest of them to make sure we fix all of the problems at one time. Make sure you give 'em a tug to check for snug fits."

Both boys nodded, but Cora Beth noticed they stayed as far apart as possible while they worked.

Mitch, however, didn't seem to be paying any attention at all to the boys. "I think these two here just need another nail or two to secure them," he said cheerfully, "but you're right, this other one is going to need replacing."

"Is that a problem?" she asked.

"Not at all. I just need to get a piece of wood cut to fit and painted up to match. I'll take care of it early next week." He pulled a hammer and a couple nails out of his toolbox. "By the way, I got another visit from Nelda Oglesby this morning."

"Oh?" She could sense both boys' ears prick up.

Mitch positioned a nail against one of the slats and gave it a good whack. "Yep. Seems like she found signs of another intruder in her greenhouse." He kept his focus on the handiwork, seeming to merely be indulging in a bit of small talk to pass the time.

But there was an almost physical wave of tension coming from the boys.

"Odd thing was," Mitch continued, "she'd padlocked the door and the lock was still intact."

"That is odd." Cora Beth trusted Mitch. He obviously had a good reason for bringing this up here, in front of Ethan and Danny. "Did you find out how it was done?"

"Sure did." He gave the nail another whack, still not looking up. "Seems a raccoon has been getting in through a small hole in one of her panels."

"A raccoon!" It was all Cora Beth could do to keep from looking at the boys, but she managed to restrain herself.

"Uh-huh. That's why nothing had gone missing. The critter was just rummaging around for whatever tasty morsels he could find."

"Well now, doesn't that beat all. I imagine Nelda was surprised."

Mitch grabbed another nail. "Very. I don't think there'll be any more reports of break-ins to her greenhouse." Finishing with his handiwork, he finally straightened and looked at Ethan and Danny. "How we doing? Find any slats that need repair?"

As Mitch moved to examine the slats the boys wanted to show him, Cora Beth went back to her sewing. He'd delivered the news of Nelda Oglesby's intruder with just the right touch. The boys had heard the story, understood the implications and been left to draw their own conclusions. She couldn't have handled it better herself.

Yes, Mitch was going to make a very good father to these kids indeed.

Chapter Nineteen

Her wedding day dawned bright and beautiful. The crispness of early fall was in the air and from her bedroom window Cora Beth could see that several of the trees were just starting to turn lovely shades of yellow and orange.

"You make a beautiful bride." Josie stood behind her, fussily tying the sash of her dress. "I just wish Ma and Pa were still around to see this."

Cora Beth looked over her shoulder. "I have you here, and I like to think they're watching."

Josie gave Cora Beth's sash one last pat. "There— perfect." She stepped back and made a twirling motion with her hand. Cora Beth complied.

"Perfect," Josie repeated. "That color suits you. Mitch won't be able to take his eyes off of you."

"He's the one who picked out the fabric." She smiled, remembering their playacting in the mercantile that day.

"Did he now?" Josie gave her an amused look. "I always had a feeling you and Mitch would end up together. Truth to tell, I'm surprised it took this long."

That pulled Cora Beth up short. It was one thing for

her to daydream, but she didn't want to mislead anyone. "You do remember that this is not a love match, don't you?"

"Oh, fiddlesticks." Josie smoothed her own dress. "You can't tell me you don't love that man. It's there in your eyes every time you look at him."

Did Mitch see it, too? Well, trying to deny that she loved him would be a lie, so she didn't. "It takes *two* people in love to make a love match."

"It's plain as day that man cares for you, whether he admits it or not. Just look at how he came to your rescue when you needed him most. How much more romantic can a man be?"

If only that were true. "You have it all wrong. He made it quite clear that he did this for the children, not for me. He's formed quite an attachment to them—Cissy especially."

Josie shook her head stubbornly. "She's not the only one he's formed an attachment to. You can't tell me there's not something there when you two are together. It's sure as Sunday obvious to everyone else."

"Think what you will, just don't go trying to make this something it's not. I'd like to think maybe it'll grow into something more, someday, but for now, it is what it is. In fact, Mitch went to great pains to let me know that he prefers it this way." She took a deep breath before delivering the argument clincher. "He plans to set up in the downstairs room."

"Oh." Josie was silent for a long moment. Then she gave Cora Beth a smile. "I predict that, before Christmas, that situation will most definitely change."

Cora Beth felt her cheeks grow warm and Josie laughed. Then her sister took pity on her and changed the subject as she reached for the bouquet of flowers sitting on Cora Beth's bed. "Now, Sadie sent over these flowers from her own garden—she and Penny arranged them together. She sends her love and says not to worry, Mrs. Dauber has the reception well in hand."

Sadie had insisted on hosting a reception for them immediately after the ceremony, complete with a light meal for whomever cared to attend. She declared that there was no way she'd let Cora Beth go home and tend to her own meal on her wedding day, new servant or not.

Josie handed her the flowers, then slid her arm through the crook of Cora Beth's elbow. "Now, everyone's waiting. Are you ready to get yourself over to the church and become Mrs. Mitchell Hammond?"

Was she? Cora Beth stared at her reflection in the vanity mirror across the room. Oh yes, she was most definitely ready.

Fifteen minutes later she stood in the back of the church, alone except for Uncle Grover and Honoria Plunkett, who stood ready to throw open the sanctuary doors for them at their signal.

Cora Beth adjusted Uncle Grover's bow tie. Then she paused. He was *Phillip's* Uncle Grover. How did he feel about her marrying again? "You know, it means the world to me to have you walk me down the aisle."

He beamed fondly at her. "It's my honor, my dear. You know you are like a daughter to me."

She gave the tie a final tug, then laid her hand lightly against his chest. "I hope you realize that this doesn't in any way diminish the love I had for Phillip."

He gave her hand a pat. "My dear, what you and Phillip had was very good, very good indeed. It was obvious how much you loved each other. You made him very happy during the time you had together, and the two of you produced three very precious children. Nothing can diminish that."

He held her gaze steadily. "But he's gone now and I know in my heart he'd want to see you get on with your life." He gave her hand a squeeze. "Be happy, my dear. Feel free to find joy in this new chapter of your life."

Cora Beth gave him a tight hug as she felt the sting of tears. She hadn't realized how very much she'd needed to hear those words. "Thank you," she whispered.

But it wouldn't do to walk down the aisle with red eyes. So she swallowed hard, thought of Mitch, and let the joy of her wedding day fill her heart.

"Ready?" he asked as she stepped back.

Straightening, she nodded. He offered her his arm, nodded to Honoria to open the door, and the organ began to play. Taking a deep breath, Cora Beth gave his arm a light squeeze and together they started down the aisle.

Mitch watched Cora Beth approach on the arm of her Uncle Grover. The realization that her beaming smile and luminous eyes were directed solely at him, that from this hour forward she would be his lawfully wedded wife nearly drove him to his knees.

Mitch stood there waiting on her, a proud smile on his face.

Thank You, God for giving me this opportunity to find some of the happiness I thought beyond my reach. Please give me the strength to not try to greedily grasp for more, to honor my commitment to her and to always be worthy of the trust she is putting in me here today.

When she reached the front of the church and Uncle Grover transferred her hand to his arm, he felt ten feet tall. Then, staring into her eyes and seeing the look of happiness and trust there, he was humbled all over again.

The ceremony itself seemed to take forever and at the same time sped by. He barely took his gaze from hers the entire time. Before he knew it, they were repeating their vows and he was slipping his mother's gold wedding band on her finger.

When Reverend Ludlow informed him that he could kiss his bride, Mitch cupped her face in his hands and gently touched his lips to hers. It was all he could do to keep it short and chaste, but he was afraid if he did anything else, he'd once more get lost in her sweet response.

Then the ceremony was over and the two of them were surrounded by a flock of chattering little girls all trying to talk at the same time, and a circle of beaming adults.

As they faced their well-wishers, Mitch kept a tight hold of Cora Beth's hand, letting the reality of his newly married status sink in.

He'd done it! He'd gotten married and the sky hadn't fallen and no one had been hurt by it. And though it was an in-name-only arrangement, it came complete with children and an extended family and the most wonderful woman a man could ever want by his side. It was more than he'd dreamed possible and he told himself he couldn't be happier.

That little voice in his ear that asked for more was much too faint to pay any attention to at all.

Chapter Twenty

Cora Beth felt as if her face was frozen in a smile. Not that she wasn't happy—she was beyond happy. But this was her wedding day and she wanted to spend it with her husband, not accepting the well wishes of the scores of guests attending the reception on Sadie's back lawn. To say the wedding reception was well attended was an understatement—she hoped Sadie and Eli weren't being terribly put out by hosting this.

To be honest, she was very honored and touched that so many of her friends and neighbors had shown up to wish her and Mitch well. And it wasn't as if she and Mitch had other, more exciting plans for the day.

She excused herself from the conversation with Annielou Waskom and moved toward the table holding the punch bowl, trying to avoid making contact with anyone who might want to detain her and at the same time trying to spot Mitch. Ah—there he was, talking to Eli and Ry over by the pecan tree.

Deciding the bride had a right to speak to whomever she liked on her wedding day, she altered her course. Besides, as far as she could tell, she'd spoken to everyone here at least once. Maybe it was time to gather up the family and head home. And how wonderful that the family now included Mitch.

As she approached the trio, Ry noticed her first. "Ah, here she is, the lovely Mrs. Mitchell Hammond."

Mrs. Mitchell Hammond. She rather liked the sound of that.

Mitch kissed her forehead and linked his arm in hers. "So how are you enjoying your reception?"

Conscious of Eli's presence, she was careful to give a big smile. "It's a lovely gathering. I can't believe so many folks came out for it."

Eli laughed. "Even in the short time I've been here, I've learned that you two are the best known and best liked folks in these parts. Watching you get married and wishing you well on your special day is something no one wanted to miss."

Cora Beth smiled at the compliment, but she knew there was more to it than that. The circumstances around their engagement had made their wedding the town's main event.

Josie and Sadie came up just then. "Glad to find everyone together," Josie said, "so we can give you a little wedding gift."

"Oh, but that's not—"

"Hush, sister of mine, and accept your gift like a good girl."

"That's right," Sadie added. "This being your wedding day and all, we decided the two of you needed a little time to yourselves."

"Oh, but that's not—"

Again, her protest was cut short, this time by Sadie. "Nonsense. Now, we know you're not wanting a honeymoon trip or anything, but you can't say no to a nice little buggy ride out in the countryside all on your own."

Now that did have a nice ring to it.

"And before you mention the children, Uncle Grover and Mrs. Plunkett have agreed to see that the young'uns make it back to the boardinghouse. They even said they'll keep an eye on them until y'all get back." Sadie linked arms with her husband. "Eli has the carriage already hitched and waiting out front."

"And," Josie inserted, "since you haven't taken much time out from being sociable, I made sure there was a picnic basket slipped behind the seat. Now you two just scoot. We'll make your regrets to the remaining guests."

Mitch quirked an eyebrow at her. "Looks like we've been given our marching orders."

Cora Beth pretended to consider the matter. "It wouldn't do to turn down a gift that so much thought went in to."

Josie shook her head at them. "Enough. Just go."

Once they'd settled into the buggy, Mitch picked up the reins, then turned to her. "Where would you like to go?"

"How about we just set out toward Dogwood Hill? I know the trees aren't in bloom but it's still pretty up there."

"Your wish is my command." With a flick of the reins and click of his tongue, Mitch set the horse in motion. They rode along in silence for a while, but it was an easy, companionable silence with no pressure to break it. Cora Beth allowed the jostle of the wagon to throw her shoulder against Mitch's from time to time, enjoying the physical contact.

When they reached the top of Dogwood Hill, Mitch pulled the wagon to a stop. "How's this?"

"Perfect."

Mitch hopped down, then came around to help her do the same. He placed his hands at her waist and swung her down, holding her for an extra few moments after her feet touched the ground. As they stood there, his hands at her waist, hers at his shoulders, she found herself wishing he'd kiss her again—not a chaste, almost brotherly kiss like they'd shared a few hours ago at the wedding, but an achingly sweet, powerfully claiming kiss of the sort they'd shared in her porch swing.

To her disappointment, however, he released her and turned to the buggy. "Here's the blanket Josie packed. Why don't you find us a nice spot to set up our picnic while I tether the horse and fetch the basket?"

Feeling slightly deflated, Cora Beth smiled and did as he asked.

By the time he was finished with the horse, she had the small blanket spread across a relatively flat patch of ground that was in more sunshine than shade.

Mitch set the basket in the middle of the blanket and plopped down beside it. "Let's see what kind of goodies she packed. I'm suddenly famished."

As Cora Beth started laying out the much-too-abundant foodstuffs, she suddenly sat back on her heels. "I just remembered, tomorrow is first Sunday."

This past summer Reverend Ludlow had implemented a new tradition among their congregation. The first Sunday of every month, weather permitting, everyone would gather for a picnic on the church grounds after the service. It had been a great success from the start. Nothing like a shared meal out in the sunshine to bring folks closer together.

Mitch grinned. "I think I can handle that. Nothing wrong with having picnics two days running. In fact a man could get used to that kind of bounty."

The meal was delicious, the conversation between them light and easy, and totally inconsequential. They laughed together over the antics of the squirrels in the trees and over nothing at all.

Hunger satisfied, Cora Beth leaned back on one arm. "Remind me to thank my scheming sister and equally scheming friend. This was a marvelous idea."

"I agree." Mitch lounged on one elbow. "I was feeling a bit hemmed in and crowded there at the reception."

Cora Beth laughed. "Sounds like a man used to living alone. You do realize it's not exactly a small household you've just made yourself a part of, don't you?"

"I think I can live with that."

A sudden gust of wind blew a leaf into Cora Beth's hair. Before she could remove it, Mitch sat up and scooted closer. "Here, allow me." He plucked the leaf from her hair, then teasingly wrapped a tendril around his finger. "Soft as thistledown," he mused.

Suddenly, their gazes locked and the very air around them seem charged, ready to crackle at the slightest movement from either of them. She heard his breath quicken, saw his gaze move to her lips.

Cora Beth held her breath, willing him to kiss her the way she'd wanted to be kissed all morning.

His hand swept the hair from her temple. "You know," he said huskily, "we made an important commitment today. I think maybe that kiss I gave you during the ceremony didn't quite live up to the seriousness of the occasion. Mind if I give it another shot?"

She lifted her hand to his face and stroked his faintly

stubbly jawline. "I think that would be an absolutely marvelous idea."

The kiss, when it came, was everything she had longed for. He tasted of apple cider and lemon drops. The feel of his hands at the back of her neck—warm, strong, supportive—played a perfect counterpoint to the urgency of his mouth over hers. It felt so wonderful to be in his arms this way, to feel the beating of his heart against her own, to know that he wanted her with him every bit as much as she wanted him with her.

Finally he pulled away, but this time it was no abrupt withdrawal, no sudden distancing of himself. He simply gave her a smile, stroked her cheek gently with the back of his hand, and pulled her against him so she rested in the crook of his arm. "*Now* our wedding vows are properly sealed," he said with satisfaction.

Did he realize how much he'd revealed in that kiss? Was now the time to let him know how she felt? Or would it just spoil the moment?

Saying a quick prayer that she could find the right words, Cora Beth took the plunge before she lost her courage. "About our marriage arrangement, I think you ought to know that I've changed the terms."

"What do you mean?" There was more than just a question in his tone—there was caution, as well.

"I know we promised to keep it businesslike, but I can't do that." She turned in his hold so that she was facing him. "I love you, Mitch. I know you say you can't love me, but I hope in time perhaps you can learn to."

"Stop." He gave her shoulder a warning squeeze. "Don't ruin this."

"Ruin this? But—"

He pulled away, his expression hardening. "I mean it, Cora Beth—you're mistaken, you don't love me. I'm sorry if that kiss gave you the wrong impression but we're good friends, that's all. And that's all we're ever going to be."

Why was he so afraid of accepting her love? "Mitch, it's okay if you don't love me, but you're going to have to accept that I love you. I know your grandmother wasn't the most loving of examples, but that doesn't mean you aren't lovable. Trust me."

"My grandmother—" He swallowed whatever he'd been about to say under a bitter laugh. "You don't understand."

"Then tell me. Help me to understand."

He stood and jammed his hands in his pockets. "I made a vow a long time ago that I would never, ever get married. The *only* reason I broke that vow now was because we agreed to keep love out of it."

What a terrible promise to have to live with. "A long time ago? You mean after Dinah died."

"Yes." He frowned down at her, his frustration evident. "But not for the reason you think."

What was she supposed to think if he wouldn't explain himself? She stood so she faced him more directly. "Mitch, I still haven't heard an explanation—just more nonsensical assertions."

He stared at her a moment, then sighed and raked a hand through his hair. "All right. I guess you deserve the whole story." He picked up a small broken branch from the ground and started stripping leaves from it. "According to my grandmother, my grandfather was the great love of her life. Her whole world centered around him when she was younger. And she swore that, in the beginning, he loved her just as deeply." He sent her a probing look. "I guess you know he eventually abandoned her and my mother when Ma was just a little kid."

Cora Beth nodded and he continued. "Well, since she figured *she* hadn't changed, then it had to be something else that turned him from her, caused him to abandon them so abruptly."

"I can see where she'd want to believe that."

He yanked another leaf from the branch. "What you probably didn't know is that apparently my grandfather's father did the same to his wife. Up and abandoned her with two little kids to care for. Though I take it there were some other unsavory actions laid at his door, as well."

He broke the stick in half and tossed it away. "Anyway, the whole time I was growing up, my grandmother swore it was something in the Todd men's blood, that they were bound to turn from those who loved them, no matter how deep their love might run in the beginning."

How could a woman say that to her own grandson? She put her hand on his arm. "Mitch, that's ridiculous. Such things aren't passed down from father to son."

Seeing the stubborn set of his jaw, she lifted her chin. "And even if they were, you're *not* a Todd, you're a Hammond, and I never heard tell of your father doing anything so dreadful to your mother."

He nodded, but there was resignation in the gesture. "That's what I kept telling Granny Todd. And kept telling *myself.* I was certain, no matter what she said, that I would never, ever do that to the woman I loved."

His jaw worked for a moment, then stilled. "I look quite a bit like my grandfather Todd, you know. Of course, I never met the man, but grandmother had a tintype of him up on the mantle. She would tell me over and over that if I was like him on the outside, chances were I'd be like him on the inside. There were days when I wanted to fling that picture into the fireplace."

Cora Beth was finding it hard to summon up forgiveness for such a woman. "Mitch, no matter what your grandmother said, no matter what kind of men your grandfather and great-grandfather were, you're *not like that*. If you truly don't have any feelings for me, consider your feelings for Dinah. I remember how hard you took her death, how devastated you were after the accident. And look at the way you've held on to her memory all these years. Surely that's proof of your ability to hold to a lasting love."

He gave another bitter laugh. "And there you've hit on the heart of my great undoing. You see, I *didn't* hold true to that love. Those last few weeks before our wedding day, I found my feelings for Dinah changing, starting to cool. Oh, I still liked her well enough, I just couldn't see spending the rest of my life with her. It was my worst nightmare—my grandmother's predictions coming true."

Her heart went out to the young man he'd been, faced with so terrible a prospect and no family or close friend to turn to. "Oh, Mitch, I'm so sorry. But that's still not—"

He held up a hand to stop her. "Here's the really funny part. When I realized what was happening, I prayed about it. Prayed harder than I've ever prayed about anything before or since. I prayed that God would help me to feel that love again or, barring that, to help me find a way out of my commitment to Dinah without breaking her heart. And you remember how He answered me, don't you? Four days before the wedding she trips and breaks her neck. Just like that—" he snapped his fingers "—problem solved."

Cora Beth thought her heart would break as he revealed that final bit of his terrible burden. A burden he'd shouldered so unnecessarily. "You are *not* responsible for Dinah's accident. God doesn't work that way. God didn't plan that accident in answer to your prayers."

"That's exactly how it looked from where I stood."

"Then you were standing in the wrong place."

He touched her cheek, then pulled his hand back as if it had been burned. "Ever the stalwart defender of the downtrodden." A small tic near the left corner of his mouth jumped once, twice, and then was still. "If you're worried about my spiritual well-being, don't be. My faith isn't shaken. I still believe in God, I still believe that He is the Great Creator, the Sovereign, the One who loves us above all others."

He drew his shoulders back. "I simply believe, also, that He chose this method to show me the truth of who I am, to help me to make the difficult decision I had to make. I also thought, maybe wrongly, that this marriage arrangement with you was God-sent, that He was providing a means for me to have a small piece of the family life I wanted, without anyone getting hurt. Maybe I was wrong about that, too. Maybe this marriage idea came from my own selfish desires and isn't of God at all."

She wanted to stomp her feet at him, to shake him until his teeth rattled, to make him *really* listen to her. "Mitch, for goodness' sake, listen to yourself. Saying God caused Dinah to die so He could teach you a lesson is the same as saying God abandoned Ethan and Cissy to Titus's cruelty because He wanted to teach *them* a lesson."

She took a deep breath and softened her voice. "Yes, bad things happen, and yes, God can use those things to teach us, to do His work, to eventually bring good to us or others, but He is never deliberately cruel to us. A loving God just doesn't do things that way."

"Apparently we see things differently."

"Mitch, you didn't force God's hand. Prayer is good, of course, and prayer is an effective means of communication and petition, but prayer doesn't change God. He doesn't grant us our heart's desire on a whim, and He never goes contrary to His own perfect will. His will *always* prevails, is always perfect, whether we understand it or not. Don't you see, by accepting blame for Dinah's death, you're claiming a power over God that you just don't have?"

He didn't say anything for a long moment. Other sounds seemed to be magnified—the sound of the horse chomping at the grass, the hum of insects, the trill of a bird.

And, as his expression closed off completely, the wrenching sound of her heart breaking.

Mitch stooped down and began stuffing things into the hamper. "I think we're both too tired to continue this discussion right now. Why don't we head back to town?"

It was all Cora Beth could do to keep tears of helplessness and frustration from flowing down her face.

Chapter Twenty-One

Cora Beth got very little sleep that night. Her mind kept going back to that conversation with Mitch, torturing her with things she should have said, arguments she should have made to help show Mitch how skewed his thinking was.

What a terrible burden for him to have lived with all these years—to believe not only that he was destined to eventually betray any woman he dared to love, but that he was responsible for Dinah's death. How had he borne it? And, more importantly, how could she help him see how very, very wrong those two deeply ingrained beliefs were?

From the looks of Mitch the next morning, it seemed he hadn't slept well, either. Oh, his smile was as friendly as ever, and he chatted easily with the girls, but she saw the weariness in his eyes and the way he avoided meeting her gaze.

Even the day seemed tired and weary. While it didn't appear that rain was imminent, the sky was shrouded in clouds and the air had a damp feel to it. Not the best of weather for a picnic, but maybe the day would improve as the sun had more time to do its work.

Danny was the first of the kids downstairs, already dressed in his Sunday best. "Don't forget it's first Sunday."

Was he thinking about spending time with Odine? "Don't worry, the picnic hamper's already packed."

Mitch was effortlessly drawn into their Sunday morning routine—almost as if he'd always been a part of it. He was even recruited by Audrey to help tie a hair ribbon when Cora Beth was occupied making sure Lottie got her shoes on the right feet.

They walked to church, Mitch carrying the big hamper, Cora Beth carrying a smaller basket, and the children between them.

And during that walk, all she could think about was how to set matters right between them. The problem was, she didn't want things to go back to the way they were before. She wanted a true marriage. And now that she knew what stood in the way of that, she was more determined than ever to break down those barriers.

During the church service, she found herself having trouble focusing on Reverend Ludlow's sermon. Finally, she bowed her head.

Heavenly Father, please forgive me for my wayward thoughts, but I am so heartbroken and need Your comfort and Your guidance. Thank You for showing me what is in Mitch's heart and what is walling him off from ever finding fulfillment and the love You intended for him to have. Now please, please, help me find a way to get through to him, to shatter that horrid wall and set the true Mitch free.

Raising her eyes again, she did feel a measure of peace that had been missing before. Settling more comfortably in her pew, she determinedly focused her attention on Reverend Ludlow's words.

* * *

As soon as Mitch stepped outside after the church service, he excused himself from Cora Beth and went to help the other men set up the picnic tables. The busier he kept, the better. He'd been doing entirely too much brooding since he and Cora Beth had left their private picnic yesterday afternoon.

Cora Beth's admonishments kept rattling around in his mind, refusing to leave him in peace.

Sawhorses and long boards were pulled from the back of a number of wagons and quickly converted into sturdy tables. As quickly as they were set up, the women would cover them with colorful cloths and begin to lay out the food. The meal was a community event with folks free to sample whatever items struck their fancy.

Blankets and quilts were spread out on the ground with lots of good-natured jostling for the prime spots. It wasn't long before the churchyard looked like one big, colorful, crazy quilt, with wide swaths of uncovered grass to form the green outline for the individual pieces.

While the adults visited and got everything ready, the children were left to run around and play with friends amid admonishments to not go very far off and to not ruin their Sunday clothes.

Mitch crossed the church lawn, greeting longtime neighbors and friends, but not pausing for long with any one group. He was looking for Cora Beth. Before, he'd always been a bit of a tumbleweed at these events, moving from spot to spot, receiving invitations to join this group or that, always careful not to pay too much attention to any one family. It felt good to know that this time he had a place where he belonged, a family who waited on him to complete their group.

He finally found Cora Beth. She'd spread two blankets side by side toward the back of the church property. He noticed the Oglesby family was close by. Had Danny and Odine orchestrated this or was it just coincidence?

She greeted him with a warm smile and he felt himself relaxing. They could get past their argument. She knew the worst about him now and didn't seem to hold it against him.

"There you are," she said. "I hope this spot is all right. It's not too crowded on this end of the grounds so I thought it would give our group a chance to spread out a bit."

"Looks fine to me. I saw one of the hands from Ry and Josie's place. He said to tell you they're not here because Josie's a little under the weather but it's nothing to get concerned about."

"I wondered when I didn't see the three of them. I figured it might be morning sickness kicking in."

For just a moment, Mitch allowed himself to think about what it might be like to have Cora Beth carrying his child. Then he ruthlessly wiped that thought from his mind. "I think all the food's set up and ready to serve." His voice was surprisingly steady. "You ready to fix a plate? I saw Suellen brought some of her corn fritters and I want to grab one before they're all gone."

She handed Mitch and the twins each a plate. "If you don't mind, you help Pippa and I'll help Lottie serve their plates." She glanced toward the large oak where several of the older children were gathered. "Danny, come get your plate." Then she looked around. "Now where did those other three get off to?"

"Don't worry, they won't have gone far." Mitch waved to the dozens of children chasing each other in the open area near the church building. "And they know the rules, first come, first served. Those corn fritters won't last forever."

She laughed. "Audrey understands that, but I guess Ethan and Cissy may just learn the hard way."

"It won't take but one time for them to learn."

Mitch found himself enjoying helping Pippa fill her plate, even when she spilled half of it and they had to go back through the line again. It felt good to have the girl look up to him, to trust him to help her make choices, and to take his hand when she needed help navigating the rough ground. Finally their plates were filled and the four of them headed back to the blanket. Danny had disappeared among the food tables early on.

"I still haven't seen Audrey, Cissy and Ethan," Cora Beth said worriedly.

"They're probably at the food tables by now," Mitch answered. "But I tell you what, I'll get you three ladies settled on the blankets and then I'll go look for them." He raised a brow at Pippa. "That is, if I can trust you to guard my plate until I get back."

Pippa giggled then nodded.

Mitch, Cora Beth and the twins had just reached the right pair of blankets near the Olgesby family when a muddy and soaking wet little girl came running to them from the far side of the field, crying hysterically.

Nelda scrambled up and rushed forward, her husband right behind her. "Loretta? What's the matter, what happened to you? Did someone push you in the water?"

"I f-f-fell." The girl pulled out of her mother's grasp and ran over to Mitch. "You gotta help them. The water's getting higher."

Mitch, his pulse quickening, handed his plate to Cora Beth and placed a hand on the girl's shoulder. "Help who, Loretta?" But he feared he knew the answer already as he scanned the crowd, still unable to see his three.

"Audrey and Ethan."

He heard Cora Beth's quick intake of breath, felt his own heart thudding. But he had to keep his wits about him. "Where are they?"

"The ground just fell out from under us and we were falling and—" Her teeth were chattering so hard she could barely talk.

Resisting the urge to shake the answers from her, he asked again, "Where are they, Loretta?"

She pointed over her shoulder. "Over by the far corner of the Clowsen place."

Mitch took off at a run. Three agonizingly long minutes later he spotted Cissy, flat on the ground, peering into a large opening.

As soon as she spotted him, Cissy scrambled to her feet and he saw the tears streaming down her face. "Help them!" she screamed. "Help them get out of there!"

He took one look inside the hole and his insides turned to ice. The hole appeared to be about eight feet deep and six feet across. There was water inside, lots of water. It was up to Ethan's neck and it was obvious it was still rising. But the boy was gamely holding on to an unconscious Audrey, trying to keep her head above the water, as well.

"Hold on, Ethan, I'm coming in." Mitch eased over the edge and slid into the hole, doing his best not to splash or swamp them. The water was freezing cold— no wonder their lips were blue. As soon as he took Audrey, Ethan slumped and began to tremble. The boy was exhausted.

"She's hurt," Ethan said through chattering teeth. "I think she hit her head when she fell in."

By this time several other folks had gathered at the mouth of the hole, sending clods of dirt and grass tumbling into the water.

"Careful up there," Mitch called out. "I'm not sure how stable the ground around this hole is."

"You heard the man, everyone but you and you, get back," he heard Eli say.

"Eli, help Ethan out of here before the water gets over his head."

Was Cora Beth nearby? He'd rather not scare her but there was no help for it. "Audrey's hurt. You'll need to fix up a sling to haul us both out with."

He heard some muffled conversation from the crowd above and then Eli's face and shoulders appeared above the hole at ground level. He dangled his suit coat over the edge. "Here, Ethan, grab hold of the sleeve and we'll pull you out." Eli glanced at Audrey, then looked at Mitch with a worried frown. "Doc Whitman is right here and Horace is fetching a rope from his wagon. We'll have you out of there in no time." Then, with a grunt, he focused on pulling Ethan out.

Mitch stared down into the face of the much-too-pale, much-too-still Audrey, then cradled her snug against his chest. This normally vibrant chatterbox, this bright, mischievous, curious child, his sweet pea—she couldn't be extinguished this way.

Dear God, please, please, don't take this little girl, not yet, not like this. It would drive a stake through her mama's heart.

He swallowed hard against the thickness in his throat. *And even if Cora Beth is strong enough to withstand such a loss, I don't think I am.*

Ten eternally long minutes later Mitch was back on solid ground, seated on the edge of the pit, his precious burden still cradled in his arms. He allowed Eli to take the child from his nearly numb arms and watched him place her on a blanket at Doc Whitman's feet. She hadn't wakened, hadn't stirred, hadn't made a sound.

Someone offered him a hand and he stood, scanning the crowd. A heartbeat later, he stepped toward the blanket where Audrey lay and caught Cora Beth as she tried to get to her injured daughter. "Let the doctor do his job," he said gently.

With a sob, she threw herself in his arms. He stood there, holding her close, stroking her back, sharing her worry and fears, praying with all his might that Audrey would be okay.

Someone threw a blanket over his shoulder and he was vaguely aware that the rest of the family stood nearby, but his whole world had narrowed down to Cora Beth and the still, small form on the blanket.

When Doc Whitman finally straightened, both he and Cora Beth braced themselves and he kept a tight hold of her shoulder. Whether it was to support her or himself, he wasn't certain.

"She's got quite a knot on her head."

"Is she going to be all right?"

"I wish I could tell you yes, but I'm afraid it's too early to tell. More than likely she has a concussion. Best thing right now is to get her home, get her into some dry clothes and into a warm bed, and keep a close eye on her." He eyed them both sympathetically. "I'm afraid the rest is up to the Good Lord."

Chapter Twenty-Two

Mitch stepped onto the front porch and pulled his shoulders back, trying to get the kinks out of his muscles.

It had been nearly six hours since they'd pulled Audrey from that hole and her condition was still unchanged. He leaned his elbows on the porch rail, clasping his hands in front of him.

He tried to take comfort in the fact that at least she hadn't gotten any worse. But that was cold comfort indeed.

Scout padded up and lay at his feet, muzzle to the ground. "You're worried, too, aren't you, boy?"

A few minutes later, Ethan stepped out and joined him. "Any word on Audrey?"

"No change."

"I wish I could have gotten her out of that hole faster."

"You did all you could, Ethan. You saved her life." He slid a hand into his pocket. "I never did get a chance to ask you exactly what happened out there."

Ethan reached down to pat his dog. "I was looking for Cissy, to tell her it was time to eat. I saw the girls heading for the tree line and went after them. Then they all just kinda disappeared and I heard 'em screaming so I took off at a run. When I reached where they'd been, there was a big ole hole in the ground with them trapped inside."

A sink hole, just like he'd figured. "So you jumped in after them?"

Ethan shrugged. "I didn't have no rope or nothing to pull them out with and Audrey looked like she was hurt and the water started seeping in pretty fast."

"How'd you get Loretta and Cissy out?"

"Loretta's the tallest, so I made her climb up on my shoulders and pull herself up. Then Cissy did the same, with Loretta's help. Then I told Loretta to stop bawling and run and get you."

"Smart kid."

"Yeah." Danny stepped out on the porch. "And pretty brave, too."

Had the boy heard the whole story?

"You would have done the same," Ethan said. "I just happened to be the one who was there when it happened."

"Yeah, well, still, they would likely have all drowned if you hadn't done what you did." Danny shoved his hands in his pockets. "Audrey would have for sure."

Then Danny pulled his shoulders back. "I want to apologize for how I've been treating you since you moved in here. I was wrong to believe all those things folks said about you. It won't happen again." He scuffed the floor with his toe, then looked up. "And you can move back into my room if you like."

Ethan grinned. "Thanks. But I kinda like it where I am."

Danny returned his grin. "Yeah, you have a pretty

good setup. I mean, a whole floor to yourself, and walls that you can move whenever you want to. I gotta admit, I was just a little bit jealous when I first saw it." He nodded his head toward the door. "Hey, you want to have a look at my set of tin soldiers?"

Ethan straightened. "Sure."

With that, the two boys disappeared inside the house.

Mitch was glad to see they'd finally gotten over their differences. It was just a shame it had taken a terrible accident to accomplish it.

He pushed away from the porch rail and headed back inside, determined to see that Cora Beth took a break.

Cora Beth looked up when he walked in the room, her face pale and strained. She gave him a smile that was a weak shadow of her usual bright one. "I think maybe she's breathing just the tiniest bit better."

Mitch could detect no difference, but nodded. "That's a good sign."

"If only she'd open her eyes."

"Cora, honey, I want you to go in the kitchen and get yourself something to eat. Sadie dropped off a basket of goodies from the picnic a while ago and Hannah is here and has some good broth simmering on the stove in case we need it."

"I'm not hungry."

He took her hand. "You need to eat and you need to rest. You're not going to be any good to Audrey if you make yourself ill."

"I'll be fine." She looked up at him with swollen, despairing eyes. "I just can't leave her, not while she's so helpless."

He pulled a chair up next to the one she was seated in and put his arm around her shoulder, cradling her against his side. "All right. If you won't leave her, then rest here. I'll keep watch and I promise to alert you if there's even the slightest change."

"Promise?"

"You have my word."

"Then maybe, just for a few minutes…" She snuggled more deeply into his arm and closed her eyes. A few minutes later, Mitch heard the soft rhythm of her breathing that signaled she'd drifted to sleep.

She was so fragile, so vulnerable, so very special to him. Holding her this way, knowing that she trusted him to see to her child, to support her faithfully while she slept, was both humbling and exhilarating. It felt as if something in his chest had expanded almost beyond his ability to contain it. There was nothing in this world he wouldn't do for her or for her children. He'd never in his life felt like this before.

That thought stopped him, gave him pause. Was that true? What about the love he'd felt for Dinah, before it had faded? He probed his memory, trying to dig through the cobwebs of the passing years and remember how that had felt back then.

And then the truth came to him, blindingly clear.

What he'd felt for Dinah was a young man's infatuation with the *idea* of love, the idea of starting a family of his own and of escaping the gloom and emptiness of life in his grandmother's household. He hadn't fallen *out* of love with her, because he'd never really been *in* love with her to start with. And somehow, he'd sensed that back then. That's why he'd pulled away from the idea of marrying her.

Could that be true? Or was he just looking for a way to justify what he was feeling now? But the more he thought about it, the more he compared those long ago feelings with what he now felt for Cora Beth, the more convinced he became.

Because with Cora Beth, he was in love with the woman—the stubborn, hardworking, amazing woman whose heart was big enough to encompass this whole mismatched, boisterous family that she had drawn to herself, including her latest acquisition—him.

There was no desire to pull back, no second guessing his plan to spend a lifetime loving her.

Dear God, thank You for showing me the truth, and for helping me to find my way to this place. I promise You I will strive every day to be worthy of this wonderful second chance at having a loving family that You have given me. And, Dear Merciful God, if it be in Your will, please bring Audrey through this and back to us. But in all things, help me to remember that Your plan for our lives, though sometimes hard to understand, is always perfect and always meant for our good.

Chapter Twenty-Three

"Cora, honey, wake up."

Cora Beth fought against the layers of cotton swaddling her, keeping her from opening her eyes. Mitch's voice had been thick with emotion. What was wrong?

Suddenly remembering, she jerked herself fully awake. "What is it? Audrey—"

"Is awake and asking for you."

She turned from Mitch's beaming face to that of her daughter, blinking up at her from the bed that was too big for her. In the space of one heartbeat to the next, Cora Beth was out of her chair and clutching her daughter to her.

"You're squeezing too hard," Audrey complained.

A bubble of laughter, part hysteria, part relief, erupted from her. "I'm so sorry, baby," She eased her hold but couldn't stop touching her. "Mama's just so happy to see that you're okay."

"My head hurts."

Mitch gave Cora Beth's hand a squeeze, then tapped

Audrey's nose. "Glad to have you back with us, sweet pea."

Then he turned to Cora Beth. "I'll send for Doc Whitman."

An hour later, Doc Whitman had pronounced Audrey clearly on the mend and she was sitting up in bed, thoroughly enjoying all the attention she was getting. Cora Beth finally felt comfortable leaving her in the care of Uncle Grover while she went in search of Mitch.

She found him standing on the front porch, looking at the stars studding the evening sky.

"How's she doing?" he asked over his shoulder.

"Much better. Uncle Grover's with her." Cora Beth moved beside him and felt a little thrill of pleasure when he put his arm around her as if it were the most natural thing in the world.

Don't read too much into this, she told herself. It's been an emotional day. He'll go back to normal by morning. "We can bring her upstairs to her room if you want yours back now," she offered.

He shook his head. "No point in disturbing her right now. I can sleep in a chair for one night." He finally looked down at her and traced the line of her cheek with a finger. "You look beat. Why don't you go inside and get some sleep. I'll stay up with her tonight."

She shivered at the tingle of his touch and he pulled her back into the crook of his arm.

"I'm not sleepy yet. Maybe a little later."

They stood there quietly for a while, then she finally looked up at him. "What were you thinking about before I came out here?"

"What a lucky man I am to have been given this second chance."

"Second chance?"

He turned to face her, his smile a warm caress. "At having a family. At finding love."

"Love?"

He smiled, no doubt at her dull-witted repetitions. "I was thinking of something else, too. I was thinking it might be a good idea to add another room or two to the back of the house."

"Sheriff Lemon Drop, whatever are you talking about?"

Mitch smiled at her use of Cissy's nickname for him. "You never know when you might need to make room for another boarder. And it might be nice to have our master bedroom on the first floor where we can have a little more privacy."

It took a heartbeat for his words to sink in. Then she pulled back to eye him better. Did he mean what it sounded like he meant?

His smile turned earnest. "That is, if you'll do me the honor of tossing out this businesslike nonsense and *truly* being my wife." He took her hands. "I'm through fighting this, Cora Beth—I was the worst kind of fool to even try. I love you, love you so much that the idea of ever leaving you is so painful I'd as soon pluck out my own heart with a rusty nail. If you tell me I'm not coming to my senses too late, you'll make me the happiest man alive and I'll spend the rest of our days together trying to make you just as happy."

Cora Beth launched herself into his arms and threw her own around his neck. "Mitch Hammond, you *are* a fool. As if I could ever stop loving you. Now hush all this silly talk and kiss me like you mean it."

And, with a joyous laugh that could be heard all through the boardinghouse, he did.

* * * * *

Dear Reader,

Hello! Both Mitch and Cora Beth have made appearances in the two other books I wrote set in Knotty Pine. Almost from the very first I knew I would have to give them a story of their own. However, I never dreamed it would be such a difficult story to write.

It took me some time to figure out what had kept them apart for so long when there was an obvious attraction there. Mitch was reluctant to let me in on his secret, but when he finally did it all started falling together. The appearance of Ethan and Cissy on the scene provided just the impetus I needed to stir their quiet world and force them into some uncomfortable situations. And those situations eventually led them to dig deep and make the choices they would have to make in order to earn their *happily ever after*.

I truly fell in love with these characters and all the children in their lives. I hope you, too, will find something to celebrate in their story.

Wishing you much love and blessings in your life,
Winnie Griggs

Questions for Discussion

1. Mitch and Cora Beth view Ethan quite differently at first—Mitch sees him as a troublemaker and Cora Beth as a boy in need. Why do you think this is?

2. Danny seemed to have trouble with Ethan's presence from the very first. Given Danny's own background did this surprise you or did you understand it?

3. What did you think of Mrs. Plunkett's decision to actively pursue Uncle Grover? What did you think of Cora Beth's reaction to that decision?

4. What did you think of Ethan's decision to make a room for himself up in the attic?

5. Did Cissy's quick integration into Cora Beth's household ring true to you?

6. Did Mitch's sudden decision to propose to Cora Beth after his years of refusing to consider marriage ring true to you?

7. Individual townsfolk in Knotty Pine reacted differently to Ethan's actions and his subsequent residence in their town. Can you see merit to each of the different reactions? How do you feel you would have reacted?

8. Once they discovered that Ethan and Cissy had been in the care of Titus Brown, both Cora Beth

and Mitch felt guilt for the fact that they didn't try harder to reach out to them and their mother. Was that guilt justified? What more could they have done? What would you have done in their place?

9. Once Mitch confessed his "dark secret" to Cora Beth, she did her best to help him see that Dinah's death was not his fault. Do you think she got through to him at all? Is there something else you would have done or said in her place?

10. What do you think caused the breakthrough that allowed Mitch to finally heal and let himself love and be loved again?

INSPIRATIONAL

Inspirational romances to warm your heart & soul.

Love Inspired.
HISTORICAL

TITLES AVAILABLE NEXT MONTH

Available August 9, 2011

THE CHAMPION
Carla Capshaw

THE MATRIMONY PLAN
Christine Johnson

MARRYING MISS MARSHAL
Lacy Williams

REDEEMING THE ROGUE
C. J. Chase

REQUEST YOUR
FREE BOOKS!

 HARLEQUIN® HISTORICAL:
Where love is timeless

2 FREE NOVELS PLUS 2 **FREE GIFTS!**

YES! Please send me 2 FREE Harlequin® Historical novels and my 2 FREE gifts (gifts are worth about $10). After receiving them, if I don't wish to receive any more books, I can return the shipping statement marked "cancel." If I don't cancel, I will receive 6 brand-new novels every month and be billed just $5.19 per book in the U.S. or $5.74 per book in Canada. That's a savings of at least 17% off the cover price! It's quite a bargain! Shipping and handling is just 50¢ per book in the U.S. and 75¢ per book in Canada.* I understand that accepting the 2 free books and gifts places me under no obligation to buy anything. I can always return a shipment and cancel at any time. Even if I never buy another book, the two free books and gifts are mine to keep forever.

246/349 HDN FEQQ

Name _____ (PLEASE PRINT)

Address _____ Apt. #

City _____ State/Prov. _____ Zip/Postal Code

Signature (if under 18, a parent or guardian must sign)

Mail to the **Reader Service:**
IN U.S.A.: P.O. Box 1867, Buffalo, NY 14240-1867
IN CANADA: P.O. Box 609, Fort Erie, Ontario L2A 5X3

Not valid for current subscribers to Harlequin Historical books.

Want to try two free books from another line?
Call 1-800-873-8635 or visit www.ReaderService.com.

* Terms and prices subject to change without notice. Prices do not include applicable taxes. Sales tax applicable in N.Y. Canadian residents will be charged applicable taxes. Offer not valid in Quebec. This offer is limited to one order per household. All orders subject to credit approval. Credit or debit balances in a customer's account(s) may be offset by any other outstanding balance owed by or to the customer. Please allow 4 to 6 weeks for delivery. Offer available while quantities last.

Your Privacy—The Reader Service is committed to protecting your privacy. Our Privacy Policy is available online at www.ReaderService.com or upon request from the Reader Service.

We make a portion of our mailing list available to reputable third parties that offer products we believe may interest you. If you prefer that we not exchange your name with third parties, or if you wish to clarify or modify your communication preferences, please visit us at www.ReaderService.com/consumerschoice or write to us at Reader Service Preference Service, P.O. Box 9062, Buffalo, NY 14269. Include your complete name and address.

HH11B

DEA Agent Paige Ashworth's new assignment is to work undercover at a local elementary school to find out how her partner and his girlfriend died while trying to take down a drug ring. Read on for a sneak preview of AGENT UNDERCOVER by Lynette Eason, available August 2011 only from Love Inspired Suspense.

Pain. That was Paige's first thought. Her first feeling. Her first piece of awareness.

It felt like shards of glass bit into her skull with relentless determination. Her eyes fluttered and she thought she saw someone seated in the chair next to her.

Why was she in bed?

Memories flitted back. Bits and pieces. A little boy. A school. A crosswalk. A speeding car.

And she'd pedaled like a madwoman to dart in front of the car to rescue the child.

A gasp escaped her and she woke a little more. The pain faded to a dull throb. Where was the little boy? Was he all right?

Warmth covered her left hand. Someone held it. Who?

Awareness struggled into full consciousness, and she opened her eyes to stare into one of the most beautiful faces she'd ever seen. Aquamarine eyes crinkled at the corners and full lips curved into a smile.

The lips spoke. "Hello, welcome back."

Another sweet face pushed its way into her line of sight. A little boy about six years old.

"Hi," she whispered.

The hand over hers squeezed. "You saved Will's life, you know."

She had? Will. The little boy had a name. "Oh. Good."

Her smiled slipped into a frown. "I was afraid I couldn't do it. That car…"

"I'm Dylan Seabrook. This is my nephew, Will Price."

The name jolted her. Doing her best to keep her expression neutral, she simply smiled at him. She wanted to nod, but didn't dare.

Closing her eyes, Paige could see the racing car coming closer, hear the roar of the engine…

She flicked her eyelids up. "Did they catch him? Whoever was in the car?"

Dylan shook his head. "No. He—or she—never stopped."

She sighed. "Well, I'm glad Will is okay. That's all that really matters." Well, that, and whether or not she'd just blown her cover to save this child—the son of the woman whose death she was supposed to be investigating.

For more, pick up AGENT UNDERCOVER
by Lynette Eason, available August 2011
from Love Inspired Suspense.